UFOs Over Ohio

A novel

Take but degree away, untune that string,
And hark what discord follows.

William Shakespeare's *Troilus and Cressida*

UFOs Over Ohio

A Novel

Linda Oxley Milligan

UFOs Over Ohio

Library of Congress Control Number: 2020911297

Beak Star Books, Powell Ohio

ISBN: 978-1-944724-04-7

Beak Star Books
Powell, Ohio 43065
www.beakstarbooks.com
Cover Designed by Andy Bennett
www.B3NN3TT.com

Preface

"Are we alone?" This is the fundamental question that drives our space exploration and fills our movie and TV screens with science fiction glory and horror. The search for answers informs our legends and sells books that offer insights taken from first hand witness accounts or speculations from researchers.

This obsession is reflected on all levels of culture. It crosses national, gender, educational, and age related demographic lines. Who are they? Where did they come from? How long have they been here? How did they get here? And most importantly, what are their motives?

This obsession likewise is a response to enduring questions about ourselves. Who are we? Where did we come from? What planets will we visit? Who might be there to greet us? And what will they think of us and we of them when such a meeting finally takes place, for surely it will?

As a sequel to *Cygnus*, *UFOs Over Ohio* is an imaginative response to these questions. It is a journey that takes the reader on a ship through outer space to the planet Avian, a planet associated with the double star Albireo at the beak of the constellation Cygnus. Avian is a place fantastical. Less fantastical but more comical is the planet upon which we reside.

UFOs Over Ohio seeks to render both. Parts of it are drawn from widespread legends that express hope, fear, and paranoia as legends often do. It draws upon this author's imagination. No part of the space drama is based on fact. It is a fiction. And yet some small part of the novel draws upon events that actually happened. The winter solstice celebration at the Great Serpent Mound (*sans* UFO) is a portrait of an event this author happily participated in for a number of years until it was banned. What a loss, but I happily record it here.

Join the ride.

Contents

For Don Jernigan (1934-2011)

Who never stopped believing.

UFOs Over Ohio

Chapter One

Welcome Committee

Stillness settled on Barry Short's street in the small town of Delaware, Ohio after holiday lights blinked off —house, by house, by house. All were fast asleep except Neighbor Bill, who brought his white lab Shadow outside for a moment of relief. Blocks away and under his blanket, young Paul struggled in the dark to text Andy the big news, "Uncle Barry is back!!!"

Bill stood in his backyard looking up at fast moving clouds while Shadow sniffed the grass searching for the perfect spot. Before Shadow could take care of business the clouds opened wide. Big, wet snowflakes began to fall.

"You're slowin' down on me Shadow. Hurry up. It's gettin' cold," Bill said as Shadow walked round and round sniffing the ground. Bill looked up. "Holy Cow! What's that?"

A stairway appeared out of a cloud situated above Barry's rear yard. Bill rubbed his eyes and Shadow began to bark. When he opened his eyes a golden stairway mounted to nothing hung suspended in air.

"I knew they'd be comin' back!" Bill opened his back door, "Shadow, you get inside the house and be quiet now. I'm gonna take a look."

He tiptoed into his neighbor's yard and hid behind a tree. Two people walked down nearly imperceptible steps seemingly out of the cloud, one gingerly helping the other who looked hesitant as she took each step. The stairway disappeared, as did the fast moving cloud above it when they had reached the ground.

I'll be damned, space aliens! I knew they're still around here, Bill thought while keeping very still and quiet.

He watched as the couple walked through the yard to the front of Barry Short's house. Moving forward from tree to tree, he kept concealed while keeping a careful eye on the intruders. He watched as the two space aliens went up to Barry's front door and knocked. Under the porch light they look pretty regular, he thought. The door opened. Barry greeted them heartily. Then the door shut, and Bill could hear or see no more.

"Holy Ships!" he shouted into the cosmos. "I've got to get ahold of Walt!" he said as he ran to his house.

"I'm tellin' you, I saw what I saw," he said to Walt, having awakened the pilot from a sound sleep. "You know I don't drink that much. Okay, I'll be expectin' you and Quentin tomorrow after you get back. Sure, I'll keep an eye on the place."

He watched Barry's house until he saw the lights go out and decided it was safe enough to catch a few hours of sleep. Shadow woke him early the next morning asking to be taken out. Bill broke a long-standing rule and took the lab to the front yard rather than to the back so he could get a glimpse of the front of Barry's house. In the gray morning light it looked peaceful enough. He made some breakfast and stationed himself on the couch next to the split in the living room draperies while the TV broadcast morning news and weather. Just before noon he spied Barry climb into his jeep and return a half hour later with three bags of groceries and a Christmas tree. "Some cooking and celebrating going on," he recorded in his log. The house remained quiet for the rest of the afternoon until Barry came out and took his "House For Sale" sign down and brought in his mail. "Guess he's planning on staying awhile," he wrote just before his phone rang.

"Anything happening?" Walt asked.

"No nothin'. He just went out and bought a lot of groceries and took down his sign."

"That's interesting," Walt said. "Have you made a report to WUFOC?"

"I was just thinkin' about it."

"Hold on until we get out there. We'll be over in about half an hour."

At 5:45 p.m. Quentin's blue metallic electric car pulled into Bill's driveway. Two men climbed out, Walt in his tan khakis, white polo shirt and brown leather flight jacket and Quentin nearly concealed under his long, wiry hair. They looked casually through the darkness over at Barry Short's house. Had there been something to see, it is doubtful they would have seen it. The porch light was out.

"Anything happen since I talked to you?" Walt asked when Bill opened his front door.

"Come on in," Bill said. "It looks like they're holed up in there."

"That may be why he took the sign down," Walt said. "He's not looking to have strangers coming through."

"So exactly what did you see?" Quentin asked. "All the details please."

"I took Shadow out back late last night, and lo and behold a big cloud moved in droppin' big, white snowflakes."

"It snowed last night in Columbus too," Quentin said. "What else?"

"A stairway appeared in the sky comin' from a cloud."

"How were you able to see it if it was dark?"

"It was lit up. Two people walked down, a man and a woman. He was helpin' her down."

"How'd you know it was a man and a women?"

"I followed them round to the front of Barry's house. I didn't see much of them until they came under the porch light. And there they were, a man and a woman. Nothin' unusual about them except they didn't have on coats, and it was cold last night."

"So there was nothing odd about their looks? They weren't Grays or anything?"

"No, they were human. Or at least they looked that way. His front door opened and they went inside. Haven't been out since."

"So they're in there right now," Quentin said. "What happened to the lighted stairway?"

"It disappeared as soon as they came down it along with the cloud."

"Hmm," Quentin said, applying his scientific mind to the problem at hand. "How well do you know the guy who lives over there?"

"Barry? Not real well. I've said hello once or twice down by the mailbox, but we haven't talked much. He's overseas a lot. Just got back from France. "

"Do you have anything around here we could give him, a cake or something like that?" Quentin asked.

"I've got some cookies I baked yesterday."

"Good. That's just what we need. Here's what I propose. You wrap up those cookies and we all go over there for a neighborly visit, the cookies being a welcome home gift. That will be our excuse to check things out."

"Good plan," Walt said.

Cookies packed in a tin, the three men sauntered over to Barry Short's house, knocked on the front door, and greeted him with smiles when he answered.

"Oh, I thought you were someone else," Barry said surprised.

"Are you expectin' company?" Bill asked and looked up and down the street.

"Why, yes I am."

Neighbor Bill held out his tin of cookies. "I won't keep you long. I've been meanin' to bring you somethin' since you got back. A little welcome home gift."

"Why thank you Bill. You needn't have done this. So happens I've got guests here who will really appreciate your offering."

"You've got guests? Oh, I'm sorry."

"Look's like you've got some as well," Barry said.

"I should have introduced you. These are my friends, Walt and Quentin."

"I like your hair," Barry said to Quentin, noting his wiry curls. "It gives you that electric look. Oh, wait! I know you two. Paul wrote me about you and that mouse incident. You and Bill here have a UFO club, don't you?"

"I'm not in that club," Quentin said. "I'm a graduate student at Ohio State studying physics and electrical engineering. But, yes, I was with these two when they investigated the incident. I examined one of the Bio-Nano Robots myself."

"Well, here, come on in. I've got a fellow scientist inside. You might have something to talk about. We were just having hors d'oeuvres before our other friends join us. These cookies will be a treat for dessert. Sit down with us for a while."

Summer and Roland were sitting at the dining room table eating cheese and drinking wine.

"Summer, Roland, meet my neighbor Bill here and his friends. Did you say Walt?"

"Yes, Walt."

"And Quentin here, a fellow scientist."

Roland rose and held out his hand.

Summer followed and said, "I know you guys. Paul wrote about you."

Quentin looked embarrassed. "What did he write?"

"He wrote about the extraterrestrial mice invading Barry's house," Summer said. "I've looked all around and can find no traces of where they hid."

"That's because they all left," Walt said. "They rose up in a beam of light into a ship just outside in the backyard."

"I'm not gonna beat around the bush any longer," Bill said. "I was out in my yard last night when you two got here. You didn't arrive by conventional jet. I saw it myself."

"Well," Barry said scratching the back of his head having no explanation to offer.

Roland spoke up. "We came over here from CERN where I'm a resident scientist."

"Are you saying that was some kind of secret aircraft?" Walt asked.

"You must understand. I cannot speak about it."

"I'm a pilot," Walt said. "Corporate jets mostly. I would certainly like to know more about that craft."

Quentin nudged Walt and said, "He can't tell you, man! He works at CERN. It's top secret."

"Some of it, but not all of it," Roland said.

"Yeah, I just read an article about the elusive God Particle you guys discovered over there," Quentin said with admiration.

"Roland worked on that," Summer said, taking her husband's arm.

"Only some of the time," Roland said. "Most of my work has been with neutrinos and the speed of light."

"Speed limit: 186,000 miles per second," Quentin said.

"That's what we're trying to verify. Some think neutrinos have traveled faster."

"It's the law, man!" Quentin said.

"It wouldn't be the first law that's been broken," Roland replied.

"Say, what are you doing visiting here anyway?" Bill asked. "No big science going on around here."

"Summer tells me this is the home of Big Ear," Roland said. "That's a pretty adventurous research project."

"It was, but they tore it out and turned it into a golf course," Quentin said.

Roland looked astonished. "I'm sorry to hear that."

"That's what a lot of folks say," Quentin said looking slightly forlorn before speaking up. "So what are you doing here, man? It's smalltime around here compared to CERN."

"If you must know, Summer and Roland are newlyweds," Barry said. "Her sister and brother-in-law are on their way over to meet Roland for the first time."

"Congratulations!" Bill said. "Are you gonna be stayin' here then?"

"I thought I could put them up for a little while," Barry said. "I've got the extra room."

"Great!" Quentin said. "We can have plenty of time to talk about what they're doing over there. Maybe you can help me get an internship."

"I'd be happy to try," Roland said warmly. "I remember my own days in graduate school. I'd stay up half the night talking with the other students about what I'd learned that day."

"Well, we'd better get goin' then if you've got company comin'. Summer, please eat some of my cookies. They're my mother's recipe, oatmeal and brown sugar laces. So nice to meet you," Bill said as he shook Roland's hand.

"Yes, this was really cool," Quentin said.

"Anything you can think of that you can tell me about that aircraft, please do," Walt said. "I try to keep up with these things."

"Bill, thanks for the cookies," Barry said as he opened his front door and let them out.

The trio left content that the mystery had been solved. Roland sat back down at the table looking worried.

"What's wrong?" Summer asked.

"I'm supposed to stay in the shadows for now. I never expected the local UFO club to show up."

"Oh, they won't say anything," she said. But as soon as she said it, she thought otherwise. Another knock came at the door.

"Oh my god, you're here!" Rosalind said and dropped her shopping bags full of lights and ornaments to embrace her sister. "I thought you were lost in the Swiss Alps!"

"We were."

"They arrived late last night," Barry said. "It was a surprise for me too."

"How did you get here?" she asked.

"We were rescued in the mountains and dropped off here by Roland's friends," Summer said.

"All the way here?"

"Yeah, I know. It seems pretty fantastic. I would tell you more except that I slept through the whole flight. But here we are."

"Really!"

"It's kind of hard to explain," Barry said. "But don't stand in the doorway. Come in and meet Roland."

"He's with you?"

"Of course! Roland, my sister Rosalind and her husband John."

He's handsome, Rosalind thought. He looks intelligent too, but there's something else I can't put my finger on. Maybe it's his eyes.

She is Lira's cousin too, Roland thought as he looked on at Rosalind looking at him. She has Lira's discerning look and the same expressive eyes.

"Come join us for cheese and wine," Barry said. "We'll have soup later. And we can't forget dessert. My neighbor just brought over some cookies."

"That was nice of him," Rosalind said slightly distracted since all of her attention was focused on Roland's unnaturally deep blue eyes. Refocusing herself, she said, "Come on now. What happened that brought you here so unexpectedly?"

"We were lost in the mountains after having a paragliding accident during a storm," Roland said. "Fortunately, we were found by my friends. They brought us here employing their own aircraft to do it."

"A private plane flying all the way from Switzerland to Ohio?" Rosalind said with a touch of skepticism in her voice.

"Oh, this one's pretty special," Barry said. "Experimental, I think Roland said."

"Very advanced. They were able to bring us all the way to Barry's house at Summer's request."

"I don't remember any of it," Summer said while rubbing her forehead. "The only thing I remember is this very long stairway we climbed down into Barry's backyard. Now the accident I remember because, well, it was terrifying."

"What happened?" John asked.

"I took her paragliding as a honeymoon gift when an unexpected storm blew up," Roland explained. "I thought we would be struck by lightning or blown away if we didn't go down, so I took us down very fast."

"We spun through the air at lightning speed," Summer said. "I'm not exaggerating at all. We went so fast our bodies were horizontal to the ground. I could look down the whole time I was spinning round and round. I thought we'd get caught in the trees or drown in the river, but Roland somehow managed to land us safely in the grass, but it was a really hard fall."

He grabbed her trembling hand and kissed it. "It was a hard landing, but it saved our lives." He turned to Rosalind. "I want you to know that if I had had an inkling of warning there would be bad weather, I never would have taken your sister up. The forecast called for perfect weather. It wasn't until we had flown a great distance that a violent storm blew up very suddenly out of nowhere."

Rosalind hugged her sister once more. "You must have suffered a minor concussion that has affected your memory. Thank god you're here now and all right!"

"The weather's been unpredictable around here too," John said. "It's gotten hard to plan anything outside. It's become so erratic that the long term forecast holds up less than fifty percent of the time."

"It's been that way in Europe, at least where we were," Summer said.

"Do you think the cause could be climate change?" John asked.

"I don't know," Roland said. "We visited a Swiss observatory just before it was destroyed and...."

"I read about that," John interrupted. "The destruction of the observatory at Jungfraujoch."

"We were there when it happened," Summer said.

"You were!" Rosalind said and squeezed her sister's hand. "Wasn't it lightning that caused the fire?"

"Now they're thinking it was some kind of terrorist attack," John said.

"It did seem like an attack," Summer said. "But there was a lot of lightning too."

"Interestingly enough," Roland continued, "the fellow who was working at the observatory that day—I should tell you first it's a meteorological observatory—he was studying this very problem. He was trying to determine if their equipment had gone faulty or if something else was going on since these weather anomalies have become so frequent."

Rosalind turned to Summer. "How did you ever get down from way up there with all of that going on?"

"We took two trains down the mountain to the car and drove away from the area as fast as we could and hid in a tunnel."

"A tunnel!"

"Lightning was everywhere!" Summer said, reliving the trauma as she retold it. "We had to find shelter. It actually struck the car and set it on fire soon after we went into the tunnel. If we hadn't gotten out when we did...."

"Thank god you're alive!" Rosalind interrupted.

"Change the subject. It's upsetting her," Roland said.

"They found the car the next morning," Summer continued, "a burnt out hulk. They thought I might be dead!"

Rosalind hugged her again.

"I need to say one last thing before we move on," John said and turned to Roland. "It isn't the observatory weather equipment that's at fault because the same thing is happening here. It's something else!"

The room grew awkwardly silent until Barry spoke up. "We should decorate the tree now before I've had too much wine. I've made you some wonderful soup we can have afterwards."

"I can smell it. Um, it's Luc's recipe," Summer said, picking up the scent of rich chicken broth, spinach, and parmesan cheese.

Rosalind looked at her sister with apprehension. First it was that stuffy French nobleman; and now this crazy scientist who flies her around in experimental aircraft, drops her from the sky, and.... She tried to suppress the image of the smoldering hulk of a car her sister described. She rubbed her head in frustration. If she was so intent on marrying young, she thought, why could she have not chosen a regular guy? It sure would be a lot safer.

As Summer and Roland strung lights and put colored bulbs on the tree, Rosalind noted how he would give her sister encouragement, take her direction, help her string a light or lift a bulb to a branch that was just out of her reach. Oh, well, he loves her, she thought.

She took her camera from her bag and took a picture of the tree with he and Summer standing next to it. "I'll have prints made," she said, "so that you can remember your first Christmas together and the first time Roland ever decorated a tree."

"Was it that obvious?" he said.

"It was sweet to see you help my sister."

He blushed and the two of them embraced.

"Soup is served," Barry said.

"I have an idea that would be fun," Rosalind said just after they sat down at the table. "They will be lighting the Serpent tomorrow night. If you don't have anything else to do, we could drive down there and help."

"A serpent?" Roland asked.

"It's a rather interesting ancient effigy mound," Barry said while ladling the soup and passing the bread. "They don't know too much about it, but like many other ancient sites, it's oriented to the sky."

"They do a lighting ceremony on the winter solstice," Rosalind explained. "People who claim ancestry to the early Native American Indian tribes who used to live there hold the event."

"That could be interesting," Roland said.

"It's a great idea! You will love it," Summer said. "Rosalind, do you have any clothes I could borrow? All I've got is what I'm wearing."

"Oh, Summer."

Chapter 2

The Great Serpent Mound

Barry's jeep rumbled along the snow covered roads of Southern Ohio carrying five passengers to the Great Serpent Mound. "I wish I could take you in by helicopter," he said to Roland after he turned off the highway on the far side of Chillicothe. "It's most impressive from the air."

"It's pretty impressive anytime," John said from the backseat. "Particularly when it's lit."

"At least they haven't tried to turn the mound into a golf course," Rosalind said.

"What did you say?" Roland asked, thinking the road noise must have affected his hearing.

"The Mound Builders Country Club installed a golf course on top of the Newark Earthworks. Can you believe it?" Rosalind said. "Like turning the Vatican into a fun park."

"It's a desecration alright," John said. "They tee-off right on the mounds."

"The Newark site has enormous historical value," Barry added. "It's a lunar observatory, and the whole complex taken together was a huge Hopewell ceremonial center. They say its alignments with the moon are more precise than those at Stonehenge. And here it is in our own backyard, only fifty miles from my house."

"Why hasn't something been done?" Roland asked.

"Because the people who care don't have the money, and the people with the money don't care," Rosalind said.

"Have you no ministry of culture?"

"Yes, we do, but they're underfunded. The Earthworks is actually owned by the Ohio Historical Connection," John explained. "The same people who own Serpent Mound. Years ago they signed a lease with this country club who maintains it because the historical society couldn't afford to maintain it themselves."

"Maintain it!" Rosalind laughed. "A few years back they arrested a Native American woman for praying on one of the mounds."

"What's this obsession with golf?" Roland asked. "First you told me they tore out an important radio telescope to construct a golf course, and now this. It's outrageous! What could these men be thinking?"

"I'm afraid the men we are talking about are not thinking too much," Rosalind said. "It's more about what they take pleasure in. They love golf!"

"Well, at least they haven't tried to mess with Serpent Mound just yet, and there is talk that the historical society is going to court to try to wrest control of the Newark complex," Barry said as he drove the jeep along the gravel road leading into the packed parking lot.

"Only because it's out here in the sticks," Rosalind said. "Besides, if they did, they might launch an Indian war."

"And it wouldn't just be the Native Americans coming to the serpent's defense," John said.

The snow stopped falling and the sky momentarily cleared. John wandered off to watch the solstice sunset while the others were about to join the crowd who had gathered until he shouted for them to follow him over to the serpent's tail.

"Look at this alignment," he said, and pointed to the tail of the serpent and then to the setting sun. "If ever I had any doubts that this was designed to follow the sun, they've ended now."

"I see!" Roland said. He looked back and forth between the sunset and the serpentine tail. "It's in perfect alignment. Too perfect to be an accident. Too exact. How old did you say this effigy mound is?"

"There's a controversy around that I will tell you about later," Barry said. "Right now we'd better get over there if we want to light this thing."

A man with a ponytail and an angular jaw approached them with candles as they tried to join the circle. "Light these from the sacred fire once I've made my prayer." He turned to the larger gathered crowd. "Make a bigger circle now," he shouted. "Move back so these others can join. There's no time to spare. Another winter storm is coming."

Men and women, young and old, their features made uncanny by the fiery light, gathered around the blustering bonfire. The silhouette of the dark haired man blessed the fire in the name of the Great Spirit before he brought the fire to the candle of a person standing in each quadrant of the circle, who in turn shared the flame with the person standing next to them. The flame quickly traveled around the circle until all candles were lit. The candle bearers then moved towards the serpent to light paper bag lanterns that lined the serpent's seven coils, its head, and its curled tail that pointed to the winter solstice sunset.

"It truly is a wonder," Roland said to Barry after he reached his melting candle down to light a lantern. "Can you tell me now when it was built?"

"It depends on the methodology used, and there's a lack of agreement there. The estimates range anywhere between 1000 and 10,000 years ago."

"That's an extremely broad range."

"It means no one really knows," Barry said.

Summer ran over and grabbed Roland's hand after all that was left of her candle was remnants on her gloves. She guided him to the serpent's mouth, positioned near the edge of a drop-off that looks west up into the big sky and down into the Brush Creek Valley.

"The head points right to the summer solstice sunset," she said.

"It's quite magnificent," Roland said standing at the head and looking back at the now fully lit effigy. "But what is this oval here at the mouth?"

"An egg, I've heard."

"I see," he said taking a step back. "The snake's jaws open wide as she gives birth."

"I never thought of that," she said. "I've been focused on the astronomical positions. But you're right. That makes sense. If the serpent is a calendar, what is it a calendar for? Let's climb up on the observation tower and get a really good look."

They wandered up the path towards the lookout and climbed the slippery steps to the first deck and then further up to the top. John was already there snapping photos of the serpent glimmering white under fresh snow with the stars above.

"Look, you can see the Milky Way," he said pointing up to the sky. "It looks like a river. Some say it's a sky representation of the Nile."

"Yes," Roland said, his head arched back as he stared. "I can see that."

"And there is Cygnus," John said. "There above us. It's so clear in this sky."

"Yes," Roland repeated as he squeezed Summer's hand. "As above, so below. And what of this serpent? I've never seen anything like it before."

"Neither have I," Summer said. "That's what keeps bringing me back."

Their eyes continued to take in the beauty of both the stars above and the lighted serpent below when the solemn moment was broken with John's shout. "What the hell is that?" He pointed his camera to the sky and wildly snapped.

Roland looked up just in time to see a silvery ship slip behind a cloud that had just moved in. "Did you get a picture?" he asked.

"Yes, here, several" John said, and began to review his photos through the camera's LCD panel.

"It looks like a flying ship!" Summer said.

"It sure isn't an airplane!" John said.

"I didn't mean that kind," she said. "Roland? What do you think?"

"I think you are right."

"Are you saying this thing is a flying saucer?" John asked.

"For now we will call it a UFO," Roland said.

"Okay, I'll be politically correct, a UFO. I can't believe this. I must be seeing things."

"Can you tell whose it is?" Summer said, her voice quivering but not from the cold.

"What do you mean whose is it? How would he know whose it is?" John asked.

"He tracks them."

"Summer!" Roland said silencing her too late.

"You're kidding, aren't you?" John thought about it for a moment and knew she was not. "Paul has said they've been flying around Barry's house, but I never took him seriously."

"Take him seriously," she said. "Can you tell whose it is?" she asked Roland again.

"I'd have to see a larger photo."

"I can blow them up on the computer screen when we get back," John said.

"Good. I will take another look at them then. For now, please don't say too much about this to the others. I don't want to frighten them, and it could be nothing."

John raised his finger to his lips. "They're sealed," he said.

The crowd had already begun to thin as winter thunder roared over the noise of the wind that had blown in.

"Let's go back down," Roland said. "I want to learn more about this serpent before we leave."

The three of them joined Barry and Rosalind who were waiting at the bottom of the lookout. They followed stragglers towards the parking lot, but before they sought the shelter of the jeep, John led them over to a nearby plaque that recorded the mound's history and background. "Here, this will tell you something," he said to Roland.

One of North America's most spectacular effigy mounds, Serpent Mound is a gigantic earthen sculpture representative of a snake. Built on a spur of rock overlooking Ohio Brush Creek around 1000 A.D. by the Fort Ancient culture, the earthwork was likely a place of ceremonies dedicated to a powerful serpent spirit. This site is located on the edge of a massive crater possibly formed by the impact of a small asteroid around 300 million years ago. Frederick Ward Putnam studied Serpent Mound between 1886 and 1889. Due largely to his efforts, Serpent Mound became the first privately funded archeological preserve in the United States.

The Ohio Bicentennial Commission
The Ohio Historical Society, 2003

"It's at least three times older than that," said a voice coming from behind them.

Barry turned to the ponytailed man who had blessed the flame and a fair-haired companion. "How so?" he asked.

"They think the Fort Ancients built it based on carbon dated charcoal," the ponytailed man said.

"Isn't that how it's usually done?" Barry asked.

"That's why archeologists sometimes get it wrong," the fair-haired man answered. "The site was inhabited and then re-inhabited by later tribes. They're confusing the later with the first."

"Barry is an archeologist," Rosalind said as an aside.

"I meant no offense," the fair-haired man said.

"I'm not offended," Barry said. "I'm curious. Do you mind me asking to whom I'm speaking?"

"Between us," the man with the ponytail said referring to himself and his friend, "we've done a lot of research on the subject. He's studied the science of the place and other historical facts. I've looked into the legends and myths. Together, they tell a different story."

"I'd be curious to hear it."

"The Adena people may have built this mound thousands of years earlier than this plaque claims."

"I've heard of the Adena," Summer said.

"That's the name they were given," the man said, "after the name of the farm where their artifacts were first discovered. But the elders among us call them the Andaste."

"Evidence of habitation dates back to the Paleolithic period," said the fair-haired man. "We see it again in the Archaic period, which began way before the Woodland period, which is the period this plaque cites. But who built the mound? Iroquois legend says the tall men."

"The tall men?" Barry said.

"The Allegheny people. A race of giants. Fredrick Putnam unearthed the skeletal remains of a seven-foot man right over there in that burial mound next to the serpent. I've got a picture of it," he said and pulled a very old picture postcard out of his pocket. "Look, you can see where the legs were severed from the knee down. They've seen a lot of that around here, in Pennsylvania and Indiana too."

"So big!" Summer said. "Why would they have cut off his legs?"

"To take him down a peg or two I guess," the man said and laughed. "If these were descendants of the Andaste, that could explain it. They were not known for their kindness and were disliked by other tribes."

"However unkind they may have been, these astronomical markers suggest tremendous skill," Roland said.

"You're right," the fair-haired man said. "The astronomical knowledge of whoever built it was astounding."

"The Serpent Mound was their grand temple to the sun," the ponytailed man said. "Seth here thinks the mound could be five thousand years old, built when the constellation Draconis was highest. The serpent represents Draconis and the spirit animal lodge way back when the medicine brought here by the Great Spirit abounded. Myself, I think one of the Thunderbirds is up there right now spitting lightning into the serpent's head. And I'm going to catch it."

"Thunderbirds!" Summer said as she thought back to the UFO John had just photographed. "Are you an Andaste?"

"I'm Cherokee, but we're one family. We're intent on recovering the knowledge that was lost."

"How was it lost?" Roland asked.

"It was scattered to the winds like my ancestors when the Europeans pushed westward. All that is left to us are fragments of stories that once preserved their historical records." He looked at Seth. "My friend here and I have made it our business to find and reconstruct as many of these stories as we can." He waved his arm as if pulling back a stage curtain as an apt metaphor for what he was about to say. "All of these trees block the sky. Until they are removed, we will never see it as the ancestors did."

As if to answer his pessimism, an unexpected bolt of winter lightning struck the ground, shaking it with its thunder.

The ponytailed man turned and raised his arms to the sky. "You come to us. In spite of a barrier of a thousand years, you come to us. Could the time for rebirth be near?"

"We'd better get out of here," Barry said. "This weather has turned nasty. I can't remember ever seeing it like this at this time of year."

The wind kicked up and the sky turned white with winter lightning. The few people left looked like ghosts under the eerie light as they searched for their cars in the parking lot. Deeply moved, Roland embraced the ponytailed man as the French are given to do. This man, sensing Roland's sincerity, returned his embrace as if he knew that however foreign Roland seemed he was a brother in spirit. Then the two strangers walked off, disappearing behind a wall of white falling snow that separated them from Roland. "A barrier of a thousand years," Roland uttered under his breath.

Wipers flapped back and forth, back and forth making a low scraping sound as the silent passengers huddled inside the jeep. There was little evidence that the highway road crews had tried to plow; it was early for snow, and perhaps they had not gotten fully into gear. Barry turned the radio to a bluegrass station to try to break the silence as they approached Columbus. When banjos and violins had not breached the deafening quietude, he said, "I'm starved. How about the rest of you?"

"I could use something," John said.

"You live around here. Any suggestions?" Barry asked.

"This late at night our best bet is pizza. I know a good place. Not much for looks, but it's near the highway we're on. And they have the best pizza in town if you like Italian style."

"Do I hear any objections?" Barry asked.

A half hour later they were gathered round a table at Jimmy's Pizza drinking cold beer and waiting for their pies.

"It'll just be another five minutes," the friendly waitress said. "Can I bring out more beer?"

"I can use another," Barry said.

"So can I," John said. "Oh, heck, bring another pitcher for the table."

"I will have another hot tea," Summer said.

"Make that two," added Rosalind who sat shivering from an early cold snap she had not yet adapted to.

"Can you tell me more about the discrepancies in the dates?" Roland asked.

"You saw the situation first hand," Barry said. "It all depends on your point of view, or I should say worldview. The plaque represents one perspective based on one set of partial facts and those men we spoke to represent another. There's nothing definitive unless you've got some kind of time machine."

The waitress put a fresh pitcher of beer on the table. "Your pizzas are coming right out."

"But that one is a descendant," Roland said. "That should give him greater insight. And as for folktales, well, they might seem like soft evidence to those of us trained in the sciences. Yet I have learned—reluctantly I must admit—that these old tales may contain more truth than many of us would like to acknowledge."

"Don't forget," Barry said, "they lost much of their past including the tales. Even now they're trying to reconstruct them."

The waitress placed two steaming pizzas on the table.

"Look at these pizzas!" Barry said.

"I told you they make great pizza here," John said. "They've been in business as long as I can remember."

"And now?" Roland asked, not giving up on the conversation just yet. "Are they given no respect now?"

"A lot more than they had before," Barry said, just before he took a very large bite. "There are some good people working in this area on both sides of the date issue."

"What about the people you were working with over in Pennsylvania?" Rosalind said.

"That's what I mean, good people. In my line of work legends and myths are not proof by themselves, but they can be a starting place. Right now they're looking for evidence of an ancient Atlantic crossing. Some of these Native Americans who lived in the East may have been descended from their ancient European counterparts."

"That's what you were supposed to be doing, wasn't it?" John said.

"I'm afraid I let them down. I got distracted."

"I wouldn't call rescuing Gitane Marie a distraction," Summer said.

"You're right," Barry said. "She is evidence that all of us have lost parts of our past."

Chapter 3

Photo Graphic Evidence

John downloaded his photos into Barry's Mac. "Only three shots caught anything of that ship, and only this one is discernible," he said.

"Can you enlarge it?" Roland asked. "Can you hone in on just that part?" A detail popped out.

"Are they the ones who tried to kill us?" Summer asked.

"I think so," he sighed. "What were they doing there?"

John grew noticeably rattled. "Hey, what's this all about?"

"It could be nothing," Roland said. "Will you keep these to yourself?"

"Will do if you think I should."

"We shouldn't frighten them just yet. Can you print me a full screen copy and a detail?"

The sound of the printer drew Rosalind's attention away from the Christmas tree she had been fussing over. "What are you doing?" she asked.

John quickly swapped a screen shot of the serpent for the detail of the ship he had just printed. "Roland wants one of my pictures of the serpent."

"It's beautiful," she said, looking at the image of the lighted Serpent Mound now up on the screen.

"Coffee's ready," Barry said. "I hope you don't mind decaf. I have some leftover cookies."

They gathered round the table, drank coffee, ate Bill's oatmeal brown sugar laces, and talked about the weather along with the evening's adventure at Serpent Mound.

"I'm beat," John said after he drained his cup. "What time is it?"

"Midnight," Rosalind said. "We'd better get along. Don't forget your camera."

Barry took the cups back into the kitchen and begged off for the night. Roland and Summer followed him upstairs to bed.

"So, what do you think?" Summer whispered as she lay in darkness next to Roland.

"About which thing? My mind is full."

"About the ship. Why would they be watching such a remote place? Could they be abducting people over here too?"

"They could be, or maybe they're tracking us."

"Or both!" Summer said.

"I don't know which is worse," Roland groaned.

"I'm scared!"

"We're safe now," he tried to assure her, although he was unconvinced himself.

Summer dozed off, but Roland could not sleep. The whole point of their being brought to Barry's house was for concealment, to lend credence to the story that the two of them had perished in the river in Switzerland after they fell from the sky. That ploy sure didn't work if they've already found us, he thought as he turned over in bed for the hundredth time. More to the point, he felt vulnerable, he being a stranger and having no access to safe rooms here. Barry's was to be the safe house, but not now.

He went downstairs, turned on the computer, and studied the detail of the photo of the ship lit up brightly on the screen. There was only one thing left to do, make emergency contact. He gathered up copies of the photos John had printed off, deleted the images of the ship, put on the jacket Barry had loaned him, and went outside.

Neighbor Bill happened to be scouting Barry's house through the opening in his living room drapes when he saw the figure of a man turn in the direction of the backyard before he disappeared into the dark. "Stay here boy," he said to Shadow. He slipped on his coat and quietly went out the back door and made his way to the tree he had hid behind when he first saw Roland and Summer arrive down the lighted stairway. Once his eyes had adjusted to the dark he could make out the figure of a lone man, sitting cross-legged in the snow as if he were waiting for something. Nothing happened for a good fifteen minutes until a blast of light shot down from the sky. Roland rose up through the beam and disappeared into the bottom of a ship.

"Damn, just like those mice," Bill mumbled. "My, my, they got stairways and they got elevators too. I knew it!" he said, slapping his leg as he ran towards his house. "He couldn't fool me. That's a spaceship!"

"Walt, you better get over here right now. And bring your night camera," he said into his kitchen phone. "Another ship out there, and it's no experimental aircraft. It's a UFO if ever I saw one, and that Roland fellow just got sucked right up into it just like those mice did."

Summer snuggled closer to Roland only to find an empty pillow. He must have gone downstairs, she thought. She looked for him in the kitchen and then the living room. The computer was on. Serpent Mound, all white and outlined in lantern light shown beautiful and strange on the screen.

He must have stepped outside for some fresh air, she thought, or to look at the stars. Indeed, she saw fresh footprints made in the snow on the front porch steps leading into the yard and ran back upstairs, quickly dressed, and grabbed the coat Rosalind had loaned her. She made her way out into the cold night, following Roland's footprints into the rear of Barry's yard.

A hand reached out of darkness and clutched her throat, silencing her before she could scream. It felt more metal than flesh against her flesh, causing her to briefly imagine it was some kind of machine until she felt the steam of its putrid flesh as it pressed its chest tightly against her own, binding her arms behind her. A light descended fast from the sky as if it would fall on top of her. She realized what was happening; she was being taken. With the only part of her that remained free, she kicked the creature mightily where it hurts most. It kicked her back so hard her leg went limp and she crumpled to the ground, which momentarily freed her from its grip. She tried to let out a scream that sounded more like a gasp, but it was loud enough.

"Who goes there!" shouted a voice rushing towards them from across the lawn just as the metal hand reestablished its grip around her throat, squeezing very hard. Another voice yelled, "Stop! We've got you covered."

Camera lights shattered the dead of night nearly blinding her. A dog barked, then growled and snarled as it grew near. Her abductor abandoned her in the snow, running into a thicket of trees on the far side of the yard, the dog chasing behind him.

"Are you all right?" Bill said as he helped her up.

"I think I am," she said hoarsely while rubbing her throat. "Oh, my leg hurts," she said sobbing when she tried and failed to put her weight on it. "Where did he go?"

"Walt and Shadow are chasing after him. He looked pretty ugly."

"I couldn't see him, but I could smell him," she grimaced.

"We took some pictures with Walt's camera."

"Have you seen Roland?"

"I saw him out in the yard about an hour ago sittin' in the snow right over there. I saw a beam of light take him up into a ship."

"Oh, my god they've abducted him!" she wailed and began to cry harder.

"It didn't look like that," Bill said as he tried to console her. "It looked like he wanted to go, like he'd been sittin' there waitin' for them."

She calmed herself. The Alliance, she hoped.

"He got away," Walt said when he came out of the woods the creature had escaped into. "But not before Shadow took a big bite out of him. Look at what he got." He held out a hand full of sinewy wire mixed with blood.

The earth beneath them shook when a rumble of thunder and a bolt of lightning shot across the sky. They looked up in astonishment but could see nothing.

"Young lady," Walt said. "You might as well tell us the truth. We know you didn't arrive here in an experimental aircraft."

She began to cry again.

"Come on over to my place until your husband gets back," Neighbor Bill said. "I'll make you some hot chocolate. Shadow, you stay out here in the yard and guard the place."

"He didn't tell me he was going anywhere," she cried. "I hope he's all right."

Walt downloaded the photos he had taken into Bill's computer and brought up the whole scene. "My god he's an ugly one!"

Summer looked on with horror seeing herself half strangled and in the arms of a creature with a pale, vampirish face, scaly skin, and fearsome yellow teeth.

"Look at his hand, better to say his claw around my throat. It felt metallic and cold, and it is!"

"It's a prosthetic," Walt said, "designed to capture its foe by the look of it. Tell us what you know right now or I'll call the police."

"I don't know much," she sobbed exhausted. "I suspect that thing was sent here from the Endron. Ugh! I've never liked scaly things, and to think this one touched me. I can still smell its foul breath!"

"Who are they?"

"All that I know is they've come from somewhere else and they want to reduce us. They took a man I knew, and when he was returned he was a shadow of the man he had been, in intelligence at least and in kindness."

"They abducted him?" Bill asked.

"And he didn't even know it at the time," she whimpered.

"They erased his memory?"

"They tried to, but eventually it came back. But almost as soon as he remembered he tried to pretend it never happened. And that's when he started to change. Roland said he was mind-stripped."

"Mind-stripped?" Bill said. "What's that?"

"I don't understand it entirely. It made him less of a human being. He looked the same, at least the last time I saw him. But he turned harsh and mean and full of brute lust. The Alliance thinks that's part of the Endron's plan, to turn us into their beasts. Maybe like that creature that just nearly kidnapped me," she sobbed louder.

"Who's the Alliance?" Walt asked. "Are you getting all this Bill? Okay now, who is the Alliance?"

"I don't know. All that I can tell you is they look like us, not like that thing. And they're trying to protect us from them."

"Them!" Bill said, thinking of what that ugly creature might have done to Summer had he and Walt not been there to stop it. Would they have mind-stripped her too? he wondered. His brief meditation was broken when he heard Shadow barking from outside in the yard. "It's back! Maybe they will try to mind-strip all of us," he shouted in a panic.

Walt, camera in hand, spilled out the back door while Bill and Summer slowly followed behind, neither wanting to come face to face with such horror. But no horror had returned. Instead Roland stood next to Shadow, petting the dog.

"Roland!" Summer shouted as she ran to him, half limping, half walking, and fell into his arms.

"What happened to you?" he said, trying to soothe her while evaluating her condition.

"Something tried to take her," Walt said. "It was an ugly looking thing. If it weren't for this dog here, she'd be gone. And god knows what that creature would have done to her. He didn't look too friendly. We've got a photo inside."

"He had metal hands!" Summer cried, "and scaly skin that was almost green."

"Look at this chunk Shadow took out of him: flesh and wire," Bill said.

"They must have sent one of their cyborg henchmen," Roland said, tears welling up in his eyes. "Thank you," he said, and reached down and patted Shadow on the head. "And thank you too," he said to Walt and Bill. "So you know."

"Couldn't fool us for long," Bill said. "I never believed your story about that experimental aircraft from CERN. But that Quentin there, nearly a Ph.D., and you bamboozled him good."

"What are you talking about?" Summer asked. "It was an experimental aircraft! You told me so. Didn't you say that's what it was?"

"I had to say something."

"Then how were we brought down into Barry's yard?"

Roland lifted her chin searching her eyes. "We must leave now. The Endron have found us, and we're putting our friends in danger. You will understand it all. I promise, but you've got to trust me."

She began to weep again. "But we just got here."

"I'm sorry," he said. "I wish I'd never involved you in this."

"Don't say things like that. I'll be all right," she sobbed.

"Where will you be going?" Bill asked.

"To the safety of the ship for now. I learned there is business I must attend to; and after that, well, I don't know."

"Can we go back to Luc's?" she asked. "I want to see Luc."

"Someday," he said and kissed her tears.

"You two just got married, didn't you," Bill said.

"Yes," Summer said and wept some more.

“Well, you take good care of each other,” he said. “We’ll handle the rest down here. And if you do come back, we will be happy to see you.”

Roland took off his jacket and handed it to Bill. “Give this back to Barry, will you? And tell him thanks. And tell him I will be looking for him in Italy. He will know what I mean.”

Neighbor Bill and Walt watched as Roland took Summer to the place where Bill had seen him ascend earlier that night. They sat together, she on his lap, he looking up as if meditating on the stars. Within seconds a bright beam shot down and pulled them up. The ship that had appeared quickly disappeared behind a sky door.

Walt slapped his leg. “We hit pay dirt! Got all the evidence we need!”

“I wonder if anyone will believe us?” Bill asked.

“They’ve got to now. We have the photo. We’ve even got evidence of an attempted abduction. We’ll be famous!”

Chapter 4

Departure

Dazed and shivering, almost faint, Summer leaned against Roland as if without his support she might topple. Foreign sounds of a rich, melodic voice aroused her. "What be her condition?" the voice said. She opened her eyes rightly assuming the voice was referring to her. Before her stood a tall, majestic woman, hair and skin so radiant as nearly to cast a light. She blinked her eyes before closing them again. "Beautiful" is hardly a word worthy to describe the woman standing before me, she thought before she was distracted by a familiar voice.

"The Endron tried to take her," Roland said. "They set one of their cyborgs upon her while I was up here. Two neighborhood men and their dog saved her. I'm afraid these men know about us now."

"No matter," Summer heard another voice say. "Others do as well, but few believe them."

She glanced at the golden haired man who just spoke and thought him quite elegant in maroon velvet pants and shirt and with a bearing that matched that of the beautiful woman's.

"Can you walk?" Lira asked Summer.

"Not so well," she answered, her voice hoarse and groggy, her throat raw. "That monster kicked me hard in the leg when I tried to fight him off."

Lira saw a mass of swelling on Summer's leg and red welts on her throat. "Follow me Roland. We should take her to the baths for healing." She turned to Bryn. "What should I tell her?"

"As much as you must but nothing more. She's too much in shock. I will prepare nourishment for them. You soothe her."

Roland picked Summer up in his arms and followed behind Lira who entered the baths and asked that he put her down on a table. An attendant examined her leg and suggested soaking and a massage. A bath was drawn filled with the silver bubbles of lycmthe. Roland helped her out of her wet clothing and lifted her in. The attendant brought a carafe of heated oil, propped her leg on the side of the tub and began to rub the oil in, spoonful after spoonful of the rich smelling stuff while Lira hummed her tune. Roland himself was almost put to sleep by it, so hypnotic it was.

"She be well now," the attendant said when the last of the oil was gone.

"Thank you," Lira said. "I be needing no more of your attentions just now."

"Roland," Lira said, "Here be a silver coin that will give you entrance to my room. Go there and bring something for Summer to wear. You will find a blue shift on the shelf. While you be away, I shall wash her beautiful hair."

Roland gone, Lira hummed her tune as she gently massaged lycmthe soap into Summer's hair. Softly she rubbed her temples, neck and crown then whispered a song into the dreams of the sleeping girl.

Know who you be oh Summer my dear,
My sweet girl, know who you be.
You be the golden star to his blue,
You with him and he with you. So be strong.
Be strong my dear.

If horror should hold you in its fearsome grasp,
Or false longing should tempt you away,
Look to your ring and he will return,
For you like the yellow and he like the blue stars of Albireo,
Shall preserve the whole to bring the joy to destiny.

Know who you be oh Summer my dear,
My sweet cousin, know who you be.
You be the golden star to his blue,
You with him and he with you. So be strong.
Be strong my dear.

If he should falter in his task,
Or from you be taken away,
Look to your ring and he will return,
For you like the yellow and he like the blue stars of Albireo,
Shall preserve the whole and bring the joy to destiny.

Know who you be my Summer my dear,
My sweet princess, know who you be.
You be the golden crown on his head of blue,
You with him and he with you. So be strong.

Lira paused for a moment then whispered emphatically into the sleeping girl's ear, "You be strong my dear!" She raised Summer's left hand and kissed the blue and yellow sapphire wedding ring on her finger. Then she kissed the top of Summer's head before she began to rinse her hair. When the last of the lycmthe was rinsed out, Summer awoke from her dream.

"She be ready now," Lira said when Roland returned with the shift. "Help her dress and then come to the dining room. I be waiting for you with Bryn."

Roland marveled at Summer's beauty, so radiant she looked. Tears all gone, she embraced him with a kiss and time was lost as both fell under the spell of lycmthe.

"We must go now," he said, tearing himself from his beloved after the minutes had past. "They have prepared us a meal."

They left the room and entered a long, wide hallway with metal walls and floors polished to a near mirror finish.

"Who are these people?" she asked.

"They were my instructors when I received training as a watcher, particularly Bryn who to me is like the father I never had."

When they entered the room for dining it was as if Summer saw the alien couple for the first time: master teachers, she thought. Lira, pleased with what she saw, smiled when they arrived. "The color be good on you," she said. "It brings out the blue in your eyes."

"Thank you for loaning me your dress," Summer said, running her hands across the silken cloth.

"It be yours, my dear. It be made for you. Come sit. We shall eat and Bryn will tell you his news. I think you will like what we've prepared," Lira said, taking hold of Summer's hand as she helped her down upon a pillow. She passed a plate of fruit and cheese. "They be very good together."

And indeed they were. The fruit tasted something like sweet cherries but had more the look of blackberries, only larger. The cheese was sharp and contrasted nicely with the berries. There was hot vegetable broth filled with dumplings and bread as fresh and warm as any Summer had tasted. The meal reminded her of dinner with Luc Renard. Yet there were neither shelves full of books nor maps on the walls, just this sparsely furnished room for dining. She missed the comforts of Luc's home.

Lira's expression changed from exuberance to worry. "You miss your home," she said.

"How did you know what's on my mind?" Summer asked feeling violated.

Roland grabbed her hand. "Lira and Bryn are elevated even among their kind. That is why they are teachers. The have certain capacities few others have."

"You are a sensitive?" Summer said looking into Lira's eyes.

"I am. And so be you. There is much to tell you; it's hard to know where to begin. But let us begin with your well-being."

"Lira, when her mind be focused, can see into things, forward into time a year sometimes two," Bryn explained. "What she sees be not immutable but what will be if the current time path be not altered. She sensed from your face your distress and the rest from circumstance." He took his wife's hand and squeezed it with, as Summer noted, a good deal of affection.

"Can I ask you a personal question?" she asked. "How long have you two been together, married I mean."

"Yes, married," Lira said. She looked at Bryn. "Last month marked our 50th year."

"But you're so young!" Summer said.

"We be! Oh, I see, you be comparing us to those from Earth. We have perfected the art of long life," she explained.

"You mean you've overcome disease?"

"Many have, yes, but more. We've learned how to live." Lira could see that Summer was puzzled. "We've found the joy! Now Bryn should speak."

"I've just had word that a mediation be going on as we speak on Avian. The Endron demand Roland's presence if an agreement be reached."

"What for? What agreement?" Summer asked.

"I have not told you yet," Roland said. "Bryn has been making an arrangement to save my life."

"They've agreed to spare him if what we have stated be true," Bryn said. "That at the time Roland turned over the coordinates of their base, he did not know its full nature or that a visiting royal be there. Nor did he know that we would destroy it."

"But how should I prove?" Roland asked.

"You be put to their test, but no harm will come to you they promise."

Roland turned pale. "How can I trust?"

"I be with you to watch that they don't probe too deep. If you had such knowledge, not far they must go; it has been argued well."

"I trust in you," Roland said, only partially relieved. "But what else?"

"One hundred prisoners of theirs we have to return and two hundred bags of gold to give."

"I am humbled you would give so much for me," he said, "and for my Summer."

"You be precious to us," Lira said.

"For me?" Summer said.

"You be to them one now," Lira said. "What they would do to him, they would do to you, which is to explain their goal to take you captive and why this agreement must be honored so dangerous it has become."

"You mean to mind-strip him, don't you?" Summer shouted as she now realized the plan. "I lost one man that way; I cannot lose another. Not Roland. I won't permit it!"

"You must!" Roland said. "They were to take you only hours ago. They will not relent. And me they will murder if they continue to believe I plotted to assassinate one of their royals. It violates the rules these two parties have established in their aggressions and could swing the balance. Earth being what is sacrificed if such aggressions should increase and our home get caught in the middle of their war. No match Earth would be."

"Summer dear," Lira said, trying to comfort her. "Roland will be safe with Bryn and you be safe with me."

She listened carefully as Lira spoke then looked back at Roland who did not sound as familiar as he had once seemed. She detected Lira's and Bryn's odd phrasing in the patterns of his speech, and for the first time fully comprehended that her dear beloved husband belonged to them and their people as much as he would ever belong to her. "Then you must take this risk I suppose, though it will break my heart to see."

"You cannot be there Summer," Bryn forcefully said, although he was struck by her quick turn to courage and sacrifice. "You must let Lira educate you. You have much to learn, but I be impressed that you be prepared so quickly."

"She be very bright and passionate," Lira said.

"I can see she be," Bryn said approvingly. "Lira will take you on a tour of Avian while Roland does this deed." He turned to Roland. "In honor of your willingness to perform such service, the counsel has agreed to make exception this once and let you see what you asked in the Historical Time Machine, but only you and only once."

Roland looked at Summer. "I had asked special permission to see Serpent Mound, its descendants needing the truth of who built it that they may restore their history unjustly taken from them."

"This be a remarkable exception given," Lira said. "None be allowed to enter this time place."

"How will you go back?" Summer asked. "I'm frightened twice for you now."

"No, no my dear Summer. It be not like that," Lira said. "Roland will not go back, but time will be brought to him, at least that be how I've been told it works."

"And that be how it works," Bryn said. "For now, both you and Roland go to sleep and prepare for when we put down. But before you leave me dear Roland, I wish to speak with you alone a few minutes."

"You chose well Roland," Bryn said at their private meeting.

"She is beautiful and sweet with a heart brave enough for adventure," Roland said. "I knew when I met her she was for me."

"I heard you fought for her."

"In my own way. She was about to make a sad mistake with a man unworthy of her."

"She be more than what you see," Bryn said. "Roland, we have told you little of your father. Herold only told you what had become of him to make him act against your mother as he did. But I should tell you more. Your father be a great man among us, a leader of high repute. He never married so busy he be guiding our affairs. Some would say his heart be too great to give to one. He gave it to the many. It be a tragedy what happened to him, to bring a great man low. Which be why we believe the Endron returned him to us in his diminished state rather than kill him outright. They hoped to bend our hearts towards ill. But we endured and so did he until he died, winning dignity still in his lesser state. But until we learned of you, we thought he had died childless. He had a great estate where now his sister lives. And she offers you this gold to assist you until you come into your full estate. The Endron be turned upon you, but we hope their wrath will fade soon or at least be redirected."

"Why do they hate me so?" Roland asked. "I am surprised at how relentless they pursue. Was it the lake base I found?"

"It be that too and something more. That lake base be an important one, so deep it penetrated into their nether world. We took it out at a great loss to them and their plans. But more than the loss of their base, they lost the secrecy of their plan when you discovered and reported that they be mind-stripping humans. We did not know, but now that we do so much be explained. The sudden and rapid decline we have observed in what had been an evolving species. We thought perhaps a virus had begun to depredate their brains, but this explains it better."

"What do they hope to learn from tapping into human minds?" Roland asked. "They are not at war to learn their secrets."

"It be not for that reason they do it. It be for the unfortunate side effects. They be at war with us because they want to enslave them."

"To bend them to their tasks."

"Make them brute beasts. They mean to put back our work of

thousands of years of hastening human evolution by turning their minds to sieves, by making them intemperate towards each other, unable to self-rule, turning their entire planet into chaos. We have wondered at human's inability to even save those things in nature their lives depend upon. So reduced some have become. And with the effects of mind-stripping, those most reduced be the most aggressive in forcing their foolish intemperate wills upon the gentle multitudes. Now we understand, and it be through you we learned. Thus, the Endron upon you have turned their wrath. "

"What am I to do?" Roland asked.

"You do little for now but keep your Summer safe. Teach her our ways. After the trial be over, we will put you down in some obscure place until their tempers soothe. This gold will provide for your sustenance if managed well. Go be with her now."

Summer lay dreaming on a woven mat suspended in the air, draped over with a silken sheet, which provided more warmth than its weight would suggest. Lira must have given her something to rest her spirit, Roland thought. He stood looking at her pretty face framed in golden waves and wondered at the beauty of the girl, so miraculous. He reached down and kissed her ear. "We're flying," he whispered.

"I thought we came down," she said, eyes beginning to open.

"We're flying higher than that."

She looked about. "Where are we? I thought we slept under the trees. Was I dreaming?"

"You must be dreaming now. The trees were days and days ago."

She sat up and spied a window across the strange room she found herself in, a room all silvery with smooth curved walls and a polished mirror-like floor. She noticed the mat she sat upon had no legs but was suspended in the air as if levitating. "I want to see out the window," she said.

"I'll take you to it." Roland helped her jump down from the mat. "Welcome to the universe," he said.

The window revealed the blackest sky Summer had ever seen sprinkled with shimmering white dust.

"Nanodiamonds!" she said as she gazed out of the window.

"It's the Milky Way. Those bright stars out there are the constellation Cygnus. Their home."

"It's beautiful," she said. "Now I remember. That's where we're going!"

Now fully awakened from her dream of love under the trees and seeing the man she loved most, she reached up to him and held on to him tight, so grateful she was for such a perfect state. He drank the scent of lycmthe in her hair and folded her into his arms. The mat like a wave on water undulated beneath them.

Chapter 5

UFO Story Mix-Up

Barry had just gotten out of bed when Neighbor Bill arrived at his front door with the jacket Roland had borrowed.

"He asked me to give this to you before they took off in that spaceship last night," Bill said.

"Why, they're upstairs in bed!" Barry insisted.

"They didn't get outa here soon enough either. That lizard man draggin' Summer off through the backyard like that. The way he grabbed hold of her neck. Why, if it wasn't for Walt and Shadow, she might have been killed."

"What the blazes are you talking about?" Barry shouted.

"Here, I'll show you," Bill said as he tried to lead Barry off of his front porch and out into his yard.

"Okay, but wait a minute while I put on my shoes."

He ran upstairs and saw the unmade bed in the now empty guest room, threw the jacket over his robe, put on his shoes, and followed Bill out into his backyard.

"You can see where he was draggin' her through the snow. Walt got some pictures. You can see them on my computer. Come on over to my house."

The two men trudged through the heavy snow to Bill's back door. Shadow barked.

"It's only us Shadow," Bill said as he opened the door. He turned to Barry. "He's been nervous after what he saw. He got a big bite outa that thing too, all wires and flesh."

"Lizard, did you say?"

"Pale as the dead. Big yellow teeth."

The computer warmed up and last night's photos popped up on the screen, and sure enough....

"He's pretty ugly," Barry said. "It looks like he's got a pretty tight grip on her neck. Is that a hand?"

"All metal. Looks like a claw. Roland called him a cyborg."

"Is she all right?"

"She was all right the last I saw her. Limpin' a little bit, welts on her. Then her husband came back down from the ship and took her up."

Barry collapsed into Bill's chair. "You mean I slept through all of that? I'm getting old!"

"We were up 'cause I've been keepin' an eye on your place. I never believed it was an experimental plane that brought them here. I saw those lit up stairs they walked down. I got Walt over here earlier when I saw Roland beam up. And it's a good thing too. He was ready with his camera and got these pictures." He paused for a moment to study Barry's reaction. "You seem pretty quiet. You look tired. Let me fix us some breakfast. How 'bout some pancakes with maple syrup."

"Any coffee?"

"Sure, I'll put on a pot. Walt will be over here soon. And I expect the boys from WUFOC too."

"WUFOC?"

"World UFO Collaborative," Bill said. "Serious guys."

"Oh, yes, that's who you mean. I met some of them once. Went to a conference they sponsored in Switzerland."

"You did?" Bill said.

"Heard Claudio Postremo speak. He impressed me."

"I've got all of his books if you want to borrow any. Walt is gonna contact *Questers* to hit the TV spot. We got the goods now, and we're gonna make sure everyone knows about it."

"To what end?" Barry asked.

"People have the right to know. That's what!"

"I suppose you're right." Barry replied. But then he thought back to the lecture Postremo gave at WUFOC. Disclosure, he had implied, could backfire terribly. "Roland is a good man. That I am sure of. So whoever he took off with must be good people or he wouldn't be associated with them. They must have their reasons for keeping themselves hidden."

"That gets discussed a lot in the literature," Bill said. "Some think 'cause we're not smart enough. Some think they're up to no good. Others think they're afraid of what we might do to them. Like dropping yourself down into a lions' pit, some of them say."

"What do you think Bill?"

"The folks in my club have been workin' on makin' ourselves smart enough so we can carry on an intelligent conversation with them. That's our goal. The evolution of the human race. So we study a lot of science and all that, but we do it with a more open mind than most of those so-called scientists. Won't they be surprised when they're wrong, and I'm proved right."

"So there's a little payback in your motive. But what if the other theories are right too? That lizard faced cyborg sure didn't act too friendly."

"Yeah, we suspect there's more than one group visiting. Some claim there's a war goin' on among them. We got the proof now."

"But what if most people can't tell the difference between the good and the bad and the lion pit theory proves true? What if our army goes after all of them?"

"They're so far advanced they'd make mincemeat outa us, that's for sure." He paused for a moment, and said, "I see what you mean. This is serious! We gotta keep this thing quiet."

"Good to see you again Barry," Walt said when he arrived with Quentin. "I'm sure Bill filled you in on all the details from last night."

"Yes, he has. It's all a surprise to me. I thought when they hadn't come down yet this morning, that they were still upstairs sleeping."

"I'm surprised you slept through it," Walt said.

"So am I."

"Well, stick around here if you can. I'm sure these guys from WUFOC will want to talk to you. They should be here within the hour."

"If you don't mind, I'll just go over to my house and dress."

"Be quick," Walt said. "You don't want to miss all the action a second time."

"No I don't. Fifteen minutes," Barry said as he went out the back door.

"I don't know about him," Quentin said. "He knew the truth. What's he trying to hide?"

"He's okay," Bill said. "He just told me he was at WUFOC's conference in Switzerland."

"Good, we can check up on him," Walt said. "Let me do it now." He sat down at Bill's computer and ran Barry's name through the WUFOC's membership link. "No Barry Short here."

"He wouldn't have to be a member to go to the conference," Bill said.

"But he would have had to register. Hmm, it says here that Ray Lepont organized that conference. I know him. I'll just go into the kitchen where it's quiet and give him a call on my cell."

"So, what did he say when you told him what happened?" Quentin asked Bill.

"He looked sorta flabbergasted. Sat right down where you're sittin' now. Then he looked kinda resigned and said we should be cautious about tellin' everyone."

"See, he knew all along. He's been holding out on us, but he can't hold out any longer."

"He thinks if our army starts messin' with them we could all be wiped out. It made a lot of sense when he said it."

"That could happen if they're hostile," Quentin agreed.

"He said Roland's guys are okay, but the other ones..."

"Lepont didn't recognize the name," Walt said when he came back into the living room. "He said he kept a close eye on the conference attendees though, and I should email him a photo. I'll get my camera ready."

Bill's doorbell rang. A good-looking brunette stood at the door when he opened it.

"Hi, Gail Barnett," she said as she extended her hand. "WUFOC sent me over here to take a report. Said you had a UFO in your backyard last night?"

"Not exactly. Come on in, come in," Bill said, looking surprised. "It's just that I was expectin' the regional guys from around here."

"I was in Columbus on business and said I would take the call."

"What kind of business are you in Gail?" Walt asked.

"I'm a journalist—science writer. Out west mostly, but I'm expanding. I was just at the university for a demonstration of a new wind turbine design. It looks very promising, very innovative."

Quentin put out his hand. "I'm a graduate student there, working on a masters in electrical engineering and a doctorate is physics."

"And you're a very intelligent looking guy too," she said and smiled. He blushed and shook her hand.

"Sorry for not introducing myself properly," Walt said. "I'm a pilot, corporate jets mostly."

"Oh," she said and smiled. "Maybe if my plane's delayed, you could give me a ride back to Denver."

"At your service!"

The back door slammed, and Barry came in from the kitchen. "Sorry it took me so long, but I had a phone call from Summer's sister and had a lot of explaining to do," he said and smiled at the new visitor. "Sorry for butting in. I didn't know you had guests."

"You know these guys," Bill said. "And this is Gail Barnett. WUFOC sent her over here to take a report."

"Oh, so you are my interrogator," Barry said as if he enjoyed the prospect.

"I wouldn't put it like that. I'm only here to take a report that will be used to determine if any follow-up is needed."

"You mean justified," Quentin said. "Well, if this case isn't enough for a real follow-up investigation, nothing is."

"How 'bout we sit down and talk," Bill said. "I've got some coffee if you'd like some."

"That would be nice."

"Let's get some photos first for our newsletter," Walt said. "Barry, you sit over there on the couch next to Gail."

Barry was happy to oblige, and Walt got his photo, which he promptly uploaded into Bill's computer. "Looks pretty good," he said.

"Any picture would look good with Ms. Barnett in it," Barry said. "It is Miss, isn't it?"

"I'm afraid so. Settling down and journalism, at least the kind I want to do, are not very compatible."

"You like to travel?" Barry said sympathetically.

"Yes, I do. And I want to get into documentary style journalism. That takes money, time, and dedication."

"And a story. Well, we've got a story for you," Bill said, altogether forgetting Barry's admonition to keep a lid on it.

Neither Barry nor Gail noticed that Walt had attached their photo to an email he had just sent to Raymond Lepont.

"So, what exactly did you see?" she asked.

"Throw up those pictures since you got the computer on," Bill said to Walt.

"Oh my god! What is it?" Gail said, staring in horror at the screen.

"We don't know exactly," Bill said. "I just call him lizard man."

"Where's the woman he's got the stranglehold on? I would love to interview her." She paused for a moment. "She survived, didn't she?"

Walt spoke up. "Yes, I chased him off with the help of Bill and his dog here, Shadow."

"Well, where is she then?"

"I don't know where to begin this story or even if it should be told at all," Barry said.

"Heck, I'll tell her," Bill said. "She took off in a UFO with her husband. Both of them are friends of Barry here."

Gail turned on the couch, eyes fixed on Barry. "She took off in a UFO?"

"It's complicated, and I don't know all the details."

"I've got time," Gail said as she turned on her recorder.

"I don't know who that lizard faced creature is or why he tried to snatch Summer. He's not one of the folks Roland is associated with."

"Who is Roland?" she asked.

"Summer's husband. All that I can tell you about him is that he's a scientist at CERN, but I recently learned that additionally he monitors UFO activity. He calls himself a watcher if you've ever heard of them. I didn't know this about him when I was the best man at their wedding, just a month ago in Switzerland. You heard about that big fire over there at the observatory at Jungfraujoch, haven't you?"

"Why of course. Everyone has. You're not saying that had anything to do with..."

"It was some kind of alien attack. Apparently there's a conflict between alien visitors. That cyborg is probably part of the conflict. But why he would grab Summer, I do not know. I actually wasn't there to see it. I was still asleep in bed."

"Oh, so you were sleeping."

"Through the whole thing," Barry said.

She turned back to Bill. "So, this UFO she left in, did it, well, did it land back in that field behind these houses?"

"It didn't land. It hid behind a cloud and sent down a lit up staircase. That's how I found out, but they didn't see me watchin' them. "

"When we confronted them later, Roland tried to say it was an experimental aircraft from CERN," Quentin said. "We believed him for a little while."

"No, you believed that story!" Bill said. "I never did. So I kept watchin' the house and lo and behold, I saw Roland sittin' out there in the snow last night lookin' like he was meditatin'. Here, I'll show ya." He sat down on the floor and awkwardly put himself in a lotus position. "See, he was sittin' like this, and the ship came back and lifted him up in a beam. That's when I called Walt here."

"And when I got over here with my camera that thing there was dragging the girl off. That's how I was able to get these shots. It was pretty darn ferocious. We probably saved her life."

"And how did she leave?" Gail asked. "Did she get in a lotus position too?"

"Heck no!" Bill said. "No, Roland came back down and found her here all limpin' and beat up. He took her back out where I saw him beam up earlier. They both went up together that time."

"Can we go outside so you can show me where all of this took place?"

"Sure," Bill said. "You better put on your coat."

Gail and all four men went outside and trudged through the snow into Barry's backyard with Shadow running beside them.

"This is the tree I hid behind when I watched," Bill said.

"But you never saw the ship?"

"Nope. It was always behind a cloud. All three times."

"Well, we saw one once," Quentin said. "That was the other time."

She looked over at him. "The other time?"

"This didn't just happen once," Quentin said. "Late last summer we saw a ship right here above this backyard beam up some Bio-Nano Robotic mice that had invaded Barry's house."

"I wasn't living here at the time," Barry said. "I was in Europe."

"They were livin' inside the walls. Could walk right through them," Bill said.

"You're losing me here," Gail said. "Let's go back inside. I'm cold as ice."

Bill served the rest of the coffee with some of the fresh cookies he had made.

"Well, I will submit this report right away."

"Don't you want to hear more?" Bill asked.

"I think this is enough for the initial report, and I've got a plane to catch so I had better get going." She quickly packed up her recorder and went to the door. "I want to thank you for being so forthcoming."

"Here, I've printed off a copy of my photo of that thing," Walt said, handing it to her.

"Thanks, this will help," she said as she considered that the creature looked a little overdone, a little over-the-top, maybe photoshopped. "I'm sure WUFOC will get back to you for more follow-up. Again, thanks a lot," she said as she shook hands and exited the front door.

Barry returned to his own house shortly after Gail left. Walt waited at Bill's for a reply from Raymond Lepont. It came quickly.

"Listen to this," Walt said as he read Lepont's reply out loud to Quentin and Bill.

Recognized him immediately. He tried to trick me into believing he was Brad Blanton from Chicago before he realized I know Brad personally. Having failed at that subterfuge, he quickly registered under the name Bob Connors from Chicago. I did my routine questioning that I always do when I see a new face at one of these things. He said he just happened to be in France when he learned about the conference. Said he is in the antiques business. Said he was interested in abduction, but didn't seem to know much about it. So, he's really Barry Short from Delaware, Ohio. I knew he was a fake.

Keep an eye on him. I don't know what he's up to, but you can never be too careful. Keep me posted if you learn anything new.

"I knew there was something fishy about him," Quentin said.

"He seems like a nice enough guy," Bill said.

"A nice enough liar!" Walt said. "Bill, you're just too nice. You lack the critical faculty. We've got to go until tomorrow, but I want you to promise to keep an eye on his house. *Questers* will be here. I don't want him to mess that up. It's our best chance to get this story on television."

"I never stopped lookin' at his house," Bill said. "I been lookin' at it ever since that Roland fellow appeared out of the sky. I won't stop lookin' now!"

"Call us if anything happens over there," Quentin said as he and Walt headed out Bill's front door.

"Harrumph!" Bill said as he shut the door behind them. "I'm not critical enough! Those guys bought that whole experimental aircraft story hook, line, and sinker. I wonder if Barry wants some lunch?" he said to Shadow. "I believe I will ask him to go with me over to Mighty Burgers. Lunch on me. I'll get to the bottom of this."

Gail dropped the car off at the airport car rental, checked in her luggage, and headed for the airport lounge where she wrote up her report on her laptop while she waited three hours before her flight would board. When she was finished, she signed it and included her summation. "Not credible," she wrote, pressed the send button, and ordered her third glass of wine.

Chapter 6

Heart to Heart

"Tell you what. I'll let you buy the burgers if you let me buy the beer," Barry said to his neighbor sitting across the booth.

"I could use a few myself," Bill said. "I don't usually touch the stuff, but after all this, whew."

"It has been intense," Barry said. "Waitress, two half pints to start."

"And two of your Mighty Burger baskets. Maybe some pie later." Bill turned back to Barry, "You can't beat 'em. The best burgers in town."

"This will be my first."

"You haven't been around here much since you bought that house."

"No, I haven't. Been in Europe mostly. Egypt some. I was working a site over in Pennsylvania for a while."

"Are you in construction, an engineer?" Bill asked.

"Oh, no! I guess you don't know too much about me. I'm an archeologist; at least I was when I had a job. I just got back from Paris where I helped curate a museum that houses one of my most important finds."

"What's that?"

"A statue of a goddess found in Egypt. One of my associates actually found her hidden away in the cellar of an old monastery over there. He called me down to help get her out and discover her identity. He was sure her origin was European, and it is...I think."

"So you been in Egypt."

"More than once. I used to have my own dig site there out in the desert near the Pyramids of Giza. I had to leave there too."

"You had to leave?"

"The kind of work I'm in gets complicated. Who has rights to what, and who owns what when it's found. It's complicated."

"You got yourself into some trouble?"

"Sort of, I mean yes I did, but not for the reasons people think. And what about you Bill? What brought you to Delaware or have you always lived here?"

"No, I grew up in Cincinnati. Came to Columbus when I was a young man and newly married. I worked down there 'til I retired. I taught high school math. I moved over here to Delaware because it's easier to get along here on a teacher's pension."

"Math, huh. Not my best subject."

"That's what everyone says. A thankless task teachin' it, but I tried to make it interesting. Some say I did. My students always liked me."

"Any kids?"

"No. Marriage didn't work out. How about you?"

"Never tried marriage. Too busy with my work until now. I'm trying to get hired on to another expedition in Italy soon if I can ever sell this house."

"So, if you're an archeologist and all, what got you into UFOs?"

"Man this burger's good, but the fries are too salty," Barry said. "Waitress, could you bring us more beer and some ketchup?"

"I told you so," Bill said. "The beef's local. Grass fed. So, what got you into UFOs?"

"It was sort of an accident," Barry said. "I wasn't too interested until I heard Claudio Postremo speak. I told you I heard him at that conference in Geneva."

"What brought you there?"

"Well, in part it was you and that near nephew of mine Paul. He sent me a letter recounting the whole event surrounding the Bio-Nano Robots that got into my house. I read it out loud to friends in Paris. Summer was there. And the next thing I knew, just a few weeks later, one of those friends was abducted. At least that's what we thought. So, we went to the conference to learn what we could about abduction. Not much there really, but I happened to hear Postremo. He struck a cord with me."

"So what happened to your friend? Did you figure it out?"

"Sad to say he's not my friend anymore. Oh, maybe I shouldn't say that. He was Summer's boyfriend at the time and then she met Roland and the whole thing broke up. I was forced to choose sides."

"But was he abducted?"

"Yes and worse. He was mind-stripped."

"What? Mind-stripped?"

"I don't know if I should be telling you this, but I will if you keep it in the strictest confidence. Yes, something called mind-stripping. I just learned about it myself. These aliens probe into the mind. The results can be quite damaging. His whole personality changed and not for the better. At first we didn't know what was wrong with him, and I'm afraid the personality change in large part accounts for why he and Summer split up. It was dramatic."

"Mind-stripping, did you call it?"

"Yes, barbaric. They don't all do it. Roland's people don't. But these other ones—probably that cyborg guy you saw—they do it with abandon I've been told."

"Oh, my! What are we in for?" Bill said shaking his head.

"I hope nothing. I hope it was an isolated incident. But if you see any spaceships around, run the other way."

"Was it the guys that put the mice in your house?"

"No, not them. Those were Roland's people. Hey waitress, could you bring us another round of beer?"

"You say Roland's people like he's one of them."

"They hired him on as a watcher to keep tabs on what those other ones are doing."

"A watcher," Bill said and let out a long sigh. "I hope you're right about that."

"Roland? I know I'm right about him. There are few things I would say with complete confidence; but this I can say, Roland is a good man. If anyone can help us out of this mess, he can."

"Hmm, I hope you're right about him too. *Questers* is comin' here tomorrow. You can tell them all about it."

"Bill, promise me not to mention this to *Questers*. If word got out, it could cause an unimaginable panic."

"Okay, but they want to know what went on here. That's all. Your nephew Paul will be there with his friend Andy."

"Paul? Andy?"

"Yeah, they're excited about havin' the kid's angle. They tell me they've got a lot of young viewers. It will help make UFOs hip."

"Hip! I just told you what they did to this man, and they're going to make them hip!"

"This is television we're talkin' about now."

"Oh, I see," Barry sighed and rubbed his chin. "They want entertainment."

"It's television, but it's the best way to get the word out. Get the word out so people will demand the truth from the government."

"So you think they know?"

"Sure they do."

"I'm not so sure," Barry said.

After eating slices of fresh apple pie, Bill left Barry at his front door and called Walt.

"Had a long talk with Barry over lunch. He's okay. Had a friend abducted. That's what brought him to that conference. He's cautious. Has employment problems. Probably didn't want anyone to know he was there. But here's the news—come to think of it I can't tell you on the phone. Don't want to take any chances. What he told me is so mind-boggling it's to be held in the strictest confidence."

Chapter 7

The Time Machine

The ship hovered above the port in the Northeast Quadrant, Region Four of the planet Avian long enough for Summer to climb from her mat and look down through the window at the whole architectural marvel with its silver towers, intricately landscaped garden, and flower shaped docking facility. The silvery flower construction gradually opened its petals, and the ship descended slowly into a large hanger full of ships and the men and women who keep the fleet maintained.

Lira explained while they disembarked that the Northeast Quadrant Port is also the Center of Interstellar Relations where all planning takes place among the Alliance participants and where Roland would be taken to have his memory tried. But as the agreement stipulated, in exchange for Roland's willing testimony, the council had agreed to allow him a look inside time, a privilege nearly unheard of. They traveled across moving sidewalks to the Library of Time, which was housed in a heavily fortified building made of lavender stone.

"I wait for you outside," Bryn said, as the four of them stood in front of the massive door. "Make your goodbyes to Summer."

Roland kissed Summer before entering the vault where he was greeted by the timekeeper, a wizened old man who looked particularly out of sorts.

"I be given only the vaguest direction," the timekeeper snapped. "Earth's North American continent be all that I be told, and it be stipulated that I'm to only give you access to one locale."

"If you have a map, I will help you find it," Roland offered.

A map of the continent instantly appeared as if projected onto thin air in an otherwise empty cavernous chamber.

"It's below these lakes here," Roland said.

The timekeeper pointed his hand with thumb up. An enlargement emerged.

"South of this one, further south," Roland told the timekeeper who mapped his directions. "We are looking for an earthen mound in the shape of a snake nearly hidden by trees."

The timekeeper focused in by moving both hands forward. He slowly went over the enlargement inch by inch.

"That's a small city," Roland said "I think we are near. Maybe further south yet and to the west. There, you've hit upon it."

An aerial view of a large snow covered earthen snake appeared on the screen that looked just as Roland had seen it on the winter solstice. The timekeeper set it in place, focused, and enlarged the image.

"How will this work?" Roland asked.

"Once the locale be marked, I will enter the proper file that contains a set of discrete photos organized to go back in time. When you hit upon a photo where further detail be required, I call it up, in which case a moving picture will emerge depicting the action at that particular moment. You must be selective in your search, however, since time be infinite but our time be not. I might be better able to assist if I know more precisely what you seek to find."

"Where do these photos come from?"

"From our files, as I've already stated."

"I meant before that. Where do you get them to put in your files?"

"We don't make them ourselves if that be what you want to know. All time be recorded. It be an inherent universal process that not even we understand. After we discovered how to retrieve and file these photos and saw for ourselves the aftermath from many past disasters, our job was to learn how to tune time, which we mastered many millennia ago. I must admit at this task we quite excel."

"If you don't take the photography, who does?"

"That's the same as asking who and not what causes gravity."

Perplexed, but eager to move on, Roland asked if it were possible to make copies of the photos.

"It can be done with proper authority. But it be highly irregular, and yet it be highly irregular that you be here at all so I will make this proclamation. I will make photos at your request, but I will leave it to others to decide if you may have them."

"Fair enough," Roland said. "What I seek is knowledge of who built this mound and when and who may have inhabited it since."

"Hmm, that could be difficult. How old it be?"

"I don't know. Some say one thousand years old while others say nine thousand years older. That's one of the questions I hope to resolve."

"Quite a range," the wizened timekeeper said. "As we know, the pictures closest in time will be more accurate."

"Why so? Should they not be equally accurate regardless of age?"

"Of course not!" the timekeeper answered indignantly, and then studied Roland's face. "You be not from here, be you?"

"Of course not!" Roland answered equally indignant. "I'm from this planet we look at now."

"That would explain why you would ask such a preposterous question."

"Preposterous! You think it preposterous to assume pictures in time would be equally accurate of the time rendered? Why do you call that preposterous?"

"I be sorry to offend you. I sometimes forget how ignorant the many be. Hmm, where shall I begin? You do understand that time must be tuned now and again?"

"Tuned, did you say?"

"Yes, that be what I said, did I not?"

"Like a violin is tuned?"

"Something like that. Of course we do our best not to disturb the timeline when we must tune, but it cannot be helped sometimes. The greater the number of adjustments, the greater the likelihood that the picture from the past will be an approximation."

"Call me ignorant if you will, but you must explain yourself better. You say you must tune time, disturb the timeline?"

"To avoid final chaos. Don't you see? Can a violin be harmonic if it never be tuned?"

"Of course not, but a violin is musical instrument. Time is an entirely different matter."

"Consider this analogy. Think of time as a force that plays upon the strings of the universe. The universe, although finely made, like a violin be subject to distortion. When distortion occurs harmony goes adrift. If it goes adrift too far, we set the course right again with our timely tunings. And it be right and proper that we do; but alas, there be some loss following the drift into chaos and the ensuing tuning. Such loss be nearly imperceptible to those affected, so minor it may be. But after countless tunings over thousands of years, well, these losses add up, so they say."

"So what you are saying is the past that you show me may not have occurred."

"What I have said be the further back I take you, the greater the approximation will be from what occurred in that actual moment in time."

"Well, take me back anyway, and let me see for myself what you are talking about."

"I will proceed. Since your initial goal be to see the mound's coming into being, I will begin by taking us back before it existed and then move forward. This may take some time if you would like to visit the drink bar."

"I have brought no money with me," Roland said.

"Here, take my card," said the timekeeper who longed for a few moments of peace, so unused he was to company, particularly company such as Roland's whose understanding of the universe, from this timekeeper's perspective, was no more than a child's.

The bar was fully automated. Not a soul was there so Roland sipped a large glass of mead quite alone before returning to his task.

"This photo I found before the mound came into being," the timekeeper said. "Few trees I note, a barren ridge overlooking a valley."

"How far back are we?" Roland asked.

"I measure seven thousand, three hundred and fifty-six Earth years, but that be an approximation."

"An approximation?"

"I estimate the timeline be adjusted three hundred times or so from this point. That could create considerable distortion. I will go forward slowly." Only seasons changed as scene after scene flipped before them. "I will increase the time intervals between files."

"Stop! Something has changed," Roland said. Before them was the same ridge but with what looked like a large pile of rocks. "A stockpile," he said. "We must go slower now. The building is about to begin."

File pictures flipped forward, the scene unchanged, until everything changed suddenly. Construction was clearly underway.

"Can we open this file and take a closer look? And could you make a copy?"

The file opened and all came to life. Women and men, young and old labored to move the stone. They were small and thick in stature, and they looked strong, very strong as the labor did not look to strain them. They were a handsome people, with thick straight hair and chiseled features. Roland's attention shifted to the construction site cut deep into the ground, outlined by a fibrous rope of some kind tied to rough wooden stakes. He noted they did not work section by section but worked on building the whole effigy at once, starting with small stone on the bottom then larger, and filling in the gaps with even smaller stones and clay soil. And then he noted the appearance of a man who looked different from the rest. Tall he was and majestic, he thought, and clearly in charge. He wore some kind of brightly colored woven cloth and had large feather plumes in his hair while the others dressed plainly in leather. It was two peoples who constructed this mound, Roland thought. But who were they?

"Where are we in time?" he asked the timekeeper.

"Some five or six thousand Earth years back."

"What is that rope made of, and who are these people?"

"Only pictures you see and must deduce from that. And too you must consider this be an approximation."

"What do you mean an approximation? I see them before me as in life."

"You see what would have been with the three hundred or so adjustments we have made. It be hard to say exactly what it be without them."

"You need to explain better. How could your tuning have changed what I see here?"

"All be harmonious," the timekeeper said, "but that harmony may have derived from the tuning. The tuning we do when chaos threatens. At such times, we retune the forces that would otherwise lead to chaos and extinction."

"And you've done this three hundred times since this approximate scene occurred?"

"Approximately three hundred times."

"We were that close to chaos and extinction that many times?"

"Yes, many things can severely unhinge the natural harmony bestowed by the universe, particularly with intelligent minds at work."

"What do you mean?"

"Without humankind, the delicate strings be subject only to natural disasters: floods, fire, the shaking of the earth. In the most severe manifestations a large meteor strike could throw Earth into chaos. Before we learned the art of tuning there be many extinctions brought about by such natural disasters. But with the introduction of human beings on Earth, the episodes increased as a result of the destructive force of manmade conflict and war. It seems to some only a coincidence that we learned the art of tuning with the introduction of human beings, but I and many other timekeepers think rather it be providence. Providence cannot be proved, however, so it be open for debate."

Roland looked at the peaceful scene before him as he struggled to understand. "Are you saying that without your interventions humanity would have gone extinct?"

"That's precisely what I've said. You be turning into a better student than I first expected."

"And this peaceful scene I'm seeing could have been full of bloodshed had these tunings not occurred?"

"Precisely. When we tune a slight adjustment occurs that ripples back. We cannot know for sure what this scene would have been without those adjustments. That be lost because in essence we change all events in time, in most cases very slightly. But what you see in these pictures reflects the accumulative change of three hundred tunings. That be quite a lot."

"So I cannot know the past?"

"Not exactly, but the approximations become more accurate the closer in time to us. Let me take us forward to see what we can see."

They saw the mound nearing completion, and with its completion a celebration ensued with a tall feathered man standing at the head of the snake while others sat along the length of the snake's coils. Roland spotted another tall feathered man standing at the coiled tail. A storm blew up and the man at the snakehead seemed to draw lightning down with an upward held staff. The head was struck in a giant flash of light and yet no one took cover.

"Can I have a photo of this?" Roland asked.

"I will have one made; but be advised, it be only an approximation."

The scene was so like what Roland himself had seen when he visited the Serpent Mound on winter solstice that he was convinced there was far more accuracy in these pictures than not. He marveled to himself of the power of strong traditions to stay intact over so many years, in spite of these people being forced off of their lands and in spite of all the time-tuning and adjustments.

The timekeeper went back to file mode and began flipping through other scenes of celebration, some similar and many taken at sunrise and sunset in better weather with the tall men standing at the snake's head and tail. And then nothing. No one was there, file after file, scene after scene was empty of people. Roland detected a gradual eroding of the mound.

"Where are we in time?" he asked.

"We be two thousand years back," the timekeeper said.

"What happened?"

"I do not know. Maybe the passage of time and the change that comes with it. Rituals change and people change too. Or maybe there be some sort of catastrophic event and these people gone. No wider a range than the mound you be authorized to see."

"Well, take another photo here, and mark the date and flip forward fast."

"I mark the date on all."

The mound remained void of life for many, many years except that the trees grew nearer, when all changed again. The trees were cut back, the mound restored, people had reappeared.

"Where are we in time?" Roland asked.

"A thousand years back."

"Hmm, just as they thought. It's being re-inhabited. More tall men I see, and the ritual has been restored. How would they know from so long ago?"

"Examples we sometimes see in the Library of Time. Traditions are stubborn things to kill. Men die, but tradition not always."

"Photograph this for me, and let's move forward."

The timekeeper having recognized Roland's passion to know had become much fonder of the man. "These photos I take for later consideration I will recommend that you be given."

Scenes similar flashed before them, and then they changed. There was abandonment again.

"Where are we now?" Roland asked.

"Some two hundred years past. We are nearly now."

"Take us to the present then."

And there it was, the Great Serpent Mound just as Roland had seen it. His visit in time had ended.

Chapter 8

Avian

If the silvery port of the planet Avian was all metallic and bold in design, Lira and Summer's boat was quite the opposite. It was made of painted wood and weathered steel and powered by a simple paddle of the old fashioned kind, a rear water wheel that pushed the boat forward once it was set in motion. The boat was mostly flat and painted white with a large platform made comfortable by cushions and covered with a mint green canopy that shaded the women from two afternoon suns, the fullness of one sun seeming to follow the other as the first lowered on the horizon. They relaxed and enjoyed the scenery as the boat glided slowly along the twenty-five mile cruise to the city.

The land was marshy and flat, abundant with graceful trees whose limbs hung down to weep over the many flowers that grew freely. Lira pointed to the white lycmthe growing wild in the green marshy fields as far as the eye could see. Near to the shore were enormous white lilies mixed in among the reeds, very Earth-like but larger with their great, wide stalks to keep them upright. Scents of the lilies and lycmthe clung to the air making each breath a balm. Countless birds fluttered past while others perched in trees, except for the swans, most regal in their bearing, which floated past their boat as it moved silently toward the city. Summer could barely speak so transfixed she was by the beauty.

"Avian be a water planet," Lira explained. "We inhabit islands between great bodies of blue, but as you can see even this island we ride through be much composed of it."

"Do they flood like in Venice?" Summer asked.

"Temperate be our rains, as mists they come, and they come often but never heavy. So, to answer your question, no. We have no floods."

Summer looked over the side of the boat into the clear water. "It's so clean!"

"What would you have?" Lira asked. "Would you choose to live in a dirty room?"

"Not by choice, of course, but oil leaks and coal blackens."

"It does," Lira said, "so we see on your Earth. But here our power comes from our abundant water and our two suns."

"You power your spaceships that way?"

"We've learned to store the sun."

"What are they?" Summer asked pointing to a herd of horned animals.

"Like your deer they wander everywhere."

"I see no farms here."

"They be largely located in the Southeast Quadrant along with what be associated with them." Summer looked at her curiously. "We organize differently than you do on Earth. The Southeast be our best land for agriculture. On the margins of those lands be our food packing industry along with our cloth making industry, along with our clothes making industry. All that be grown on the land and made from what be grown comes from there, except for the house gardens people make for themselves. Our science, art, education, and technology institutes and governing bodies be here in the Northeast for so much water be here it be not good to grow. Next to us in the Northwest, metal and wood industries thrive and below in the Southwest we leave wild."

"This looks pretty wild to me," Summer said.

"It be as much as can be. We think it better not to try to bend nature when it be as gentle and sublime as it be here. That be not always the case on other planets we've visited where nature be threatening by the forces of its own being or sometimes driven to ruin by the Endron. That be the saddest to behold, and that be what they would do to your Earth. But here we exist with each other harmoniously, and see no reason to do otherwise."

"If you can do that, why not they?"

"The Endron? That has puzzled us for centuries. Many papers be written on that subject and delivered to the places of governance here. Many proposals have been tried, but all have failed. I am of the opinion that it be as much in their nature to be as they are as it be ours to be as I am. And I'm not easily changed for it be my character. That be the conundrum we find ourselves in plain and simple. In the last century we have at least been able to fashion the rules to which we be both pledged to abide. That has lessened the tension if not stopped the war."

"And if Roland had broken those rules?" Summer asked.

"It would be ruinous."

"And what would happen to him?"

"If he was to be proved to have done such a deed, he would be sacrificed."

"To the gods?"

"No, we don't abide such things. To the Endron."

"It seems to me that doing such would be as bad as throwing him into a volcano".

"You do have your opinions!" Lira said and smiled. "Roland be innocent. He will not be harmed."

While Summer was convinced of the former, she was still in doubt about the latter in spite of Lira's protestations otherwise.

Roland was taken aback when he was placed under arrest like a criminal. Bryn had not prepared him because Bryn did not know Roland would be treated as such, the council members from Avian being so convinced of his innocence. What he had not counted on was the Endron's success at politicking the other planet members who themselves knew what calamity would befall them if Roland was guilty and not prosecuted with swift justice. To appease the Endron terror, they had convicted Roland already in their minds if he could not prove his innocence.

The trial began with the Endron pleading their case. Witness after witness testified as to the fine character of the deceased royal, incinerated by Alliance warships unjustly and against the rules. After hearing a variety of witnesses from the court upon which the royal had sat, his family was brought on. Aunts and cousins, followed by parents and grandparents and his own children grieved for him before the council's eyes. And then at the end of such testimony his own dear widow, so wracked with pain she had to be helped up to the testimony pulpit where she wailed and cried of her loss so eloquently that the members of the council were themselves in tears.

And if the judges were not moved enough by this spectacle, the prosecution brought on witnesses that were at the scene of the assassination, as they called it, who had survived. They gave witness to what they had seen, the gruesomeness by which their royal had died, blown nearly to smithereens as he valiantly fought to put out the flames that engulfed him. And once he became smithereens, the rest that followed reduced him to ashes. There was so little of him left his family could not put on a proper burial. The family all began to wail again as they heard this testimony. Inconsolable, they looked at Roland with hate in their eyes.

To close, the prosecution projected photographic evidence high up on a screen for all in the courtroom to see. Roland, in the company of several men, had been caught by the base's security cameras searching about the lake's rim. On a second occasion he was filmed there unawares, alone with a woman who later would become his wife, as if that fact were evidence of some sort of strange calculation. Close-ups were projected of the device he used for measuring followed by the final proof, a photo of Roland knee deep in water, standing at the drop off to the Endron base while taking the full measurement down.

"Conclusive proof!" the Prosecutor shouted. "It be this man seated before you who be responsible for the gruesome death of our dearly departed royal. He be a deceiver! He violated all custom and rules! Case closed!" he declared.

The council judges were so overwrought the Presider called for a continuance until the next day. Roland was lifted off his seat by guards to be taken into confinement in jail.

Bryn was overwrought but for different reasons. The testimony had taken a different turn than he expected, tainted with the grief of loss to bolster weak evidence. He should have known, he thought, that the Endron would be up to their tricks. What else, he wondered, would they have in mind to undermine Roland's credible testimony? Or worse yet, would they seek to destroy his mind when he was probed as they had probed his father. He would have to guard him well. He sent a message to the town port where his wife would soon dock. "Do not return," the note said, "The trial unexpectedly will continue yet another day. Find a place to stay for the night."

As the trial was closing, Lira and Summer floated towards the town. Seeing it ahead it reminded Summer of somewhere else she had been.

"It looks like Holland. Look at all the windmills!"

"Watermills my dear, if you look closely. We grind our wheat near our cities, the demand being great for flakey pies and buttery shells."

The similarities became even more remarkable once the canal entered the town and intersected with other canals jutting off from side to side leading down similar streets, all lined with tall townhouses with pitched and gabled roofs and windows with flower boxes abloom.

"I love it here!" Summer said. "If I did not know better, I would think I was in Amsterdam where I lived for a short time."

"We borrow dear from our sister planet when we delight in what Earth invents, and then we modify to meet our needs. We dock soon, so prepare to visit an hour or two before we return."

Lira received the note from Bryn when they put in to dock. Not wanting to trouble Summer more she made nothing of it.

"Since you so like this place, we shall stay the night so I might show you more of life here. I will call for rooms at the inn."

"But what about Roland? He will be expecting me."

"He will be fine. I will tell Bryn our plan."

Lira waved a bicycle taxi to carry them to the inn.

"This is so pleasant," Summer said, her hair blowing in the breeze. "How do you keep this place so clean?" she asked noting how clear the water remained even inside the town, how sweet the air still smelled, how little litter she saw laying on the ground.

"By not getting it dirty in the first place. Or when we do at celebrations and such, cleaning it up."

"That makes sense," Summer said, embarrassed at how ridiculous her question must have sounded to someone so highly evolved.

"We shall take to our rooms for a little while so we can get refreshed. Then I take you out for dinner. Here be the coin that will open your door. I be just down the hall. When you hear me knock, we will go."

Summer went to her room and collapsed on an old fashioned bed. No mat suspended in the air here. Not recognizing how tired she had become and thinking she would only rest a bit, she fell soundly asleep.

Lira meanwhile set out to speak with Bryn. She phoned several inns at the Port, but he had not checked in. Finally she called a council member friend who told her Bryn had scheduled meetings with the Avian council throughout the night and would probably sleep in a chair in the lounge.

"Why so?" she asked. The councilwoman told her what had transpired in court that day. Lira sighed and grew grim.

"Be assured," her friend said. "Roland be innocent and would prove his case once he be able to speak."

"He has not spoken yet?"

"He be shut out by the wailing of kin."

Lira sighed again, and then told the councilwoman where she was staying and to tell Bryn.

Lira tapped on Summer's door and grew panicked when there was no reply. Would she be safe, she asked herself, if Roland failed to convince? She tapped again and heard the girl say weakly, "Come in."

"Up, you must be. You can sleep when we return from our meal. I want you to taste the local delicacies. Pastry pies you must try. They be very delicious, and my cook lacks the skill to make them on the ship so I look forward too."

The two women left the inn and were out upon the street when for the first time Summer realized there were no vehicles with engines.

"Our weather is temperate and we build our cities small and compact. No need for such things," Lira explained. "Our principle be to go fast, very fast when we must, but otherwise the opposite. It keeps the blood pressure down, and be one of the ways we learned to keep a long life."

"It's more quiet too," Summer said, "and keeps the air clean. But what's this?" she said looking into a shop window filled with hand painted pictures of birds.

"Oh, they be tatouage," Lira said, looking slightly embarrassed. "A custom we have here I have seen nowhere else."

"What is the custom? I might want to practice it myself. They're beautiful to look at."

"Look more closely."

"The birds seem all to be mating and nesting," Summer said upon closer inspection. "What did you say the custom is?"

Lira looked about the street and spied a place across the canal where young people were gathered outside the door. "You will see. I will take you over there before we eat."

They crossed a bridge over the canal and walked back down the street to the establishment and entered into the crowd. "You sit here," Lira said. "I will get us mead to makes us less conspicuous."

Summer looked about while Lira went to get them glasses of mead and soon realized she was in an Avian bar with live music of an acoustic kind, romantic croons, and lovers dancing. And then she spied what she had seen in the window, lovely pictures of beautiful birds. But these were painted on the up pushed breasts of young women, girls some of them, teenagers in looks. The shifts they wore were much like her own, long and A-line, with sleeves straight from the elbow down and delicately puffed at the shoulders and in all the rest. But in hers the neckline was modest while in theirs it was low, some extremely so. They all wore the birds painted on their chests, as she would wear pearls.

"You've noticed, I see," Lira said when she set the mead down.

"A fashion style?" Summer asked.

"More than that, a courting fashion. They wear them to attract a partner."

"But some of these girls are so young. Look over there. She looks no older than sixteen if that."

"And well she might be," Lira said.

"At least her painting is more tender," Summer said. "Her birds are delicate like love birds I suspect although I don't know your species here. But look at that one over there, her breasts large and nearly bare, her birds all gold and yellow and red. They are copulating!"

"You be shocked, I can see," Lira said.

"I didn't expect this. I thought you a higher type than ourselves."

"Biology be biology no matter where you be. We've adapted to it, and these children have made this ritual their own. See how the boys flock about and look before offering food to a girl of their liking."

"You encourage this?"

"Yes and no," Lira said. "For those who be afflicted young with urges strong we do. We encourage them to marry early."

"But their education?"

"Nothing be sacrificed in that. They can go as far as they can compete. We provide for them all in that regard, single or not."

"But if they should have children? These nests full of eggs I see upon some breasts would indicate that desire."

"And it be so for many," Lira agreed. "But we provide for their children as well. We are organized differently here than on Earth, you see. We learned long ago not to try to fight biology because to do so can lead to behaviors far less acceptable than early marriage. And yet there be risks involved."

"Early marriage, early divorce," Summer said

"Not so drastic as that. Well trained they all be in the art of blissful marriage, which some have argued has increased youth's longing for it. But even with all of their training, some marriages prove more blissful than others. See how cautious the boys be as they look about, cautious and tantalized both."

"Boys on Earth are not cautious when girls present themselves such," Summer said.

"Boys on Earth be not afflicted as our boys be, which makes our boys far more cautious since all of their happiness depends on the choice they make."

"Do you not allow divorce?"

"We do, but that would leave a man in a loveless state, so divorce be not sought after much."

"What do you mean?" Summer asked. "They could find someone else. Look at all of these girls here advertising themselves as willing and ready."

"Our men," Lira explained, "be able to only love one. Once they have chosen a mate and consummated that love, there can be no others. Emotionally, biologically, they be not capable. So you can see they be in earnest to make a wise choice. Many will wait. Better the odds of achieving sacred love all statistics show as one matures and becomes more able to choose well. But for some the urges be so strong that waiting becomes an impossibility. Which is why these girls display themselves so, to tempt these boys out of good sense. Of course, many of these boys never had good sense to begin with. But since the risks to them be far greater, they be more cautious."

"And if these girls could not attract a mate?" Summer asked.

"That be rare, but they have been known in the past to sell themselves for sex on planets where the men be not so afflicted or to offer themselves as concubines to warrior men who live as outcasts in camps, so dangerous they be to civil life. And dangerous too to the women who venture there I have been told. Which is why early marriage here be condoned, permitted, and encouraged by the most enlightened among us. And we go to great lengths to educate the boys and girls in marriage so that even if the match be less than perfect, they will be happy enough, attentive to each other's needs for the sake of their own happiness if nothing else."

"Who are these warrior men of whom you speak?"

"Those who have been reduced through mind-stripping as Roland's father be, who have formed a society of their own more conducive to their liking."

"And they're different from the rest? They can love more than one?"

"As many as they want, if you call that love," Lira said. "They be like our ancient forefathers, primitive men, driven by impulse and lust. They lack high intellect, the reason given for the affliction of our men. As the intellect increases, prurience decreases, leaving in its wake pure love, but only for one."

"And why are not the women afflicted too? Do they lack high intellect?"

"A hotly debated point you bring up. Some of our greatest thinkers be women, and they be most revered in spiritual life too. I will take you to these in the morning. But look around you at some of these girls. That one you pointed to who bears her breasts with brightly painted copulating birds. It be a measure of the urge that be driving her to do so for she be not taught this. And that is how it be explained. Nature has made some so, not all, not even many, but enough like her to guarantee the continuance of our race. And look how the boys flock to her, suitors all. She will have her pick, be well cared for, and produce many children. And thus we would rather have her wed early than tempted into a low state."

"And the sacred love you spoke of," Summer asked.

"It can only be achieved with a perfect match. The wise say there be only one perfect match for each of us, so it be rare that they find each other. And then the male must have studied hard the art of love without the experience. So that makes it doubly rare. But when it be achieved—tell me Summer, you have experience enough to compare."

Summer turned red. "Is that what it is. I have no words for it."

"That's what it be my dear and so you be blessed."

"I once showed Roland a painting while in Paris of Leda. She and her swan touched minds, and all their physicality was painted so they were perfectly in sync, although he a swan and she a girl. And the angels were coming to place the crown of heaven upon them."

"Yes, my dear. That's what it be. You have more delight than any of these girls will ever have. Come now. We will eat pastries filled with the most succulent sauces, dumplings, and vegetables you can imagine. And we will drink more mead and sing."

"I'm already dizzy it's so strong!"

Summer rose late the next morning, so tired she had been that Lira let her rest awhile longer. She went to the window and delighted in what she saw, the clean, clear canal below busy with boats, walkers, and bicyclists. She was eager to join the day's activities so she quickly dressed and went to Lira's room.

"You be up!" Lira said. "We will have a roll and be off."

"Have you heard from Bryn?"

"Not today. I'm sure all be fine. You will love our breakfast rolls if you like croissants; they be flakey and buttery too."

And indeed Summer liked them as she liked nearly everything about Avian, except she was not sure what she thought about the girl who painted her breasts for display in so obvious and coarse a manner. The other girls' chests were pretty enough. A nice accessory, she thought, those painted love birds, suggestive in their own way but not too much.

"You be still troubled by that?" Lira said. "Where I take you today may give you insight, although I like you would never wear such garish birds. But we be many and varied and have different roles to play."

They walked along the canal, Summer peering into the windows of shops filled with books, pastries, fashion, and more tatouage. Most were the same as she saw the night before, hand painted birds in various stages of love and procreation, but some were of a different type. She recognized the graceful swan but not the others. Some held out furled scrolls within their beaks, and some looked to be warbling a tune, but there was a painting high up that caught her eye. Was it bird or woman? It was hard to choose. Plumage substituted for hair, and yet the features were that of a feathered woman, with large oval eyes and an aquiline nose.

"Who is she?" Summer asked.

"A rendering of the Bird Goddess. I will take you there."

They crossed the canal on a pedestrian bridge and walked out into a large green space surrounded by lovely buildings whose architecture spoke of their importance.

"These be institutes of higher learning," Lira said. "You might call this a campus. I will take you to the museum of culture, a sacred place and very old, so that you will better understand us."

They followed a walkway that took them to a brick hub in the center of the green from which pathways shot out like spokes. A large brick and stone edifice stood down the pathway they took that to the very last detail looked like the medieval architecture one can see on Italy's Campo in Siena including the buca pontaia: scaffolding holes left as part of the construction process. Summer saw birds nesting in the buca pontaia and more birds perched in the weeping trees that surrounded the palace.

"They're everywhere!" she said.

"Yes, The Palace of Birds. You must slip off your shoes when we enter."

Frescoed bird scenes adorned the high vaulted ceilings. Elsewhere birds were carved, chiseled, and painted on pillar and post. The floor where they walked was composed of mosaic scenes of women with birds and birds with women as if the two were one. The whole grand hall was surrounded with small alcove chapels each with a golden bird carved at its entrance.

"Why birds?" Summer asked.

"Come, I take you on a tour and explain. Think of what they do?"

"They fly, they coo, they nest," Summer said.

"And more. Why do trees invariably grow along a fence if left unattended? And why does a new pond without fish become stocked once the birds start to visit? It's miraculous when you think about nature's birds. They spread the seed of life from place to place. And they be known for even more. This should not seem foreign to you. Our two worlds have shared more than seed over time, and your religion celebrates the dove."

"Now this one I would like to wear, so beautiful she is and graceful too," Summer said as she stood with Lira before a beautifully carved statue of a woman, all feathers and plumage.

"Ah, but most be not allowed to paint her upon the breast as common birds are painted."

"Why not? "

"She be the Bird Goddess! Not for procreation she be used like her common sisters. She be the Bird of Life. Only a very few be permitted to render her or wear her upon their chests. Look at mine," she said, and opened the buttons on the top of her dress.

"Why, she's beautiful!" Summer said, looking at the portrait of a goddess, her features lovely and refined, her plumage soft blues and yellows and greens. "She looks nothing like what we saw last night."

"I wear her close to my heart to keep my heart full, not to display or attract."

"And not everyone can?"

"Only those whose hearts have been tested and have earned the privilege. She be permanent tatouage. The other, what the girls wore last night, be only paint. They will wash it off when they've achieved their ends. Here, I show you renderings of the lessor goddesses they invoke."

Lira brought Summer to a painting in one of the alcoves whose colors were garishly bright. "Some think she be tasteless," Lira said.

"Her plumage looks quite tropical, but I still don't understand."

"It be biology my dear, crude sometimes it be. Bright plumage attracts."

"But why don't they simply wear provocative clothes, brightly colored if that's to their taste?"

"The birds suggest fertility."

"The nests full of eggs," Summer said. "I see, but I don't understand."

"I will make myself plain. It be the plight of our planet that few fertile girls remain, and yet they all want to be and advertise as such. That big bosomed girl with bright copulating birds on her breasts, she be a good prospect and wants it known."

"Oh, I see, that she can reproduce."

"I do not doubt. She looks readily made for it."

"Has it always been so?" Summer asked.

"It began only a few hundred years ago. It be not always so clean here. We poisoned our race before realizing what we had done, the decline being so gradual. Have you not noticed how uncrowded it be? And small children rare? Girls like you saw last night be our salvation, and those of you from Earth we mate with. You cannot know how special you be Summer, Roland too, and the two of you together."

Summer was afraid to ask for further explanation. Instead the two women wandered from alcove to alcove, looking at different renderings of lessor goddess birds. Until at the end of the procession Summer spied something astonishingly different, what looked like a pregnant Black Madonna on a golden pedestal in a clam shaped alcove.

"Who is she? I've seen her likeness before."

"She be the Virgin Expecting," Lira said.

"Like Mary?" Summer said.

"Older, older than even the Bird Goddess. It be said that she keeps all the worlds within her womb. Some call her the future. In the past she let the present be made when she gave birth to the Bird Goddess and then reached into her womb and took some seeds, which she gave to her before sending her out into the void. The Bird Goddess took the seeds from here to there, dropping them along the way. That be the beginning of all that we know. The rest that keeps the virgin so full and round be the future that lays hidden. Only the Bird Goddess knows, and she keeps the Virgin's secrets."

"That's an interesting creation myth," Summer said.

"Myth it may be, but its meaning be true. The essence of woman in her higher state be to spread the seeds of life and wisdom so others never do what my ancestors did to Avian, that we never poison the life that we make. To guess the future and act before it be made we are called upon. You could call this women's intuition or insight or some such phrase. We call it prophetic sight and praise the practice and all those who practice it."

"Who practices it?"

"As many as try. I do, and so should you. It be our gift Summer, my dear cousin."

Summer thought about what Lira had just said. And as if it had suddenly grown dark and chill, she felt the cold veil of night drop over her. She looked at her ring and became faint and would have fallen had Lira not grabbed her and held her up.

"Be you all right?" Lira asked.

"I am," Summer said as she righted herself. "But Roland is not. I must go to him."

"We will leave now."

"Do you know a faster way than we came?"

"I do," Lira said, noting the seriousness with which Summer spoke. "We can take the portal."

The women rushed from the museum and Lira led them back to the center of the green and down another path that led to stairs and an underground station. She bought their tickets for the first train to the port. "The train arrives in ten minutes. Another fifteen minutes we be there."

"So fast!" Summer said. "Why didn't we use it to come here?"

"Fast, but not as pleasant. Think of all you would have missed!"

When Roland returned to the courtroom he saw the mind-stripping device in place, a long glass tube cell surrounded by a glass screen not yet activated. He recognized it from the drawing Etienne had made and knew the damage it was capable of both from his studies and what it had done to his own father and Etienne. All animation left his deep blue eyes, leaving only steely trepidation as if he were looking at the means of his own execution. He flinched and turned away.

Bryn tried to comfort him with a consoling gaze, but Roland's eyes did not see, his head bent so low to see nothing but the floor. So Bryn used the words of his opening remarks to try to do what his eyes could not.

"The court must recognize the horror of this device to this man who lost his father to it. And yet," he said to comfort him, "Roland would not exist if his father had not been lost that way."

Roland looked up. Bryn walked over and stood next to the machine. "This device can reveal the truth for all to see. Pictures from his mind will play upon the screen, more complete, more thorough than the photographic evidence the prosecution has selectively shown. This be why we have allowed it. But I want those of you here as witness to make no mistake. This machine used improperly be very, very dangerous. So dangerous, the Alliance refuses to use it even in interrogating prisoners from combat. For if it probes too deep, it unhinges, leaving the victim's mind severely deformed as a consequence."

"Nonsense!" the Prosecutor shouted.

"Nonsense, no! Our doctors who have treated these victims can speak to this. So I have asked the court that I may monitor close and release this man at any sign such may be the case."

"You only choose to stop it if it incriminates!" the Prosecutor said.

Bryn looked up at the Presider.

"That be not what we be here for," the Presider said. "We want truth. But Bryn be correct. This experiment could be dangerous. Thus, his wish I have granted. He has the right to petition to intervene. Without that guarantee, this machine will not be permitted."

The Prosecutor remained silent after that threat. Seeing there were no more objections, the Presider nodded towards the guards, who lifted Roland from the accused's chair and brought him to the long glass tube, opened it, and pushed him inside. The machine was activated.

Rows of large watery eyes appeared nearly surrounding the tube; there were eighteen in all. As the probe began, Roland could feel the eyes boring into him at first not painfully. But as they went further back into his mind to capture the past, some pain began.

Projected onto the screen for the courtroom to see in fast motion were photos taken from his mind, the most recent first, then gradually going back in time. The pictures were of him, what he thought and what he felt, and intimate they were. Every detail of his lovemaking was large upon the screen so paramount it had been since he was wed. But along with kisses and caresses his heart could be seen in the tenderness with which he looked upon Summer.

Everyone present saw all of this. And they saw him at Serpent Mound too, a place altogether foreign to them. And they saw him engaged with strangers there, and the compassion with which he responded to their account. And all nearly screamed when they saw what he saw when he plunged back to Earth from the sky with only a wing and holding his beloved to protect her dear life from the fall. And after that they too saw the warship in the sky peering out from behind a cloud. Their honeymoon night the courtroom saw too, and the couple's wedding so simple and full of love.

The Prosecutor could see that all in the courtroom except Endron were falling in love with this man, and he started to worry. Further back the mind pictures went to scenes already revealed in prosecution photos of Roland taking measurements at the lake. I've got him now, the Prosecutor thought. But what was revealed here that was not in the photos earlier shown was the measurement Roland took of Summer that fateful day as he followed her out to the lake. It was she on his mind, not the lake, not the base, nor thoughts of revenge. It was just as true in the next photos flashing on the screen of the day in Switzerland when he first took the case. Not the case, not the lake, not the Endron occupied his mind as much as Summer, who he had only just met.

The courtroom sighed in joy, tender love in such detail they had never before seen. At such swooning and sighs, the Prosecutor feared he had lost the case through his own device and plotted his final strategy to take revenge.

"This be enough!" Bryn said. "There be no more evidence to show."

"Further we must go!" the Prosecutor demanded.

"But that be the beginning of the episode. There be not more to it," Bryn argued.

"I demand to see if that be so!"

"If it will satisfy," the Presider said, "continue further back."

Deeper the eyes probed past his work at CERN, which to Roland was of little consequence, to another eventful scene. A grieving boy at his mother's funeral taken away by strangers, he by her side and fetching medicines when she was still alive, and then the moment of her rape as she had described it to him. A pretty girl, still a youth, attacked from the sky by a lascivious swan that with no mercy ripped opened her dress and penetrated deep.

The courtroom was aghast and cried out in anger at the scene playing before them. Tears flooding his eyes, fists clenched as he endured excruciating pain, Roland went limp and fell against the glass.

"Stop this madness now!" Bryn demanded.

"Why? What are you afraid of?" the Prosecutor shouted back.

"He be innocent!" someone shouted out from the courtroom. The Presider pounded his gavel finding it hard to gain control.

"You do this with intention!" Bryn shouted and looked to the Presider.

"I must consult with council judges," the Presider said.

"You said I be the judge of what will harm him!" Bryn demanded.

"What you ask disrupts serious testimony. I must consult."

The courtroom jeered.

A woman appeared with the accused's now empty chair held high over her head and flung it hard at the glass tube. The tube shattered into a web of cracks and fell to pieces scattering across the floor, freeing Roland, who being no longer held up by glass collapsed into Summer's arms.

Outraged voices among the Endron were muffled by sobs and cheers as the courtroom applauded the heroic act. The Presider pounded his gavel and ordered the guards to arrest Summer while Lira looked on from the back of the courtroom pleased. She thought back to the girl she had first met, alternately homesick and weeping, now true to her heart and strong.

The council judges rose from their seats and made a pronouncement, deliberation having been swift, only five minutes long. "Not guilty," they said over the objection of one judge who dissented, an Endron.

"Not just!" he shouted back, "this trial be not ended."

"It be ended because we declare it so," another judge argued. "He shall go from here free and she too," he said and ordered the arresting guard to let Summer go.

The Presider put his gavel down and the courtroom clapped. The Endron, outnumbered, continued their verbal attack as Lira, Bryn, and a guard helped Summer take Roland from the room.

"We must go now while we can," Lira said as she hurried Summer along, the weight of Roland leaning hard upon her. Bryn came to her aid, and the four of them quickened their pace to the ship.

The dash for the ship is the last thing Summer remembered of that day. The rest was veiled in fog, with only the high melodic humming of Lira's song wafting through the mist.

Chapter 9

Questers

Questers, the bus advertised in gigantic red letters as it rumbled along Barry's quiet street. Blinds came up. Neighbors peered out of their windows, rushed outside onto front lawns now soggy from melting snow. Its brakes rubbed and squealed when the yellow monster parked itself in front of Neighbor Bill's house, taking up a full traffic lane. Barry looked out of his window then stepped outside onto the porch just as Paul and Andy rode up on bicycles.

"Hi Uncle Barry. Wow, look at that!" Paul said, his bike spilling to the ground, and he taking off to get a better look at painted images of planets and asteroids hurtling through space, flying saucers, big eyed ETs, a hairy Bigfoot, and even the Loch Ness Monster poking its long neck out of the Scottish lake by the same name. Andy nodded and leaned his bike against the porch railing before he ran after Paul.

"What have I gotten myself into," Barry muttered, as he stepped back inside to answer his phone. It was Bill telling him to come on over. Walt and Quentin were already there, along with *Questers'* production manager and directors.

"Come in, come in. I've got coffee and cookies," Bill said to Barry. "Don't be shy. I want you to meet the show's impresario, Wes Barnes."

"Sir, call me Wes," Mr. Barnes said as he stood up to shake hands dressed in his stock-in-trade plaid shirt with bolo tie, cowboy boots, and tan suede jacket. "I hear y'all got quite a story for me."

"Oh, sit down," Barry said, "there's no formality here among friends."

Paul and Andy had been in the middle of giving their account of what had happened the night they discovered the alien mice residing in the walls of Barry's house when Barry's entrance had interrupted. They began again.

"They were bigger than a mouse and kind of angular not round. And there were a whole lot of 'em," Paul continued. "And they had real big eyes with rims around them like a raccoon."

"And they moved together in unison like a peloton of bikes," Andy said.

"That's a good image," the show's art director said. "I think we can recreate that. You say they scurried through the walls, not holes in the walls?"

"Just disappeared into them," Paul said. "We looked, and there weren't any mouse holes."

Wes turned to Barry.

"I didn't see any of this," Barry said. "I was out of the country at the time. Paul here sent me a letter describing the whole event."

"But it's your house," the set director said. "Do you mind if we film there to lend a degree of verisimilitude. You do know our show creates reenactments. The more realistic the details, the more believable it will seem to our audience."

"No, I don't mind. I'm trying to sell the house. If you could get a plug in, that might help."

"Take note of the man's request," Wes told his writer.

"So your dog here flushed out these—what did you call them— Bio-Nano mice? And a saucer hovering over the backyard beamed them up?" the set director asked.

"Bio-Nano Robotic mice," Quentin said. "And actually it was my ultrasonic equipment that did the trick. We learned from the dog here that these things were sensitive to high frequencies, so I borrowed the equipment from my lab and set it up. That's what drove them out."

"Okay, first the dog's howl and then the device," the set director said. "And then a few months later you saw another saucer located above the same backyard only this time a man and a woman were climbing out of it?"

"His friends," Bill said pointing his finger towards Barry. "They come walkin' down a lighted stairway like they were comin' out of a cloud. I hid out there behind some trees so they wouldn't see me. And that's how they left too. Only they got beamed up just like the mice."

"So you think the same extraterrestrials were responsible?" the writer asked.

"Sure of it," Bill replied. "They came back, and they'll come back again."

"And what do y'all think?" Wes asked.

"Well, I didn't see any of it," Barry said. "Roland told me they flew over here in an experimental aircraft. As far as I know, they left in one too. Roland's a scientist, you know."

"No sir, I didn't," Wes said.

"He works at CERN," Quentin said.

"CERN?"

"The European Organization for Nuclear Research. They've got that Hadron Collider over there."

"Oh, I see, a scientist. What about that picture you took of a cyborg or lizard or something?"

"I've got it right here on this computer," Walt said as he put it up on the screen.

"Look at that thing's eyes! Red as the devil," Wes said.

"I think that's the effect of the camera flash," Walt said.

"And those teeth! Did you get all that?" Wes said to his art director. "Big yellow teeth, red eyes, and it's sickly pale and scaly."

"Yeah, I got it."

"The girl?" Wes asked.

"That's Summer," Barry said.

"Pretty. Real pretty. Here's our story men. What everything else will lead up to. Cyborg man and beautiful blond. Give me a sketch of this," he said to his art director. "Perfect, the story everyone loves: Beauty and the Beast, Fay Wray and King Kong. It gets 'em every time. Ugly cyborg falls for beautiful blond Earth girl."

"He wasn't actin' like he was fallin' for her," Bill said. "I thought he was gonna kill her."

"Y'all want an audience for your story, don't you?" Wes said. "This is how you gotta play it. Good story, good production values is the name of our game. Pull their heartstrings and inflame their fear, and I guarantee you we will have America watching. We'll play this angle up in ads for a month or two in advance."

"Okay, as long as you get to the heart of the story," Walt said.

"Can our makeup people replicate this thing?" Wes asked his art director. "That scaly skin, red eyes, and yellow teeth?"

"Sure, make me a copy of this photo?"

"I'll print it off now," Walt said.

Wes closed his laptop and returned it to his beaded leather bag, signaling to his writer, set director, and art director that they were done for the day. "Thank you boys. This will be great," he said. "We'll get to work on it right away." His assistants followed suit, packing up their own.

"You're leaving?" Walt said. "But I've got a whole lot more to tell you. I've been working up some theories about all this."

"Don't want to confuse the audience with too many details," Wes said. "Keep it simple but with lots of punch. That's what I say. I can see the promo now, 'Fire breathin' cyborg man carries off beautiful girl! Will he kill her with his kiss?' Brilliant!"

"What about the mice?" Paul said.

"Don't worry about that son. The mice, what did y'all call them?"

"Bio-Nano Robots."

"The Bio-Nano Alien Robots disguised as mice were the first clue that something strange has been happening at this—I've got it!—mystery house in Delaware, Ohio."

"Genius!" Wes's writer said. "You've broadened the whole concept...a mysterious house inhabited with a full array of extraterrestrial creatures who come out at night, walk through walls, and if they so desire, will spirit you away."

"Or kill you with a kiss!" Wes said.

"This will be our blockbuster of the season for sure. I can guarantee it!" the writer said.

Who would want to buy my house after this? Barry thought. And who would want to hire an archeologist associated with said house or this story? He realized it was time to leave Delaware, job or no job.

When the *Questers* bus pulled away, Bill, Walt, and Quentin sat together in Bill's living room looking quite deflated. Paul and Andy, on the other hand, looked elated when they left to go home.

"There goes the generation gap," Walt said as he waived goodbye to the two boys.

"Well, it looks like this is going to be some kind of production all right," Barry said.

"I had no idea how little control over it we would have," Quentin said, he too perhaps thinking about the effects such a TV show could have on his future employment.

"They have a way of coming up with their own narrative, that's for sure," Walt said.

"Fay Wray and King Kong. Give me a break!" Bill said. "The real story is much more interesting."

"The kids seemed to like what they were hearing," Barry said.

"Yep, that's the demographic they're after all right," Walt said. "They'll probably succeed, but I'm not sure to what end."

"That Roland being a watcher and all. Now that's news!" Bill said.

"What did you say?" Walt asked.

"Barry told me that," Bill replied.

Walt bore holes through Barry until he spoke up.

"I don't know much about it," Barry said. "A friend told me that he's keeping tabs on what's going on down here. That's all I know."

"I've heard about these guys," Walt said. "They come at you dressed in black suits, don't they? And they try to shut you up?"

Barry had to acknowledge that when he first met Roland he wore nothing but black suits, but he didn't remember him trying to shut anyone up until he recalled how he had warned Etienne to keep his story to himself lest he risk dying in some sort of planned accident. This is poppycock, he thought to himself and said, "I haven't heard anything like that. I can tell you this. Roland is a good guy. If we need watching out for, he's the man to do it."

"Hmm," Walt said as he and Quentin left Bill's house.

Before leaving himself, Barry turned to Bill. "Hey Bill, I'm going to leave you the key to my house so you can let them in when they come to do their filming. I will be headed out of here by then."

"So soon?" The expression on Bill's face turned to worry as if he could mentally fast forward to the consequences of Barry's leaving. "I'm sorry to hear that."

"I'm sorry too, but I need to get back to doing what I do," he said awkwardly aware of Bill's disappointment. "I would only get in the way. If you can, try to keep them from tearing the place up too bad. I'm still trying to sell it."

“I’ll keep an eye on it. I’ve gotten pretty used to that,” Bill said. “It’s too bad you’re leavin’. We were just gettin’ to know each other.”

Chapter 10

France

"Luc, are you still up?"

"I was just thinking about you," Luc said. "You and Roland and other things."

"Hey, I was wondering if you could put me up for a few weeks before I head off to Italy or somewhere else."

"Of course I can. Has something happened?"

"It's turned into a zoo over here, that's all. The sooner I get out of here the better."

"You're welcome to come. With Roland gone, I feel so...."

"Speaking of Roland," Barry interrupted, eager to unload the news. "He and Summer disappeared again several weeks ago while I was asleep. I meant to call you but..."

"Disappeared!"

"I knew you'd be upset. Yes, gone. One of my neighbors tells me they were taken up by a ship."

"Not again!"

"I'm afraid so. If I had known what Summer was getting herself into with this marriage, well.... Oh, well, there's nothing to be done about it now. I'll tell you more when I get there."

"When should I expect you?"

"I'll make a few phone calls, see what I can arrange, and get back to you."

It was not Barry's surprise request or the fact that Roland and Summer had gone missing that kept Luc up later that night. Taken up by a spaceship or put down, Roland's story had unsettled him. But what had disturbed him more were the revelations, fears, and doubts that had infected his mind after the visit he had paid to Etienne earlier that day when he dropped into Le Musée to see Gitane Marie before catching the return train from Paris. The man had deteriorated to an unimagined state.

He had not seen Etienne since he had counseled him to good effect, so he had thought. Now, he was not so sure his counseling had accomplished much, so changed Etienne had become. Madame Conti's growing remorse over her own interference caused him to question his own involvement. Had he advised Summer well? The whole experience made such a deep impression on him that he lay in bed neither dreaming nor fully awake, rather ruminating over the scene of that day's events again and again.

What an enigmatic face, Luc had thought while watching the sun dance upon her crown. How old she must be, and what she could tell us of the past if only she could speak. As he studied her goddess features bathed in sun, a passing cloud cast its shadow over the oculus just as a shadowy figure cast itself before him. It was Etienne.

"Monsieur de Chevalier," Luc said and stood up. "I came to Paris to buy some herbs and thought it an opportunity to see the Gitane Marie once again. I did not expect to see you here."

"I keep my office here now," Etienne said. "Women in the home are too much of a distraction. Let's go to the back and talk."

Luc followed Etienne from the vestibule back to his office, noting that his suit fit too tightly in all the wrong places and he had taken up the regrettable habit of cigars.

"I read about your wedding in the paper. Quite an affair," Luc said.

"Yes, and quite pricey. Grand-mère would not have it any other way."

"And how is your wife?"

"In confinement."

"Confinement! So soon! Is she all right?"

"Do not worry about Juliette. Grand-mère will let nothing happen to her. You do know that Juliette's grandmother picked her out for me or should I say picked me out for Juliette."

"I didn't know," Luc said. "I had thought you picked her out yourself."

"So had I!" he laughed. "Juliette informed me we were victims of a little subterfuge designed by her grandmother, who happens to be my grandmother's best friend. I should have known as much. Coincidence often disguises truth. Oh, me." He puffed his cigar. "Juliette's grandmother thought it would be proper to join our two families."

"She is very beautiful," Luc said, looking at her framed picture on his desk.

"And expensive to keep. No one ever told me that if I married, I would have to keep two." His laughter ended abruptly with a great snort.

"You mean now that you are about to have a child."

"That's not what I mean. She can be no comfort to me now in her condition. A man like me has needs. I like exclusivity, and for that you must pay. So I married one and keep another."

Luc's face reddened.

"I'm sorry if I have embarrassed you, you being a priest. Now Summer, she never cost me much," he said taking a long draw on his cigar. "Did she tell you about the ruby necklace I tried to give her?"

"No, she did not."

"Oh, she hasn't, well," Etienne said, coughing a bit from having taken in too much smoke. "Long before I quit the engagement—before we were engaged—I took her to my jeweler and she refused it right in front of him. Embarrassed me like that. Now that one," he said pointing to the photo of his wife, "has had an ongoing relationship with my jeweler since the day we were wed. Better to keep them than to marry them," he winked. "The other one is content with what I give her, and she gets plenty enough. I want my women well adorned when I take them out. Summer never learned how to dress. I'm taking this one with me to Canada next week. She's quite excited to travel. Did I tell you I just bought into Canadian oil?"

"No, you haven't," Luc said further sizing up the man sitting across from him at the desk. The mental breakdown he had suffered when he had arrived unexpectedly on his doorstep last autumn seems to have passed, he thought, but it left in its wake a coarser man no longer recognizable as the man he had once been.

"If you like I can get you a few hundred shares before the price goes up. So if you like..."

"That's very kind of you," Luc interrupted, "but I never risk much. Maybe a game of bingo now and then."

"I suppose being a priest you do not have much to risk."

"Not of that order."

"Have you seen her lately?"

"Who? Summer? No, not since her wedding."

"He hasn't a euro to his name, has he?"

"You might have read they've shut down the Hadron Collider for a year of maintenance, but he has some savings."

"She always liked a pretty dress." Etienne reached into a drawer and pulled out a five hundred euro note. "Take this," he said.

"She won't accept it."

"It will be our secret. Buy her a new dress."

"That's very generous of you," Luc said now standing up. "I must be off. I have a train to catch."

He paused in front of Gitane Marie before leaving and read into her glance, "Be not too proud to allow others to show a generous heart." Were these her words or a projection from his own heart, he wondered? What he was sure of was that despite Etienne's apparent worsened condition, there was still hope, the universal nectar.

A voice spoke from behind him. "You question her power?" it said.

"Oh dear Madame Conti, you startled me. I did not realize you were here."

"I saw you talking to my grandson."

"Yes."

"Do you have a few minutes for me?"

The truth was if he hoped to catch the midday train, he did not. But the evening train would do, he thought, as he put on his confessor's face. "I will always have time for such a great lady," he replied.

"Do not be insincere," she said. "I know what you must think of me for what I did to Summer."

"For what you did to Summer and Etienne, you must mean," Luc said and went on to add, "No, to the contrary, I agreed with you. I did not believe the two were suited to each other as much as she is suited to my dear friend Roland."

"And she is happily married now?"

"Married and happily. I did the honors."

"I'm quite relieved to hear that. I wish her great happiness. After

Juliette came into the picture I grew to believe that Summer was not suited to the role that marriage to my grandson would have required of her. And I believed they would not have increased each other's happiness. But it is my grandson and not Summer I wish to talk to you about. Will you hold my thoughts in confidence?"

"To all but God," Luc said. "Your grandson is married to a wife you believe more suited to him and expecting a child. What concerns you?"

"Rather, to a wife, my dear friend her grandmother believed was more suited to him. I agreed finally, and yet I can plainly see that he is not happy. I hardly recognize him he's grown so fat."

"I noted the change," Luc said as he considered what he should tell her. She would never accept the truth of abduction and mind-stripping, so he told her only what she could accept. "He came to my home last autumn very distressed. The sudden changes in his life I do believe to be the cause. He truly loved Summer, and when she was lost to him, well, he was quite upset."

Madame Conti looked down at her hands resting in her lap. "I thought the breakup was for the better."

"And perhaps it was. He talked to me about the loss of his mother too. For him Summer and his mother had become intertwined. He felt betrayed by both. I was able to help him see the loss of his mother differently, which gave him some relief. And my tea helped to calm his nerves so he could see the situation less emotionally. Perhaps if I make up some of my best tea for you, you will see to it that he takes some daily. This might help to restore him."

"Anything you ask of me I will do faithfully."

"Good. My tea should at least calm his appetites. I just bought fresh herbs today that when measured and mixed in the right proportions will provide a potent combination. I will prepare them in pouches and send them to you. But you must promise..."

"Yes, Yes! I am very grateful for your generosity."

"Oh, the tea is of little expense."

"No, your generosity towards me. You could have just as well condemned me for not leaving things as they were, interfering as I did."

How could I? Luc thought, aware of his own intrusion into Roland's affairs. "You were only trying to do what you thought was best for everyone," he replied.

"Thank you," she said.

He turned back to Gitane Marie. "Her eyes have extraordinary power to fix you in their gaze."

"She could change the world," Madame Conti said.

"Yes, that's what Summer has said. But I've detected not a whit of change since she was found and put here on display."

"If people had eyes to see," Madame Conti said, clearly distressed. "They never have. So blindly we sleepwalk through life even in the face of revelation."

"Yes," was his only reply.

Luc passed many women's shops on his way to the metro when he spied a pretty spring frock on a mannequin that he could almost see Summer wearing. It was all softness in its floral design. Much better on her than a ruby necklace, he thought. At that moment he realized that even before the effects of mind-stripping had changed him, Etienne had exhibited a coarseness towards Summer that for Luc was an abomination. The thought that he would have put such a vulgar stone around her neck before a ring upon her finger sickened him.

When he looked again into the shop window he saw Summer in all her sweetness wearing the pretty floral dress. "Was I right to marry you off to Roland?" he begged to ask the vision who confronted him. He got no answer to that question but could tell immediately by the expression in her eyes that she was in tremendous danger. "Where are you?" he pleaded "Are the two of you safe?" Her face went blank as it quickly transformed back into the featureless mannequin. He wished she were off of whatever unholy ship she was on and beside him.

"How much is that dress?" he asked the clerk.

"Very expensive," she said, looking at his priestly frock. "It is from our new spring collection. I just put it in the window this morning. We have reduced merchandise in the rear if you would like to take a look."

"No, no. How much?" he persisted.

"Nearly five hundred euros I'm afraid."

"I will take it," he said. "Could you wrap it? It's a gift."

She did as she was asked with a slightly raised brow. He smiled as he considered what she must have been thinking and had to admit it gave him perverse pleasure that he could be imagined as such a man.

The dress was boxed in pink paper and tied with a bow. He handed her the five hundred euro note.

"Au revoir! Bonne soirée mon père," she said with a sly smile.

Luc placed the wrapped box in his spare bedroom having no idea when he would see Summer next. He then went to the kitchen to cut his fresh herbs and prepare large quantities of tea leaves carefully mixed for Madame Conti to minister to her grandson. After he was done and had the tea boxed and wrapped for sending, he brought two pears to the table and a large pot of tea, his most relaxing blend. But his mind would not rest.

He had been torn between two strains of thought since Roland had made his confession. On the one hand, Roland's admissions proved the existence of a world beyond common, ordinary sight. Good news for a man like Luc whose faith depended on it but whose prayers and meditations had revealed little behind the veil beyond antique second and third hand accounts in religious texts, legends, and the vaunted saints' tales. Yet Roland's accounts of himself, his origins, and the Alliance came directly from the proverbial horse's mouth, a horse's mouth Luc adamantly believed. But what Roland had claimed was not altogether pleasant and certainly far from orthodox, he having been fathered by a personage perfectly disguised as a swan, an event completely outside of scripture yet solidly placed in traditions that had survived for centuries in mythology, art, and poetry.

He thumbed through his art books at depictions of Leda and the Swan, some rendering it a consensual act, others a rape, and finally fixed on the Gustave Moreau painting that Summer so loved. It showed not the act but a holy consummation between Zeus as swan, mortal woman, and heavenly crown. He paused for a few minutes as he reflected on the painting.

Surely there was nothing holy in what befell Roland's mother, he thought. It was a rape, most assuredly, a cruel rape at that. It made her an outcast from her family whose abandonment had sent her to an early grave. "There was nothing holy in that!" he shouted and slammed the book shut. Yet there was something in Roland, not holy perhaps, but noble, he thought. How could such a vile act have produced such a man?

The unseen world became far more complex than Luc's imaginative mind had heretofore grasped. He considered the ships that had carried Roland and Etienne away, one to safety and the other to—An image of Etienne appeared as he saw him that day, now fleshy and reeking of cigar, a diminished man, all appetite, nothing left of the man he had been except for the generous gift he made anonymously to Summer. "There is hope in that," he both declared and prayed. "Two ships. One acts for good the other—If only my teas would bring him back," he prayed harder. He recalled again the Angel Boatman in *The Purgatorio.* Could he save us?

When Roland first told him his story Luc had thought it lent credibility to his own perceptions of reality. But the longer he ruminated, the further from those perceptions his mind had taken him. He was tempted to restrain his thought altogether, close the door, and sink his mind into accepted texts. But on this night as he pored over his books, he determined he must take up the challenge so he might know the world in truth. The howling wind swirled against his front door shaking it hard, reminding him of the risks of such an undertaking.

Chapter 11

Martian Cave Hideout

"This isn't working!" Summer sobbed.

"Not even the lycmthe," Lira sighed. "We must have him rest, his brain be exhausted he be so tortured. We will take him to the room you share. You must keep near to soothe and tomorrow will be signs of consciousness."

"What's happening?" Summer cried, as the ship suddenly rocked and she fell to the floor.

"I know not," Lira said, "but I suspect."

"We be under fire!" Bryn shouted as he entered the baths.

"The Endron!" Lira said. "They never relent. We must land them somewhere. We be too much a target."

"Back to Avian should we go?" Bryn asked.

"Not there, not now," Lira said. "They send murderous assassins. Somewhere unsuspected, unknown to them."

"I have a thought," Bryn said. "These people owe me a favor. Roland can rest and recover."

"If recover he will," Lira said in a note of caution.

"Can't you take us back to where you found us?" Summer cried. "We would be safer in the trees."

"Perhaps, perhaps," Bryn acknowledged. "We take you first to Mars outpost."

"Mars?"

"Be quiet girl," Bryn said impatiently. "Act not surprised."

"But we've been roving it for years. No sign of life..."

His smile opened to a grin. "You be roving the surface. Life went underground thousands of years ago." He turned to leave and then turned back. "We must gain distance from them now. Under cover of darkness, we can return you."

"Return us?" Summer said, now standing tall. "You cannot return us to a place we've never been."

Lira smiled sweetly at the girl. "Your people's origins be unknown to you. Perhaps this stop will provide needed education. But worry not. You be there no longer than required before we return you to your true home."

The ship rocked once more, took a sharp turn and then another as if to dodge the fire. Summer toppled again and slid across the floor until she found a post to hold on to.

"You go to your room now and let him rest," Lira ordered. "Quite a rough flight we must take to lose them fast. I will fasten you in"

Lira helped Summer carry Roland to the room, she holding up one side while Summer the other, as the girl leaned close against the wall to keep from falling. Lira strapped them safely into chairs while the ship shook and rattled. She held Summer's hand for a few minutes until all was steady. Then the ship launched into such speed that Summer felt her chest constrict as if all the air were being pulled from her.

"We've begun our escape," Lira said. "The force of the speed we can feel. Let the tension go. Close your eyes and slow your breathing. You be more comfortable."

Summer did as she was asked but to no relief until Lira began to hum her tune and softly touched Summer's forehead and eyelids until the girl was fast asleep. That tune was the last she remembered before opening her eyes to a whole new place, a very dark place, a place that would confine her.

They were not welcome in this underground base of glowing rock, but "safe they would be," Bryn said, until he would return for Roland. A rough looking man picked Roland up in his thick arms and motioned Summer to follow as Bryn and Lira waved them off from across the hanger cave. Reluctant, Summer followed into a chiseled out corridor, turning back several times to look at Lira, her face pleading to her cousin to not forget them.

"A victim of mind-stripping I've been told, " the doctor said who examined Roland.

"I tried to stop it before it led to harm."

He wiggled his nose as if warding off a bad odor. "Has he exhibited any untoward aggressive behavior or a change in his appetites?"

"No, he's just been as you see him now, in a deep rest."

"Hmm," he said, wiping his nose. "In rare cases the outward signs are opposite of what's expected. This may be such a case."

"What do you mean?"

"Instead of increasing the aggressive urge, the appetite, and the libido, the effect is to diminish the victim's will to live. Some have been known to let the life force slip away quickly. Sad. Such a case and for such a man."

Summer began to cry. "You can't give him up! What can we do?"

"Sadly, nothing," the doctor said. "We must wait and see and let him rest. Perhaps the psychic devils will work themselves out in good time. As for you, I have a pill or two that will keep you calm."

"I will take no pill!" Summer asserted. "I must be by his side and alert to whatever is to come."

"If that's what you choose."

"How can you live in such a cave?" Summer asked, feeling increasingly claustrophobic in the confines of this underground world.

"Well, it is a simple question to answer. We cannot live on top with the atmosphere gone. My ancestors who remained here adapted themselves to this place while many others went to your Earth multitudes of years ago after our planet fell into decline. Earth was not so populated then as it is now. Crowded it has become and so dirty," he said, crinkling his nose. "But alas, Mars is no more than an outpost, a way stop, our culture nearly gone."

"To Earth! Where? When?"

"Many places there we settled thousands of your Earth years ago. Only an outpost this place now be," he said, his head bent low as if he was lost in sad thoughts.

He doesn't look odd, Summer thought. He could easily pass for one of us, one of the short and stout variety.

"And yet I treasure this place since it is all that I've known," the doctor lamented. "Did they tell you Roland's and your presence here puts even this lowly outpost at risk?"

Noting the passion in his disposition, Summer spoke softly. "No, they said nothing to me about it, but I'm not surprised. The ship came under heavy fire."

"Happy I will be to release the patient and send you both back!" he shouted.

"Happy we will be to leave once Roland gets his rest!" she shouted.

"Harrumph!" he snorted. "Earth is only a short distance, less than a day trip by our rockets. Tonight I speak to the council."

Safer in the trees we would be than inside this god forsaken rock, she silently sobbed, now keeping her true feelings to herself. She had no desire to stir his passions any further. For he had a case to make, she realized, and make it he did, albeit to the wrong person.

All that night she fantasized about what the doctor had said. Martians had come to Earth in the early days of Earth's ancient past. Her imaginings wandered off to images of short, squat tribes across her planet. She was aware there were people who had thought such things, which she had never before considered until she met Roland. Her mind now open to what had been fantasies, she wondered where other beings on her planet may have come from, not all from the same village in Africa, she laughed. Some from Avian, she knew, and now some from the formerly inhabited surface of Mars. What a great wonder.

She longed for companions with whom she could share this news when Roland, eyes closed, began to speak. "Time machine," he uttered and repeated the phrase again and again until he added, "Take me back." His head slumped to the side and he could speak no more.

"Roland! Roland!" Summer sobbed as she tried in vain to wake him.

Later that night after she had fallen asleep, she was awakened by two stout men, stouter than the doctor, who grabbed her arms and dragged her away from her Roland.

"Where are you taking me!" she screamed.

"Back to your Earth the council has decided."

"But Roland!"

"Council did decide to take him into their care for the debt they owe Bryn, but no debt they owe you."

"No worry," the other man said. "You will be escorted safely back from where you came."

"But I can't leave Roland!" Summer sobbed.

"Quiet yourself! No choice do you have in the matter."

She was loaded onto a transport with no more care than a shipping container, which was rushed to launch first through a tunnel then shot into space. She fell unconscious until she unceremoniously landed with a thud, like so much cargo, into the backyard of Barry Short's Delaware, Ohio home.

The linnets had arisen that early morning in Evian and warbled their song to Luc who had been up all night thinking, reading, and praying. Their song offered him temporary respite and advice. "Surely there is justice in the universe!" he pleaded aloud, his tears running fast and hard. "There must be a cure for Etienne, and I will find it." Reflected in one of his own tears that had chanced to fall into his palm was Summer's face. He knew he would see her again for the visage nearly spoke to him. Calmed, he closed his books and went upstairs to retire, but just as he was about to lie down the phone rang.

"Are you up?" Barry said, "I've got a surprise."

"I was just dosing off."

"You won't believe the package that just dropped into my backyard."

"Package?"

"Summer!"

"And Roland too?"

"Roland's another matter I will have to explain later. I don't have much time. I tell you it's a zoo over here. Been that way all day. UFOs reported all over the city. Then this evening Summer appears out of the sky. My neighbor unpacked her, and his friends are going nuts filming everything in sight including *moi*. Fortunately, they didn't capture that scene. I've got to get us both out of here soon. I'll drive us somewhere until I can get us a flight."

"Is she all right?"

"Not physically harmed, mind you, but her pride's a bit hurt from being dropped out of a ship like excess baggage. And she's angry about being separated from Roland. I'll let her explain when we get over there."

"Is he all right?"

"He's alive. That's about all I can tell you. She says he's being kept in a safe place because, well, the way she explains it he has enemies who would like to destroy him. They almost did in a little game of mind-stripping they played."

A picture of the now grossly altered Etienne flashed before Luc. "Not Roland too?"

"I'm afraid so. But we don't know how far it went or his condition just yet. She tried to save him, and well, we can hope she succeeded in saving him from the worst of it. Talk to you more about this later. I need to get off this phone right now. Someone's pounding on my front door."

Chapter 12

The Circus

Barry warily peeked through a window after he heard a late night knock at his front door. "That's a good dog," he said when he opened it to Neighbor Bill and Shadow. "She's upstairs sleeping," he whispered and stepped out onto his porch. "I don't want anything to disturb her tonight."

"Sorry to bother you this late."

"That's okay. I've been having trouble sleeping myself."

"Gail Barnett—you remember Gail from WUFOC?"

"The knockout?" Barry said.

"Yeah, that's who I mean. I just got off the phone with her. WUFOC has committed its resources to a full investigation."

"Congratulations! It probably helped that the local media made such a big deal out of all these UFO sightings around here," Barry said.

"Yeah, she said they don't often get to study the phenomenon in real time."

"Well, there's plenty going on. They dropped Summer from the sky, and more ships have been buzzing my house all night."

"I heard them too. Shadow and I investigated but couldn't see a thing. They must have been using some kind of stealth shield."

"Hmm, stealth shield technology. Maybe it was only the Air Force out on a secret search mission."

"They'd never admit it if they were," Bill said. "But I wasn't thinkin' of conventional stealth technology. What I was thinkin' of is more along the lines of a cloaking device."

"A cloaking device! The Air Force isn't that advanced," Barry said, "at least I don't think they are. And now that Summer's back, well, it's enough to make me nervous. Did Ms. Barnett say when she'd be coming?"

"Tomorrow. I expect it will be later in the day since she's comin' in from out West."

"Tomorrow! Well, again congratulations. It looks like you've hit the jackpot on this one."

"It's about to blow wide open right here, right now. They'll want your story and Summer's for sure."

"Tell you what Bill. We're going to have to get out of here in the morning after what happened last night. So what can I do for you now?"

"You two goin' right now? You're my prime witnesses."

"I've got to get Summer out of here. She could be in danger."

"I see, I see, but Gail will want your testimony."

"Tell you what I'm gonna do. Tonight I will write a full report of everything I know. It's not that much Bill. You're their star witness."

"But you've got the credentials, being a Ph.D. and all. And Summer knows more than the two of us together."

"That's right she does, which is part of the problem here. The bad ones may send their cyborg back after her in an attempt to shut her up. I'm telling you, I'm worried about her psychologically too. She's been through a horrific ordeal. I won't have her reliving it through her testimony until she's fully recovered from the shock. You understand, don't you? I'll leave my report on the dining room table."

"I guess I do, but if she changes her mind about this...."

"I won't let her."

"I see, I see. Well, I'll be seein' you when you come back," Bill said before he turned and left the front porch.

Barry checked upstairs to make sure Summer was still asleep before he pulled his portable typewriter out of the closet. He could have typed his report on his computer, but in significant matters like this, old habits prevailed.

Where shall I begin? he thought. I'll begin at the beginning.

He described his reaction when Etienne first told him his story of his sighting. He explained how that had led to the mysterious first meeting with Roland, a UFO conference in Geneva, Claudio Postremo's presentation and, almost as an aside, how it all began with Paul's letter. On and on his story proceeded. But with every creak in the house and crack of a pane of glass, he would rise from his chair at the dining room table and strain to look out the dark window, half expecting to see that cyborg creature Walt had photographed. It was the ugliest thing Barry had ever seen, uglier than the mummy he had once recklessly unwrapped after excavating its tomb. No cyborg greeted him in the glass, only his own reflection. "How many years ago was that? Thirty?" he said to his own visage now flushed with embarrassment at the faux pas early in his career.

In spite of the interruptions at the window, the night flew by quickly to the music of clickety, clickety, clickety, zing, as Barry's recollections unfolded detail after detail upon a growing pile of paper. He realized as the pile grew that he had witnessed far more than what he had thought he had, and knew a lot more than he wished he did, and quite a bit more than he believed prudent to share.

The roar of a loud engine breaking outside called him to his front window. Under the first light of morning an oversized Bigfoot stared wearily from the side of the big yellow bus. It was *Questers* returned. A man wearing a fringed suede jacket and cowboy boots climbed out of the vehicle along with a cinematographer and walked towards Bill's door. Neighborhood houses began to open up as gawkers emerged from their living rooms watching the rest of the crew unload equipment. The circus was about to begin, and he could not be far enough away.

"Summer, get up! We've got to get out of here now. The show's about to begin."

She sat up and rubbed her eyes. "What show?"

"The Big Top just pulled up. Get up and get ready to leave in a few minutes if you don't want your face splashed all over the side of a bus."

He stuffed his freshly typed manuscript in his bag and fifteen minutes later the two of them were in his jeep creeping stealthily down the road towards Highway 42 with no idea of their destination.

"You're not saying much. Are you all right?"

"I'm just tired," she said.

"You slept a good nine hours."

She didn't reply.

"Xenia's just up ahead," he said. "We could go over to Yellow Springs and have some breakfast. It's my favorite town in Ohio. It makes me feel like I'm somewhere else."

Silence.

"What do you think?" he said.

"I can't remember the last time I ate."

"Fine, we'll have some breakfast."

"I'm not hungry."

"You just said you couldn't remember the last time you ate."

"I know I did. It's just, it's just that I'm so worried about Roland I feel sick." Once the stopper was pulled a gusher full of tears flooded her eyes. "It was horrible seeing him like that. So lifeless!" she wept.

"Summer, you must believe me when I tell you he will be all right," Barry said while holding back his own tears and keeping his fingers crossed.

"How do you know?"

"Just say I'm intuitive, that's all. He would want you to take care of yourself, that's for sure."

"Yes, he would," she said and began to sob some more. "He always puts me first."

"That's enough!" Barry said firmly this time. "There's nothing you can do for him now, but when there is you'll need your strength."

"Okay, you're right. You're probably sick of me crying," she whimpered.

He was sure that was true, but Barry was too much of a gentleman to admit it to this girl who had become his charge since....

"When did it happen?" he asked.

"When did what happen?"

"I don't know. It seems like you've been my charge for quite a while now."

"Like my father? Well, you gave me away at my wedding."

"It was before that, for sure."

"You gave me your apartment in Paris when I lost mine."

"It was before that too."

She considered all the countless times he was there for her when it was support she needed. "Since I met you," she said.

"That's what I thought. So it's been a long time. Have I ever steered you wrong?"

"No."

"Just you remember that. We're going to Yellow Springs. I will order."

He parked the car several blocks from the restaurant and the two walked up Xenia Avenue past all of its 1960's vintage shops. Summer showed no interest in window-shopping, which was a sure indicator of her mood.

"Give us some corn cakes, scrambled eggs, and flapjacks" he said to the waitress. "And make sure we get real maple syrup, not that phony stuff."

"That's all we serve sir," the waitress replied, which had to be true since the menu read at the top, "*We use only wholesome and natural ingredients.*"

"That's why I like to come here when I'm in town," he said to the waitress and then turned to Summer. "The place reminds me of my youth. If you don't mind, before the food comes I should see if I can get us some plane reservations." He pushed his silverware aside and opened his laptop. "I should have done this sooner," he said as he got online. "The connection's a bit slow here," he muttered. "Great! They've got a few seats left. We can go tonight."

"Tonight!"

"You've got your passport, don't you?"

"Of course. I always keep it with me."

"Good, give me a few minutes more. There, I've got it. Tomorrow we'll be in Paris."

Not a scrap of breakfast was left on either plate when they exited the restaurant. Barry noted that Summer looked a whole lot better as they walked back to the jeep.

"We can just meander our way to Cincinnati. I don't want to get there too early. Just in time in case someone or something is looking for us there. I doubt anyone will be. Not in Cincinnati, at least. But just in case, I want to arrive, hop on the plane, and be gone. It's only a seven and half hour flight."

"I have no clothes or luggage."

"You can buy some when we get there. But if you don't mind, I'd like to take a last look at Serpent Mound on our way down to the airport. I'm not sure when I'll be coming back this way, and I'd like to see it again."

"I don't mind at all," she said as they hopped into the jeep. "What are you going to do with this jeep?"

"I'll let Rosalind have it until I come back. I'll phone her after we're out of the country."

"Good, she'll like that."

Barry headed out towards highway 72.

"There's something I haven't told you yet that's pretty interesting," she said.

"Wait until I make my turn? It's pretty tricky here, and I don't want to miss it."

"Sure," she said. "I learned about it in those horrible caverns on Mars."

"We won't be traveling that far," he said with a smile as he turned and sped down the highway. "What did you learn that could be more startling than there are people living on Mars?"

"That doctor I told you about who is looking after Roland told me that long ago when their planet's atmosphere began to collapse, many of the people came to Earth to start a new life."

"Martians here! Where?"

"Well, he wasn't specific. He just said a lot of places and that it happened a long time ago."

"This Martian you talked to said that?"

"'Martian,' the word sounds pretty strange doesn't it, like something out of a Marvel comic book. But he didn't look strange at all. He looks a lot like us. So did the others I saw. They're just shorter and squatter than your average man. And they really aren't very nice, very rude in fact. Look what they did to me!"

"No doubt the effects of living underground for centuries. I have heard some people postulate that life once existed on Mars. I've always thought the notion a little nuts," Barry said, "until now, of course. But I've never heard that Martians settled on Earth. That's well, that's pretty out there if you ask me."

"Well you've heard it now, and I heard it from the horse's mouth." She paused for a minute. "You suppose these Martian Earth people know where they came from?"

"I doubt it," Barry said. "If it's true, it happened long, long ago. The only record—if there ever were one—would be very, very old. I've never seen such a record or heard of one hinted at."

"Neither have I," Summer said and paused in thought. "When you think about it most of us don't know for sure where we came from. I mean in the philosophical sense. We know our parents and grandparents and maybe even who some of our ancestors were, but in a deeper sense, our origins are a mystery."

Barry, now pulling into to the parking lot at Serpent Mound, thought back to the two men they had spoken with at the last winter solstice who imagined themselves descendants of whoever built the mound. For them their past had become lost, more legend than real.

"True indeed," he said. "We're all in the same boat as those fellows we met here at the winter solstice. Who built the Pyramids and Stonehenge and why? Could I be descended from the prehistoric people who painted the caves I've studied in France? What happened to their culture anyway? Did it just vanish?"

Summer bit her lip in an effort to keep quiet. She had a deep intuition that she knew something about her own origins, and it was not what Barry would have thought or what she would have imagined only a few months earlier. Actually, it was less of an intuition and more of a fear coming from Lira who repeatedly called her cousin. She had hoped that it was only a term of endearment but was not entirely sure that what she hoped was true. Not that she did not see much to love among the people of Avian. She had. Nonetheless, they seemed strange and foreign even to an adventurous girl.

The place looked very different than when they had last seen it. All the snow had melted and the sun shone hard on the grassy effigy.

"Let's climb up and take a gander," Barry said. The two of them climbed to the top of the observation deck and looked out upon the writhing snake nestled in the bare trees that surround it. "This is all they have of their past," Barry said.

"It's pretty fabulous," Summer said.

"The rest is veiled in mystery. But as you say, in the philosophical sense, that's true of all of us. We're only left with these monuments from a very ancient past. I've dedicated myself to uncovering them; and yet, even after they're uncovered, studied, and preserved, the mystery never leaves them." He turned away from the serpent and looked into

Summer's eyes in earnest. "Keep these things you've learned between the two of us."

"Why? Shouldn't people know?"

"Without more evidence than your testimony, they will never believe you. They will think you are crazy, a liar, or that you imagined the whole thing. You will become the butt of their jokes. The more generous of heart will only pity you. You don't want that."

"No I don't," she said.

"Then you must be very careful who you reveal this to. Promise me?"

"I suppose you're right. You always are, but it's a shame."

"Promise me?"

"Okay. I promise"

"Most people only allow what they can conceive. Remember that. It's an important lesson to learn if you don't want to be cast out."

"Cast out?" she said.

He shook his head yes, and she went very silent.

The juxtaposition of events could not have been more disheartening for Neighbor Bill who thought the final vindication of his claims and beliefs was at hand. The planets had seemed perfectly aligned when he got the phone call from WUFOC's Gail Barnett and *Questers'* Wes Barnes that they were on their way to Delaware, Ohio to study and film the rash of UFO sightings that had startled the community over the past several days. The first hint that his dreams of fame and redemption were not to be fulfilled came when Barry informed him that he and Summer would be departing without so much as giving an interview. The second and final blow was the sudden disappearance of the strange objects in the sky that had earlier swooped down over the town on two clear nights in a row.

"It was right up there over the yard the time we saw it," Walt explained. "It pulled those Bio-Nano Robotic mice I told you about right up into it. Just sucked them up."

Questers' cameramen stood waiting for hours behind their equipment to get the epic shot that would once and for all convince the world of UFOs and boost the show's now sluggish ratings.

"They're not always visible to the eye," Bill explained. "The night it put Roland and Summer down, it hid itself behind a cloud, a dark storm cloud. It had been snowin' a lot so I didn't think too much about those clouds until I saw a golden stairway descend from it and a man and woman walkin' down."

There was no snow or rain in the forecast this day they were there gathered in Barry Short's backyard. And as the hawk-eyed cameramen stared at the sky that early evening, not a single cloud appeared for anything to hide behind.

"Two nights ago when Summer got dropped off right where we're standin', no one saw a thing," Bill added. "I think they may be usin' some kind of stealth technology."

"Dropped off! From what I hear she was dumped," Walt said.

"I would very much like to interview this woman," Gail Barnett said. "When will she be here?"

"Barry took her away. I don't think he'll be bringin' her back. He said he was afraid of what it might do to her to recount all these terrible events. You see, she's lost her husband. He's up there somewhere," Bill said as he pointed to the sky. Shadow whined in sympathy with Summer's lament.

"So you didn't talk to her yourself?" Gail said.

"She wasn't talkin' when I unpacked her from the crate they sent her down in. And Barry kept her inside the house until they left. He said she was sleepin'."

"So you have no verification of what he told you. No one actually saw this ship 'dump' her off as Walt put it, and no one besides this Barry fellow spoke with her."

"I unpacked her," Bill reiterated.

"How do you know that crate came from outer space?" Gail asked.

"What are you implying?" Walt asked.

"Nothing really, but I should tell you I spoke with one of WUFOC's directors, Raymond Lepont. He's highly suspicious of this man, Barry Short."

"Suspicious! Barry's a good guy," Bill said. "He would never make stuff up."

"Apparently, he not only lied to Mr. Lepont about his motives for showing up at a conference in Europe, he tried to trick him into believing he was someone he's not."

"What do you really know about this guy?" Walt asked Bill.

"He told me he's an archeologist. He worked in Egypt. He got himself into some trouble over a statue of a goddess he found over there."

"Trouble seems to follow him around," Gail said. "One must question his character and certainly his capacity to tell the truth."

Walt hammered into Bill. "He lied to me when I first met him with that cock and bull story about the experimental plane that brought that Roland fellow and Summer over here from CERN."

"Barry didn't tell us that story, Roland did," Bill argued.

"He went along with it, didn't he?" Walt said. "He tried to make fools out of us. Of course, I didn't take it seriously, not for long. And how about the rest of it? How do we know this Roland fellow ever worked at CERN? And how can we check? We don't even know his last name."

"I guess not," Bill said.

"So let's leave it at this," Gail added to the brouhaha. "Barry Short is an unreliable witness." She scratched him off her list.

"He told me just last night that he'd write a report before he left."

"I'm willing to look at it," she said, "with my skeptical glasses on."

"Let me take a look inside his place," Bill said.

Wes Barnes came over to join the conversation with Walt. "We've been out here for twelve hours now. Where do you suppose they are?"

"I can't say that I know," Walt said. "But a lot of folks around here saw them over the past few days."

"Or something," Gail added. "I checked with the Air Force and got no confirmation of those reports."

"Well, that's nothing new," Walt said. "When has the Air Force ever confirmed the existence of UFOs? I have to admit though, it's pretty quiet around here now."

"We can't keep our cameras here all night," Wes said. "We've got a show to produce, a schedule to meet. If we can't find some good shots here, we'll have to go somewhere else. I'm sorry. We'll just have to stick with the original script, lizard man meets beautiful blonde."

"Just give it a little more time," Walt said. "The sun is just going down and most of the sightings came at night."

"Okay, we'll go into town and have some dinner and see if the action picks up when we come back."

"I will keep an eye out for you," Walt said.

Bill returned only moments later empty handed just having searched inside Barry's house. "I couldn't find his report," he said.

"If there ever was one," Gail countered. "Okay, that's enough. We'll write him off. And you say he took off with this woman, Summer so she's not available either. What about these children you told me about?"

"Paul and Andy, yes," Bill said. "Well, I contacted Paul this afternoon. He said his parents won't let him come over, ditto for Andy. They're worried about adverse notoriety. Didn't want them filmed for this *Questers* show."

"I can understand that," Gail said. "So that leaves us with you and Walt. Where is your other friend? What's his name? The wiry haired guy?"

"You mean Quentin," Walt said. "I spoke with him this morning. He's knee deep in studying for his general exams and can't make it over."

"So what can you two tell me that you haven't already told me when we met before?" she said.

They looked at each other and drew a blank.

She packed up her laptop. "Here's my card. You've got my number if you can think of anything else to add. And you can pass it along to any other witnesses who might come forward." She looked up at the sky. "It seems pretty quiet around here tonight. I think I'll go back to my hotel and get some dinner. I'll stick around Columbus for a day or two. Call me if anything happens."

Wes Barnes returned from his dinner. Neighbor Bill, Shadow, Walt, Wes and the three cameramen stood outside the whole night under a dome of stars waiting for something, for anything. Nothing could be seen, not even a falling star. At daybreak Wes and his cameramen packed up their equipment in their big yellow bus and headed out to parts unknown, looking for a more photogenic story.

Chapter 13

Recovery

"Incroyable!" Madame Conti said, flinging her head back and covering her eyes. The blast of light would have nearly blinded her if her reflexes had not been so fast. She peered between her fingers at the girl sitting on a nearby bench overlooking Lake Geneva and thought her too engrossed in a book to have noticed even a sea torch. The blast cooled into a steady beam that moved across the water until it burst wide like flowering petals, revealing a fair-haired women who sat down beside the pretty girl who was reading who knows what.

"A fairy? An angel?" Madame Conti said dumbfounded.

"Lira!" Summer said, quite startled to find this woman beside her.

"How be my darling cousin?" the voice that had just materialized into a woman asked sweetly.

"I'm still alive if that's what you mean. Can you tell me about Roland?"

"The bird of life has not left him. We have taken him to a more comfortable place to speed his recovery."

"Then he will be all right?" the girl said with a sigh of relief.

"We must wait to see. The ordeal took much from him. It will take time to restore if it will. He sent me to you with these letters, one to you and another to his friend that you stay with, a Luc Renard."

"Yes, Luc," Summer said. "He has given me a home to speed my recovery." She reached forward to take the letters; but before Lira handed them over, she took the opportunity of Summer's outstretched hand to pull her blue and yellow sapphire wedding ring from her finger.

"What have you done?" Summer cried. "I haven't taken that ring off since Roland and I were wed. Why have you done this to me? Hasn't it been painful enough?"

"Hush girl, someone might overhear your wailing," Lira said as she spotted the woman looking on.

"Wailing! You just took my ring!"

"Hush! It had to be done, and I had to do it. You would not have handed it over willingly."

Summer arose from the bench in her pretty floral dress, looked down at Lira and said most forcefully, "I demand my ring, an apology, and an explanation!"

"An explanation be all you get. This ring I charmed into a talisman that links you to him."

"It's our wedding ring! It bound us together the day he put it on my finger with no help from you."

"It has power beyond that, ignorant girl!"

"And what about your power Lira? I thought you able to foretell. Why did you not guess Roland's danger but ask me instead to trust Bryn?"

Lira uncharacteristically bent her head low. "I failed him on that account, I admit. But you foretold and saved him from a worse fate, my dear cousin." She looked steady at the girl. "You must save him from a worse fate now. If you had understood this ring's power, you would have called him to you, and that could have put an end to him. I save you from the temptation upon discovery, and more than that, I save you from the Endron. They have violated all rules and have murderous intent. If they had captured you with this ring, they would have known its true power, which I assure you be why right now they hunt you down. This tie between you and Roland I made with a charm, I must undo. It be me and me alone who must have it to hold until such time it be safe to return, if such time ever comes."

Summer looked at the hand that now grasped her ring tightly with both pathos and pity. "I hear your message and understand," she said her voice grown soft. "But how should I take your remark 'if such time ever comes.'"

"Just as I said it," Lira said. "The Endron be relentless in their madness." She rose and kissed Summer's tear stained cheek. "Now read this letter that your Roland has sent, and be sure to deliver the other to his friend. I must go now before my presence be detected by those who would destroy you," she said and transformed back into a beam of light that faded as it moved across the lake.

Summer sat down and read her letter from Roland.

My Dear Sweetness,

I've asked Lira to deliver this letter to you so that you may know I'm all right though still prone to tire easily. It is imperative that you seek out safety for should the Endron find you while I am in this weakened state and unable to defend, they will destroy you or ransom your life for mine. I could not bear it my dear one so please do whatever Luc advises.

If all works to our good fortune, in the future we will be reunited. But if fortune should not favor us, I want you to know that the time we have shared together—each minute—has been for me a lifetime of joy. I only regret that I've brought such danger into your life. I want you to know, I never intended it. If I had known such would happen, I never would have asked you to go with me to the lake, or later that day to Jungfraujoch, or to be my bride. I would have left you to other fates than those that have since dogged me.

Know that there are no words to fully express how much I love you. Carry that in your heart when you think of me no matter what befalls us. And remember too that I want nothing but your happiness. If the future should fail us, you are free from any constraint or obligation to me to seek out what brings you joy, for joy is all that I want for you.

Your Roland

She dropped the letter onto her lap and looked vacantly into the lake as she rubbed her bare ring finger and absorbed her loss.

"My dear, can I help you?" a woman asked.

"I don't think so," Summer said before she looked up and saw Madame Conti. Startled, she said, "I'm beginning to feel haunted. Where did you come from?"

"I can assure you I'm very much alive. Actually, I've been here watching you for quite some time. I witnessed that beautiful woman who came to you from the light."

"Lira?"

"A divine presence. I could see that. I feel like I recognize her from a painting perhaps. She has that otherworldly charm that you only find in great art."

"Hardly divine," Summer replied. "But what are you doing here? Why were you watching me?"

"I was looking for the right moment. I came here today to make a clean breast of it and to beg your forgiveness. I was most insensitive when I said some harsh things to you."

"Mean things really."

"I only thought...."

"I know what you thought. You jumped to the wrong conclusions, you know. But later your conclusions turned out to be right. I married Roland."

"I was informed of that. I wish you every happiness."

"It seems there's no happiness for me," Summer said and broke into sobs. She folded the letter and stuffed it into the spiritual tract Luc Renard had given her to read.

Madame Conti put her arms around her and tried to comfort her. "Did you two have a quarrel? It couldn't be that bad. All newlyweds do."

Summer pulled away. "It's more than that. More than I can explain right now. How is your grandson?"

"Etienne? He is much better since he began to take Luc Renard's teas. Summer, I know now I was wrong to ever have thought those things about you. What I did was unforgivable, but I am here to ask for your forgiveness."

"Has he been ill?"

"Sick in mind and heart, I'm afraid. I thought I knew best, but now...."

"You thought I wasn't good enough for him."

"No, I thought you unable to fulfill the necessary role. I've always liked you. It was just—Juliette was brought up to serve him well."

"And I wasn't. You're right about that. You say he has been sick in mind and heart? What do you mean?"

"Not happy, I'm afraid. Eating, drinking, smoking to excess.

Everything in excess. How crude he has become, but Luc Renard's herbs have begun to tame his appetites. He's beginning to look and act like himself again, but now his health seems to be flagging. Luc says the cause of my grandson's fever was the heartbreak he felt when he lost you and all the rest that went with it."

"He didn't tell you everything then," Summer said.

"What more is there to tell?"

"Remember when Etienne described those eyes staring into him when he was taken?"

"That was only a bad dream, a hallucination, a nightmare!"

"I'm afraid not. Come with me to Luc's and we can talk. I need company anyway, and you should know the rest."

"Is it something that angelic woman told you? I recognize her but from where?"

"She's no angel, I can assure you."

"Angel or not. That woman of the light is magnificently beautiful. Now where have I seen her before? I'm getting so old I can hardly remember such things."

"She is beautiful. I will allow that."

Roland lay on a cot in a hut five hundred light years away from Summer. He was awakened by the music of rustling leaves. Will it rain, he wondered, before he fell back to sleep and into a dream that found him in a cavern somewhere before being taken by ship somewhere else. The smell of burning cinders and stewing meat brought him back into consciousness. He could hear the crackling fire and knew the gathering room would be warm and comfortable.

"You're awake," came a voice he recognized.

Roland opened up his eyes to the familiar face of the young man, dark haired and unshaven, who had been caring for him nearly two months now.

"Eat to restore your strength," Sedwig said. "I will help you up."

"No, I'm all right," Roland said as he climbed out of bed. For the first time in a very long time he felt hungry.

"Here, taste this," Sedwig said once Roland was settled into a chair.

He sipped. "It's very good. Wild mushroom soup?"

"Yes, I'm glad you like it. Let me fill a cup for you."

The wind roared through the trees and shook the windowpane.

"When does springtime come to Avian?" Roland asked.

"You've never been in the Southwest Quadrant?"

"No, never. It's been left wild I've been told, but I didn't know it was so cold."

"Have a blanket," Sedwig said as he placed a green woolen cover over Roland's knees. "It be winter here on Avian another two months. Have you never visited in winter?"

"Never when it has been this cold. It makes me tired."

"You must rest then. The Southwest Quadrant bears winter's brunt, I'm afraid. But it be quiet, peaceful, and has its own charm. I will show you later when you be able to go out and about. For now I sing you rest."

"I've had enough rest!" Roland said just before drifting off under the spell of Sedwig's reed.

The fluted song inspired a Dionysian scene in Roland's dreams, not erotic as one might expect, but festive, pleasant, very congenial indeed. Food and wine were plentiful, and everyone gathered seemed happy and content. He walked among these good-natured people carefree until the scene began to change into something horrific. A girl screamed, and when he looked out across the pasture where her voice came from, he saw white wings flapping over her body like a vulture mounts its carrion. He ran to the girl and beat the swan off. She looked at him with terror in her eyes as if he had been her assailant.

"Keep from me!" she screamed, and rose and ran down into a valley in her torn and bloody dress. He did not try to run after her for he had seen how repulsed she was by the sight of him. My mother! he thought, and woke up weeping inconsolably.

"What have we here?" Sedwig said.

Roland did not speak but turned his face towards the window and the driving winter rain.

"Speak, you must," Sedwig said. "You must tell me."

"I cannot."

"You need more nourishment. Come closer to the fire and away from this chill. " He wrapped another blanket around Roland's shoulders and helped him to a chair by the big roaring fire. He tossed him heavy socks that Roland was happy to wear. "Sleep can bring about your cure, but without counsel dreams may become dangerous."

"What do I smell?" Roland asked.

"Forest stew. It should be ready soon. It bakes now in the oven in a flaky crust. You will enjoy it."

He has the mother's touch, Roland thought to himself. "I'm sure I will like it very much."

"What dream you had that caused you such misery?"

Roland looked at him silently and then he understood that Bryn had put him in charge for a reason. He could be trusted, and his dream would not burden him too much. What would burden him more is if his help had been refused. His natural sympathy and understanding once ignited allowed Roland to open up.

"It was my mother at the end of what started out a pleasant dream. I heard her screams and saw my father rape her. But when I came to help her, she thought it had been I that had done the deed. No, it was not quite like that. She knew that it was not I, but it might as well have been. She hated and detested me for what he had done."

"She treated you like that?"

"I have no such memory. She treated me always with love and tenderness," he said and began to weep.

"What say you of this dream then?" Sedwig asked.

Roland paused for a few minutes as he thought. "It must be not what she did in life but what I fear. She died very young. It was quite tragic. Her family had put her out and she never recovered."

"And you felt responsible."

"No, not really. I was too young. But I felt, should I say, I knew she could not look at me without thinking...."

"Of him and what had happened."

"Yes," Roland said his head hanging low. "How could she ever look at me without seeing...."

"You be not your father," Sedwig said.

"I know, I know."

"You do not. How must I help drive this truth deep into your consciousness? Let me get a mirror."

Sedwig brought a hand mirror and put it before Roland. "This be who you be. This be who she saw, and not your father. Repeat with me now. 'This be who I am. This be who she saw and loved.'"

After the words were said again and again, Roland interrupted by pointing to all the whiskers that had grown on his face over the last two months. "I can hardly recognize myself," he said. "It's hard to believe this is who I am."

"Then we shall shave you." Sedwig went away and returned with a bowl heaping with shaver's soap, a towel, and a very fine blade. "I have not done this for a while. You must bear with me." With great expertise, he rubbed Roland's face with the foaming soap and skillfully shaved off the bearded stubble. "Do you recognize yourself now? Now repeat again and never stop repeating in your mind. 'This be who I am and who my mother saw and loved.'"

That evening Roland ate two hefty servings of hunter's stew in a flakey crust. His sleep that night was undisturbed by dreams, and in the morning he felt much stronger.

"Madame, I know it's hard to believe, but it's true," Barry said. "Your grandson was taken on board an alien ship, just like he remembered."

Madame Conti looked over to Luc for assurances to the contrary that she did not get. "Well, just having seen a woman materialize out of light on Lake Geneva, I suppose anything is possible and always has been," she said.

"I wish I had another argument to make," Luc said. "But after everything else that has happened, I do not. In fact, I fear the danger could be far greater. Dear lady, Etienne is not the only man this has happened to. The decline in his behavior appears to reflect what we see all around us. It's the devil's work, I tell you."

"Roland figured it all out," Summer said. "That's what got him into so much trouble with the Endron. And look what they've done to him in revenge!" she sobbed.

"Are you saying they've done this to Roland too?" Madame Conti asked.

"I tried to stop them but not in time to prevent damage. He was weak and debilitated when I last saw him, and now he's light years away and I'm abandoned. The lady you saw delivered a letter from him that releases me," she sobbed. "Oh! I almost forgot," she said as she tried to wipe away her tears. "I've got another letter here for Luc." She pulled it out of her book and he took it eagerly.

"Well, what does he say?" Barry asked.

"We must go to Italy!" Luc said.

"Roland said that?"

"Not exactly. He says here that he's in a safe place for now trying to get back his strength, but Summer is not safe, certainly not here. He says any place she has been since she knew him puts her at risk of abduction or worse. He's asked me to take charge of her safety, and Barry, he says I should contact you for your help. Listen to what he writes about you. 'I've grown to deeply admire Barry Short having spent greater time with him at his home in Ohio. He is a man of fine intelligence and a good heart who is worthy of your friendship, my friend, if you need a confidant in the coming months or years. I cannot say if or when I will return, but if it be never, at least I am consoled that you will not lack for solid friends.'"

Luc wept and dropped the letter. Summer followed suit letting loose a torrent of tears. Barry wiped his eyes as he fought to hold back his own.

"This will not stand! We must do something!" Madame Conti proclaimed as she stood up from her chair and leaned gallantly on her cane. "I will go with you to Italy. I have my apartment in Rome, and there are good hotels nearby. You will have a place to stay, and we will find a way to fully cure my grandson and stop this! What did you call them? This Endron!"

Chapter 14

Rome

Madame Conti had not been in Rome since the night she spirited Gitane Marie away to her granddaughter's home in Saintes-Maries-de-la-Mer. Fearing she could become an object of revenge, she had thought it wiser to remain in Paris among friends until the threat had passed. Now that she was returned, she felt as if she had never left. Her housekeeper pulled the sheets off the furniture, dusted, mopped, and vacuumed until her whole apartment was restored to its pale blue grandeur, which matched the chic blue silk suit Madame Conti had chosen to wear that day. As time ticked back, she soon acclimated to her former self, a great curator of all the sights, sounds, and historical and unhistorical facts of Rome.

"I remember now where I've seen the face of that woman of the light, your friend. Did you say her name is Lira?" Madame Conti asked Summer at breakfast.

"That's her name," Summer sighed.

"You doubt me."

"I didn't say that."

"We will go out today and see for ourselves, just you and me, while the others are lunching with their friend in Trastevere. Can you be ready soon?"

"I'm ready now," she sighed again while dressed only in blue jeans.

"You don't seem enthusiastic."

"I'm sorry. I'm just—I'm ready. Let's go."

The women stepped out of the building and strolled over to the Piazza del Popolo where they found a waiting taxi. Madame Conti allowed Summer to climb in while she looked up at the Egyptian obelisk brought to Rome from the ancient city of Heliopolis by Augustus in 10 BC. The sun was blazing brightly on the side carved during the reign of Ramesses the Great. "Ah, this will be a fortunate day," she uttered and stepped into the cab.

"Via delle Quattro Fontane, Palazzo Barberini," Madame Conti told the driver.

"We're going to a palace? I'm not dressed for that."

"It's a national gallery now, my dear. Although it was originally Maffeo Barberini's palace when he became Pope. What I want to show you is historic to the original palace. It's a fresco done by Andrea Sacchi. I won't tell you anymore until you've seen it for yourself. I don't want to spoil the surprise."

They arrived, paid their admission, and Madame Conti quickly led summer up the staircase leading to the gallery. "There is much to look at here, but on this trip you must focus only on one. There!" she said and pointed up, "Divine Wisdom."

Summer's eyes moved from paintings on the walls to the fresco on the ceiling. "How fantastic!"

"Do you not see the resemblance?"

"To Lira? Maybe a little. It's hard to tell. Her face is looking away. But what I do see is Prudence and her mirror."

"Yes! That's right too."

"But why does she turn away from her mirror?"

"Study the fresco further."

"She doesn't want to be blinded by the brightness of the sun that her mirror is poised to reflect. Oh, I see! She is a Sophia! The light of the sun is a metaphor for the light of creation."

"Look what's in her other hand."

"Ah, a scepter. She's pointing it towards the Earth. It's just as you explained it to us when we first met you. The Sophia, Prudence..."

"Isis, Minerva, and Gitane Marie."

"Yes, and Gitane Marie," Summer proclaimed. "Divine wisdom, you say. They're all one."

"You are a very fine student. You remember your lessons well," Madame Conti said feeling a further twinge of regret that she had not insisted that Summer become her very own granddaughter-in-law.

"Do others know about her?" Summer asked.

"Sacchi must have. He painted her. And I believe Campanella would have too since he chose this place to perform hermetical magic to save Pope Urban VIII's life. He must have known she had great power."

"Magic here?" Summer said as she looked all about the stately room.

"I do not know the details of it, but yes, that's what I have read."

"This is fascinating," Summer said. "Barry and Luc will want to hear all about it. But as to Lira, she is not so divine."

"In that perhaps you are correct. But Divine Wisdom herself may have inspired Sacchi's rendering here. Her look is similar. They could be of the same seed."

Seed, Summer thought, seed of life. She recalled the creation myth Lira had recited to her on her visit to Avian. The Virgin Expecting was the repository of seed out of which grew creation, but it was the Bird Goddess who flew out into the void, scattering the seed as she traveled. She considered the wings etched upon Gitane Marie's back. What was their meaning? She looked up at the fresco again and noted the winged angels above and to either side of Divine Wisdom. Similar legends, she mused, but one comes from the far end of the universe, light years away.

"I read about the Ohio incident on the Internet," Dr. Claudio Postremo said to Barry and Luc while the three men sat at table inside a quiet ristorante in the Trastevere district. "Internet reports are quite unreliable in the main. So when you called and said you had actually witnessed it, well, of course I had to come. Nothing like a good first hand account to allow me to assess what has been reported."

"Oh, it was real enough," Barry said, "and thank you very much for coming. It's quite a relief for me to be able to unload this burden, but I should tell you beforehand, I feel a bit guilty burdening you."

"You cannot burden me anymore than I already am," Postremo said and smiled. Luc looked at him doubtfully. Catching the look, Postremo asked, "Why? What more can you tell me?"

"Well, it's more than a firsthand witness account of the sighting, if that's what you thought," Barry said. "There's a lot more to it that never made the news. Remember when we met after your speech at the conference in Geneva?"

"Your friend thought he had been abducted. I quite remember that."

"Unfortunately, it was true," Luc said. "What is worse is that not long after the incident his personality began to change. His appetites became excessive. All of them. He lost all refinement. He put on a good deal of weight."

"The ordeal must have been a terrible shock to his psyche."

"If it was only that," Luc sighed.

"What are you trying to tell me? Are you saying his abductors turned him from Jekyll to Hyde?"

"Precisely!" Luc said.

"Ha! Ha! I've heard a lot, mind you, charges of rape, induced pregnancy, mental telepathy, but I've never heard a victim charge he was turned into a monster. If such is true, it would be quite serious; but I'm sure there must be a simpler explanation. That has been the case in most of my investigations."

"Maybe more harm has come to others than what you know," Luc said. "A very good friend of mine, a man that I trust implicitly, has told me an astonishing story. What's more, my friend now believes that what was done to Etienne has happened to many. In fact, there may be an ongoing campaign to abduct and to mind-strip, returning the unsuspecting victims back to their homes forever diminished."

"Mind-stripped! What are you talking about?"

"Probing an abduction victim's mind to retrieve all memories," Luc said.

"Like downloading all the data from a computer?" Postremo asked.

"Something like that. Only the human mind is far more delicate than a computer. When the mind is too deeply probed, the safeguards the subconscious constructed are ripped away causing the victim enough anguish to move him to madness, violence, or eventual suicide. I was able to help this man reconstruct his understanding of the past in such a way that he has been able to survive, but not without damage to his personality. He is now a much coarser man."

"Your conjecture is based on nothing more than premises!" Postremo argued. "Your first premise is that he was abducted. Maybe he wasn't! You follow with a second premise that his abductors probed his mind as a way to explain what you describe as psychological trauma when there are far more mundane explanations available. Your friend would not be the first man to have fallen in character after habituation to one kind of opiate or another."

"He now denies that he ever was abducted," Barry said.

"When I met this man he did not deny the abduction."

"That was true then," Luc said. "But all that changed as he changed. Ironically, it was only after this new personality was established that he made these denials."

"And then there is the matter of the woman," Barry said.

"What woman do you speak of?" Postremo said.

"Right after that conference where the three of you met he had a most erotic liaison," Luc said. "I could see it myself in his face and manner the following morning. I've never seen a man so seduced as he was after only one night of sex. That in itself was transformative. He immediately broke off with his fiancée, a very lovely girl."

"But not so full of sex as the other! Uh-huh! What did I tell you? You must always apply the principle of Occam's razor to tales of the fantastic," a self-satisfied Postremo said.

"I know this sounds fantastic," Barry said. "And the principle of Occam's razor often is correct. But those damn ships were in my backyard!"

Postremo became quite uncomfortable. He began to wonder about the sanity or at least the state of the imaginations of the men he now spoke with. He knew that ufology has always had its share of kooks, but he had not thought Barry Short one of them when he met him in Geneva. In fact, he thought him to be intelligent and level headed, the kind of man worth his time. Now he was not so sure.

"Let's start from the beginning," Postremo said to Luc. "First this friend you tell me about. Who is he, and why should I trust such a story without evidence other than the current state of mind of the victim? This victim could have suffered a mental breakdown after the ordeal of an ordinary abduction if he was abducted at all. He would not be the first. This sort of mental decline has happened to others."

"That's exactly my friend's considered point," Luc said. "You've got to believe me when I say I've known Roland for many years. He is not subject to imaginative outbursts or fits of lying. In fact, he kept me from all that he knew for many, many years."

"Roland's a scientist at CERN," Barry interjected. "A very intelligent man."

"He may be as intelligent as you say, but intelligence has never prevented a man from becoming delusional."

"I've seen too much myself," Barry said. "If Roland is delusional, so must I be."

Postremo studied Barry's face closely. "What have you seen besides these sightings witnessed in Ohio."

"A number of things. Roland and his wife Summer appeared at my front door in Ohio in the dead of night having been dropped off in my backyard by some kind of spacecraft. This happened shortly after they had been reported lost in a storm in Switzerland, just after I had returned to Ohio from France. They told me friends had rescued them and flown them over. I was so relieved to see them safe and sound, I didn't think to ask too many questions but my neighbor did. He had seen their arrival and was quite suspicious. He described having seen them walk down lighted steps that appeared to come out from a cloud. When he confronted Roland on this point, Roland claimed it was some kind experimental aircraft that a friend from CERN had flown them over in. But he didn't stick to that story for long. He couldn't since a few nights later a strange craft was back. Actually, there was more than one. There was the craft that brought them to my house and subsequently took them away, and there was another from some group apparently hostile to our planet, the same group of beings who had abducted the man you met in Geneva, Etienne. This time they tried to abduct Summer. And if it were not for my vigilant neighbor and his dog, they would have succeeded. Lord knows what they would have done to her."

"You saw all of this?"

"Not all of it but enough. Earlier in the evening of the very night Roland and Summer had fled from my house, they had seen another ship on a winter solstice outing we took to Serpent Mound in Ohio. One of us got a photo. It was downloaded onto my computer. Here, I've brought a copy to show you."

Postremo studied the photo for a few minutes. "Yes, I can see it very clearly. You say it was at a place called Serpent Mound? I've never heard of it. Where is it?"

"Out in the boonies of Southern Ohio. I'm surprised you haven't heard of it actually. It's quite famous. It's an ancient effigy mound built long ago by indigenous people long before the Europeans came. It's rather remarkable in that it points to both the winter and summer solstices through the placement of the serpent's head and tail. Every year the solstices are celebrated there with some kind of ceremony. We were there for the lighting of the snake."

"Why would this craft have been at such a place?" a now very perplexed Claudio Postremo asked.

"We don't know," Barry said. "Maybe it was tracking Roland. Apparently they're after him because they blame him for the destruction of one of their important Earth bases."

Postremo raised himself up from his chair. "How can you expect me to believe this?"

"Please, sit down," Luc said rising from his chair himself. "Please, sit down. I'll order us more wine and some soup. I see they have stracciatella on the menu. I know hearing this all at once must be difficult. For us it was a gradual awakening, and that's been difficult enough. But we need all the expert help we can muster, so please, sit down and hear us out."

"You seem to imply a war is going on between these extraterrestrials. That's been posited in legend for quite some time, but only in legend," Postremo said.

"Sometimes there is truth in these myths," Luc said. "Remember the recent incident at Jungfraujoch?"

"How could I not? It was all the news. It happened at the same time I met Barry and this man you speak of, this Etienne, while the conference was going on in Geneva. Brought about by a horrible weather anomaly, I remember. Set the place on fire."

"That's how it was reported," Luc said. "And I do believe that's how the officials made sense of it, but in actuality the event was brought about by hostilities between these two warring parties. That is when this underground base was destroyed near Evian, France. The base was located at the exact place from where our friend Etienne had been abducted."

Once the soup and wine were served, the men settled down to eat. By then, Postremo realized there was no retreating from this news. He could not escape it. He had to acknowledge that in its broad outlines it corresponded with his deepest fears, but in his heart of hearts he truly believed it was all madness, or at least his heart hoped it to be. He would have to find out later for himself.

The taxi carrying the three men arrived at Rome's Termini train station where Postremo would catch the late day train back to Florence.

"Give me a few days to absorb all that you said, do a little research, and think things through," he said. "I will get back with you then. But be patient. Don't try to rush me."

"We would never think of doing that," Barry said. "And thank you so much for coming and hearing us out."

"Yes, thank you," Luc said. "You've been very patient with us and we owe you patience in return."

Postremo nodded, turned and disappeared into the crowd going into the train station.

"I guess that went as well as could be expected," Barry said.

"I myself wouldn't believe this story if I did not know it to be true," Luc said. "So under the circumstances, you are right. But I hope he gets back to us soon. There is no time to wait!"

Chapter 15

Hermetic Magic

Sunlight burst through the windows of Madame Conti's apartment, throwing her furnishings into high relief, which provoked Summer's excitable imagination to fancy that some strange creature might pop out from a dark, shadowy corner behind the glimmering sea-green matelassé couch or one of the sun drenched marine blue chairs—a fish perhaps, a crab, a shark, or a mermaid. Years back Stuart had said the apartment looked like an aquarium. He was right, she thought, far more perceptive than I had given him credit for.

She and Madame Conti were taking tea. When her mind was not wandering off, the two women chatted as they waited for the return of the other guests. Her mood had so improved that she had changed from her blue jeans to her pink floral dress.

Madame Conti rose and closed the sheers. "There, that's better," she said. She searched her books and plucked one off the shelf, which she quickly thumbed through. "I think it more than coincidence that fortune took us to the Barberini today."

"You wanted to show me the painting that looks like Lira," Summer reminded her.

"Of course I did, but it must be part of a greater puzzle," she said now stopping at a page in the book. "First I saw you speak with that lady of the light. Later I realized whose image she bears. We were meant to go there," she said as she looked up at Summer. "Can't you see that? There's a message in this somewhere."

"A message?"

"A cure perhaps for my grandson since he is all that I think about. A mind as concentrated as mine is bound to produce its own kind of magic, drawing to itself solutions to what had seemed an insurmountable problem."

"You found a cure?"

"I can't be sure, but if the magic performed at the Barberini was as powerful as it says here, enough to alter the astrological fate that was to condemn Pope Urban VIII to his death within a year, well, that's quite powerful magic. If it could do that, surely it could restore my grandson."

"How was it done?"

"This book is rather vague on that matter. It says they used perfumes and herbs and candles and music to draw down the power of the beneficial planets."

"Hmm, the power to attract," Summer said as she looked down at her now bare finger. "Lira told me that she had turned my wedding ring into a talisman that could draw Roland to me. That's why she took it. I had no idea it could do that, but she feared the Endron might have figured it out if they should capture me." She went quiet for a sad moment. "It was the most beautiful ring I have ever seen. Lira said that it is her responsibility now."

Madame Conti dropped the book into her lap. "She has that kind of power?"

"She wears permanent tatouage on her chest, the mark of the bird goddess. Few on her planet are allowed to wear it."

"Is this the mark of a magician, a prophetess?"

"Perhaps," Summer said, this revelation to herself finally settling in. "But I don't think as profound as what we saw today." She recalled the image of Divine Wisdom and her staff directing the sun's benevolent light downward towards the Earth. "Could it be that the aim of the magic was to temporarily infuse the fresco with her true spirit so that for a sacred moment a connection could have been made between that light and the Pope?" She paused long enough for the full realization to set in. "Oh, my God, that Pope was protected with divine energy! Real divine energy! They drew it down!"

Madame Conti slammed the book closed. "I do believe you have hit upon something!"

"Your guests have returned," the maid said ahead of Luc and Barry who entered the now softly shimmering room. "Shall I bring more tea?"

"Yes, do," Madame Conti said, and to the men she said, "I'm glad you are back. We have much to tell you."

"We have much to tell you too," Barry said. "Dr. Claudio Postremo has agreed to join our investigative team. He probably knows more about UFOs than anyone. He's written their whole history."

"Has he?" Summer said.

"Well, as much as has been known at least," Barry qualified. "He's done quite exhaustive studies."

"Even with all that he was hard pressed to believe us," Luc added. "But he came around."

"Maybe we overstate," Barry said. "He said he would study our story anyway, and get back to us."

"Oh, so you're not sure?" Summer said.

"Well, you have to admit that this story is a lot to swallow if you haven't had the first hand experiences we've had," Barry said.

"Particularly hearing it all at once as he did," Luc said. "He almost got up and walked out halfway through our conversation."

"Harrumph!" Madame Conti said. "That does not sound like a resounding endorsement. His mind sounds decidedly closed."

"Cautious maybe," Barry said.

"Too cautious perhaps. Our Summer here has hit upon an amazing idea." She held up her book.

"It was more your idea than mine," Summer said.

"No, dear, I give credit where credit is due. We wish to work hermetical magic in an effort to restore my grandson."

"Did I hear you correctly?" Luc asked.

"Quite correctly. And you are just the man to help us." She looked at her watch. "I believe the Galleria Nazionale will be open tonight until seven. If you can do without your tea, we can get over there in time for you to see what I'm talking about."

"I would prefer wine to tea anyway," Barry said.

"You may have your wine later. I will take you to a very nice restaurant I know near the Via Veneto, have our dinner and talk after you've seen this very fine fresco. Will that do?"

"Oh, it's a fresco. I'm yours!" Barry said and stood up.

"What fresco will we be seeing?" Luc asked.

"A fantastic one," Summer said. "You'll have to see it to understand."

Now that his initial excitement over the Postremo conquest had cooled, Barry was quite ready to celebrate his partial success with a bottle or two of very fine wine. He would be happy enough to indulge Madame Conti for a few minutes for such a reward. Luc was another story. He was a greater lover of gallery art than Barry. And since he had previously observed Summer's refined taste and her capacity to interpret the deeper meanings of an oil, he was most interested to learn what besides Moreau's "Leda" she should describe as fantastic. He was equally intrigued to learn what Madame Conti had in mind in her reference to hermetical magic.

Traffic was heavy, creating some delay in their arrival at Palazzo Barberini, but not enough to keep them from entering the museum after a bit of coaxing and a little white lie.

"You will have only a few minutes before we close," the ticket clerk said. "It makes no sense. You should come back tomorrow."

"A few minutes is all that we need," Madame Conti said. "You must let us in. I've brought these gentlemen all the way here to see what I saw earlier today, and they will not be in Rome tomorrow."

"Yes, I recognize you and the girl from earlier. All right. This is a bit irregular, but I will let you in for no charge, but only for a few minutes."

They climbed the Bernini staircase without mention of its design, rushed past paintings in rooms that led to the chamber that was adorned on high.

"Up there," Madame Conti pointed. Heads tilted up; there came a long sigh.

"What an incredible image," Luc said. "To cast your eyes up and see this daily would be good for any soul. Who did you say made this?"

"Andrea Sacchi."

"Here, this tells you all about it," Barry said reading from the plaque on the wall. "He frescoed it between 1629 and 1633 for the nephew of Pope Urban VIII. It says here she holds the mirror of Prudence and the scepter with the eye of God."

"The scepter seems to glow," Luc said.

"As does the halo around her head," Madame Conti said. "As does the powerful sun behind her."

"I see," Luc said. "It's reflected in her mirror that she does not look upon."

"Exactly! She would be blinded."

"Wasn't it William Turner who said the sun is God?" Luc asked.

"Yes, it was he as did the Romans and many more. I love his paintings," Summer said. "This fresco speaks the same thought."

"Right here it says that Tommaso Campanella likened it to a representation of the City of the Sun," Barry read. "Some believed it to represent the theories of Galileo."

"You must leave now," a voice said coming into the room. "We closed ten minutes ago. I've already given you extra time."

"Thank you very much," Madame Conti said to the young lady. "I think we've seen enough." She turned to the others. "You will better understand when I tell you what happened here centuries ago. But let us go now and have our dinner."

The Roman restaurant they entered was small, but it made up for its size in its aura of intimacy, warm wood paneling, well-dressed tables, and a jovial proprietario.

"Benvenuto," the proprietario said. "Ah, Madame Conti! Dove sei stato? E 'un'eternità dall'ultima volta che ti ho visto."

"Ah, Mario!" she said, "Not that long I hope. My friends here are American and French. If you could speak English please."

"Oh, sì, oui, yes. Greetings to all of you."

"I've been away from Rome far too long, Mario."

They kissed affectionately. He escorted them to a table, tucked away in a charming corner of the room. "You look at the menu," he said. "I bring the antipasti and the wine." He smiled and winked. "I know what you like."

Bowls and plates loaded up with olives, roasted porcini mushrooms, grilled eggplant and zucchini, prosciutto, fresh mozzarella, bruschetta, roasted red peppers and fagioli al fiasco were placed on the table.

"Just taste," Madame Conti counseled. "Remember, we are to have their Florentine steak. They are very large." She whispered to Summer who was sitting next to her, "We will share if you don't mind."

"That's perfectly fine with me. I don't eat much meat."

Forks crisscrossed the table spearing each of the delicacies.

"Now that you're busy eating, may I have your attention? I wish to share my plan."

Small plates nearly emptied, everyone stopped eating and prepared to listen.

"No, no, you may eat. Otherwise your patience may weaken."

She had no need to worry about Luc's patience. He was looking forward to whatever she had to say, the esoteric arts having always intrigued him.

"Earlier you said that you wished to perform hermetic magic. What does that have to do, if anything, with the Palazzo we just came from?" he said.

"I was just about to explain. Imagine if you will," she said with her hands waving in front of her in a dramatic gesture designed to create the stage for the scene she was about to paint. "It's 1627 and you find yourself in that very room at the Palazzo," she said in a near whisper. "You are not alone. The dark, brooding presence of that great astrologer, philosopher, and poet, Tommaso Campanella stands there with you. He wishes to lift an astrological curse from the head of Pope Urban VIII, who astrologers had predicted would die within the year. To do so, he devised a remedy that would save him, a powerful agent great enough to change the direction of the very stars and thereby change the future of this tormented pope. Imagine that! Hermetic magic that could change the fate ordained by the stars!" She paused for a moment to assure herself that her audience was fully engaged. "Fragrant scents fill the room emanating from the abundant plants and stones that were brought there to bring to the room the vernal earth. And music most joyful and beauteous to match the beauty above in that fabulous and fascinating fresco you were privileged to see. That is how it was done. So above, so below," she uttered with a grand gesture. "Summer said to me earlier this day that it was magic enough to draw down that radiant beam from the scepter held by Divine Wisdom and reverse the curse the stars had levied on that unfortunate pope."

"And did it work?" a spellbound Luc asked.

"Yes! It did." She began to weep, taken away by the drama of her own story.

"She hopes that doing something like that could restore Etienne," Summer explained.

"We must try!" the distressed woman replied. "We must try!"

Barry hardly knew what to say because if he said what he was thinking he feared Madame Conti would have a complete breakdown right in the restaurant. He thought it very unlikely that the ritual had done anything at all since he doubted the pope was astrologically afflicted in the first place. Rather, as a result of fear and superstition, he thought himself afflicted and to relieve him of that fear required a more powerfully presented superstition. That's all. But he could not bring himself to say so in the presence of this woman who like this pope, was prepared to grab at anything that could save her grandson from a terrible fate.

"So I beg to enlist your help with this," Madame Conti said. "Luc, you are a herbalist. I know you can scheme out a hermetic plan."

"I've never done such in my life!"

"Your teas have already done my grandson so much good."

"Well, yes," he said humbly. "I can at least look into it."

"And Barry and Summer, I'm depending on you to help me make a plan to secure the room for a night. And we must devise an excuse to bring my grandson there. He would never submit if he had any idea what we were doing. So it must remain hush, hush," she whispered in a quiet voice. "Have I your commitment?"

"Well, I will do whatever I can," Barry said, "to help at least."

"Of course you have mine," Summer said.

Chapter 16

Postremo's Find

Claudio Postremo returned from Rome to his home in the outskirts of Florence, a location which offered him more space than the old city with the added bonus of a small plot of land and tranquil views of the Tuscan hills. He tried to relax, but it was of no use. The story he had been told while almost impossible to believe was nonetheless compelling and more than that, quite dangerous.

He was aware of the old legends about warring extraterrestrials but thought their veracity unlikely; at least he hoped it was. Only persistent probing such as his had lifted the veil ever so slightly, only by a fraction; and these fractional findings were not enough to convince him or anyone who had doubts. While those who had no doubts, he sadly noted, were often too ready to believe almost anything with little cognizance of the facts.

After long years of investigating UFOs, he had learned much about their proponents, observing that many were driven by the most fundamental of human emotions, hope and fear. Those who hoped imagined UFOs harbored otherworldly, beneficent beings, who might offer humankind marvels of technology as well as cures for what seemed intractable problems, war being one of them. Those who feared believed the opposite, imagining our planet potentially in danger from beings that regard us as little more than ants and the resources of our planet as theirs for the taking. When these theories collided, a third explanation emerged that corresponded to the story he had just been told. According to legend, there was ongoing warfare between those extraterrestrials who would help us and those who would harm us, and that humanity's eventual fate lay somewhere betwixt and between.

Postremo was not committed to any of these views, preferring instead to remain agnostic since after reaching adulthood he had developed far too skeptical a mind to draw conclusions from so little evidence. That was not always true. When he was a young UFO enthusiast he wholeheartedly sided with the most hopeful of these perspectives, imagining all the wonders these benevolent beings could bring to human culture, which from the vantage of his youthful, futuristic worldview still resided in the Middle Ages. His pessimism towards his own kind likely arose out of his inability to forgive Florence, his mother city, for having exiled its loftiest citizen, Dante Alighieri, in a political squabble that for him was emblematic of all the political squabbles that continued to disrupt and destroy lives around the planet. He knew we needed help, and in desperation his youthful mind looked to the stars.

But by middle age he had grown far more pessimistic. It occurred to him that if these extraterrestrials' intent had been to pull us out of the Dark Ages, they would have done so centuries ago. No longer sure of their motives in visiting our planet, only sure that they had, he believed their desire to conceal themselves should be respected. After all, they had caused no harm to either our planet or us. Better to leave well enough alone. But if Luc and Barry's reports were true that entirely changed the calculus of his reasoning, he shuddered to think.

Not able to relax an iota, the only thing left for him to do was to begin his own investigation to see if there was any evidence that human beings had been abducted and mind-stripped, as farfetched as that contention seemed. He set out to peruse recent abduction reports in the private UFO files of affiliate organizations that collect such things, looking for anything symptomatic of what was described as a sudden change in personality and character.

The volume of reports was enormous, far more than what he had expected based on his own past research. Yet in spite of their massive numbers, the reports themselves were generally cursory, noting location of the event, lost time, and witness corroboration when it existed. He moved through them quickly except for the occasional report that included an abductee account. Those he read with interest, but they were few and far between and in most cases conformed to well publicized accounts, the danger there being that the victims may have confabulated what they had previously read into their own recollections. More often than not the abductees had little memory of what had occurred. If there had been no outside witness or an awareness of unexplained missing time, these victims likely would have never known anything out of the ordinary had ever happened. How many people, he wondered, could have been abducted and left unawares?

His search had turned up nothing, which to be honest was what he had expected. What a waste of my time, he thought, as he stood in his kitchen frying himself a nice little steak in butter and garlic while steaming a few fresh green beans. He vowed to give the whole project up but a voice in his head would not be quiet.

A ship, Barry had said, brought a man named Roland into his own backyard in the middle of the night. Luc, he recalled, had testified to Roland's veracity; and yet this Roland fellow had plainly lied when he claimed he was flown there in experimental aircraft. No manmade aircraft, not even an experimental one, could have flown this man all the way from Switzerland and deposited him by golden stairway into an Ohio backyard. So what it ultimately came down to for his consideration was his estimate of Barry Short. He recalled Barry's photo of the spaceship hovering over a place called Serpent Mound. There was no doubt in his mind that if the photo were real, the origin of that ship was extraterrestrial. Was Barry Short such a man that would fabricate such a lie? His instincts told him no.

After his dinner, Postremo reluctantly went back to his computer and read many more reports identical to what he had earlier read: location, time missing, corroboration or not. His search was becoming quite redundant and tiresome. The increased volume of reports, he thought, was a consequence of easy access to reporting agencies via the Internet. No such thing had existed when he had been more actively engaged in fieldwork. And he knew from his earlier fieldwork that greater than half of these reports would prove unfounded had they been investigated, and most if not all of the rest would remain inconclusive for lack of solid evidence.

This search is becoming too tedious and unproductive to continue, he thought. Just when he was about to give up, he happened on a most amusing yet interesting newspaper article tucked into a file without elaboration. It was dated only two months previous.

BLOOMINGTON - Monroe County Sheriff's Office was called to Millford RV campsite near Monroe Lake at 4:00 am Monday morning after receiving reports of lewd behavior, fighting, and the endangerment of minors.

Several arrests were made after fights broke out with police. Three nearby tent campers told this reporter they were awakened by what one described as a "glaring light beam coming down on that RV camp" from what he called a "UFO."

"It was right up there. It scared the crap out of all us so we stayed hidden in the trees and watched. After it was good and gone, I went to my truck and got my phone and called the sheriff."

All three campers said they saw people taken out of their RVs, beamed up to a ship and eventually brought back down.

"That's when the trouble began. They were nice family people earlier that evening before that." Another witness summed it up, "It was like watching 'Invasion of the Body Snatchers' in real life."

Those arrested were charged with disorderly conduct, and none that I spoke with this morning could confirm the tent campers' story. They had no memory of the events of last night.

The sheriff responded to this reporter, "I don't think a UFO was the culprit. I think they'd all been drinking too much Flying Saucer Beer."

Postremo broke out laughing then paused. In its own peculiar way this report was the first he had read to indicate signs of sudden personality change following abduction. It appeared that the newspaper clipping had been filed, but no investigation was made to test the veracity of the tent campers' claims or any follow-up of the men arrested. He thought the sheriff's explanation far more plausible, but at the same time he found the report intriguing enough that he considered whether to email it to Barry.

He googled Bloomington, Indiana and noted its proximity to Ohio. He went to Google Maps and looked up Monroe Lake and saw that it was just south of Bloomington in an area removed from any major city. On a hunch he searched for Serpent Mound and enlarged that map to include the area of Monroe Lake. They were exactly at the same latitude, he noted, and Monroe Lake was only about 300 kilometers due west. There could be a connection, he thought. He emailed his findings to Barry with a note, "What do you think?"

The next morning he read Barry's reply. "You hit pay dirt my friend. I'll get back with you later. I'm going to get on this thing right away."

"Bill, Barry here."

"Why, hello! Where are you?"

" I'm in Italy right now. How's the house?"

"That's all you're callin' about? I've been waitin' to hear from you."

"Why? Is everything okay around there?"

"It's been crazy! They came here for about a week, a whole crew of them. They were settin' up stuff everywhere. Had a man in a lizard suit. Neighbors were interviewed. I was interviewed. Walt was interviewed. Anyone who could talk was interviewed."

"Paul and Andy?"

"They wanted them real bad, but their parents kept them out. They had no trouble findin' other kids in the neighborhood willin' to talk."

"I have no doubt."

"Paul was real mad about it too. Called the other kids frauds. A fight nearly broke out. I won't know how the production looks until it airs this week. They even had these little windup Bio-Nano robotic lookin' mice their art department made up especially for the show. And you should have seen the gal they brought in to play Summer. Wow! As for your house, well, they sure made a mess. But Paul and I got it cleaned up pretty good."

"Thank you for taking over like that, Bill. I don't know if I'll ever get the place sold."

"They tell me the market's pickin' up. But enough of this. Tell me what you're up to now?"

"That's why I called. We're over here trying to investigate the abduction I told you about. A friend of mine—I think I've mentioned him to you already, a Claudio Postremo—Well, he dug up an article last night that could have some relevance."

"Postremo, he's big time!"

"I know he is. This article he found describes a group abduction at an RV park over in Indiana, down somewhere near Bloomington. It happened just a few months ago."

"That's big news! I'm surprised I never heard about it."

"It probably got fobbed off as a joke. I don't think anyone's investigated the story, but I'm sure glad someone decided to log the article because it contains a salient detail we've been looking for, evidence that the fellow I told you about isn't the only man abducted and mind-stripped."

"Mind-stripped! Over in Indiana?"

"Look, do you know anyone over there that can help us out? We need someone who can follow up on the witnesses and victims and verify the details of the story."

"Near Bloomington? Hmm, Yes! I know someone, Buddie Eller. He's a math professor over there. He's written quite a bit about abduction too."

"That's just great! Do you think he would do it?"

"Well, if I tell him this is a favor being asked by Claudio Postremo, I know he will. That's for sure."

"You've got my consent to use his name," Barry said knowing full well Postremo would not mind. "Buddie Eller, you say? I'll pass his name on to Postremo in case this Eller fellow tries to contact him. I'm forwarding the article he sent me to you right now. You can forward it on to Eller, and he'll see Postremo's name on the top of the distribution list."

"Right! It just landed in my inbox. I'll look up Eller's email address and forward this along with a note right away. Hmm, it says somethin' here about Flyin' Saucer Beer!"

"That's the joke. You'll get back to me soon?"

"Pronto!"

Chapter 17

Buddie Eller

Buddie Eller is a man with a double life. But you would never know it just to meet him. Everything about his appearance and his demeanor is as unassuming as one might expect from a math professor. He is slim, dresses nicely but decidedly not fashionably. His hair is brown, longish, and neatly combed, but something about the styling suggests that his fashion has not changed since 1985. He wears glasses, as any respectable college professor would, with full lenses and dark rims. Eller never married and has no discernible family, but that's because his double life takes up most of his time outside the classrooms and offices of the university.

Weekends and evenings Eller is a UFO investigator extraordinaire. While he is best known for his brilliant analysis of well known abduction cases, behind the scenes he has been writing the most complete, in-depth exploration and analysis of UFO mysteries and myths to rival any other work ever published, including the works of his hero, Claudio Postremo. So when Bill forwarded him the email along with a note requesting his time and expertise, there was no way he was going to turn it down once he saw the email originated from Postremo himself. He instantly replied yes to Bill, a man who he had to be reminded that he had met once at a WOFUC conference but had no memory of.

The article cited in the email took him by surprise because it had been published in his local newspaper without him having read it. "Flying Saucer Beer," he uttered softly and broke out laughing. He surmised by its comic ending that the story might have been placed in the "Leisure and Entertainment" section. That's where he would have put it had he been the newspaper editor, which would explain why he had not seen it. But why would Claudio Postremo, of all people, have taken an interest in such a farce?

Postremo's address appeared along with his name at the top of the email under the original message line. He could email him a series of questions he thought, but then he thought again.

This is a delicate matter. I might insult the great man if I treat this story like a joke. On the other hand, if my tone is too serious, he might think I'm a joke. I can't have that, particularly at the beginning of our first working relationship. No way to know without knowing what this is all about, he thought. He proceeded to write. "Got the article and was asked to investigate. Before I begin I should talk to you first. Can you email me your phone number and a convenient time when you can be reached?" There, he thought, that's done. He couldn't do much until the next day so he watched the late night news and went to bed.

"You may telephone me at 9 a.m. this morning EST," was all the reply from Postremo said. Buddie looked at his clock. It was half past eight. That would give him thirty minutes to get dressed and eat an egg before he made the call. His class was at ten, so he should have plenty of time, he thought.

"Dr. Postremo, Buddie Eller here. I thought it best to speak with you before I begin to research this newspaper story so I know better what I'm looking to find."

"It's a complex story," Postremo said. "Let me be brief." He cleared his throat. "A few days ago I had lunch in Rome with a French priest and an American archeologist who told me an amazing story. I had met this archeologist some time ago when I was a featured speaker at the International WUFOC Conference in Geneva. I will admit I was impressed with him. So when he phoned and declared he had been witness to a well-publicized sighting in Ohio, I agreed to take the train down from my home in Firenze. I expected only to confirm the details of the event that had taken place in Ohio. You may have read about it."

"Of course. It caused quite a commotion," Eller said. "I believe I read they've made a television show about it."

"I would not know about that. I was merely interested in hearing the details from someone I could trust, but he had more to tell me. At our first meeting in Geneva he had brought along a friend who claimed to have been abducted. I know from your work that you are well aware that it is hard to be certain about such claims, but I had no reason to doubt his."

Buddie Eller smiled. Until he heard Postremo utter these words, he had not known that one of the leading scholars in his field had read his published articles. "Yes, there's so much opportunity for contamination of the subject's memories," he said eruditely.

"This case was different. The abductee was never subjected to hypnotic regression or cultural contamination. There was clear-cut evidence of an episode of missing time. But what held my attention was the fact that multiple witnesses saw a spacecraft rising from a lake near the French town of Evian in the exact location where the abduction was to have taken place."

"A lake did you say?" Eller said. "You know there's a lot of speculation about so called lake bases."

"I'm well aware," Postremo said. "Which adds to my worry. It's the other claim they make I find most troubling however, and why you were contacted to investigate the story I found in WUFOC's files."

"You know why no one bothered to comment," Eller said, now feeling quite comfortable. "The story was written with a punch line!"

"I will admit it caused me a very good laugh. Your job, if you're willing to do it, will be to find out if it was a joke concocted by the reporter. If not, I need the facts of the case verified and elaborated."

"You sound concerned, and I understand. If campers were actually abducted and dramatically changed by their abductors as the reporter's witnesses contend, well...."

"That's exactly the other claim these two men I lunched with are making about their friend."

"I've never heard such an allegation before!" Eller said.

"Neither have I. They claim he was altered somehow as a result of the abduction. They say his personality changed and his character declined quite significantly. That is why this news story grabbed my attention. If both stories are true, well, that could be evidence for something quite significant going on thus far undetected."

"If it's true about the lake bases, if that could once and for all be confirmed, well, this could prove really bad."

"You understand then," Postremo said. "You're ideal for this investigation. You know the customs over there and the lay of the land."

Eller smiled again. "I'll get on it right away."

"Please keep me posted," Postremo said. "Update me on anything you might uncover."

Eller arrived at his last class of the semester just as the bell rang. His lecture was rote, having taught this course or one like it for the last twenty-five years. Lacking a comedic style, he never won a teaching award; nonetheless, his students all agreed that he was fair and a quite competent math professor. His passion, however, lay elsewhere in his second occupation for which he received no pay and of which neither his math colleagues nor his students knew anything.

He phoned the local newspaper from his office, explained that he was a professor at the university, and asked if he could speak to the news reporter who had written the story he was inquiring about. He was immediately connected.

"Frank here," the reporter said.

"Hello Frank. This is Professor Eller over at the university. Look, I got a rather peculiar request I wonder if you can help me out with."

"If I can."

"A friend called from out-of-town, actually from over in Italy, and asked me to verify whether the story you wrote about the abduction down at an RV campsite at Lake Monroe was intended as a joke."

Frank laughed. "I didn't know it had become an international story. But to answer your question, no. They won't let me do that kind of thing even out here in the Midwest. The report was a true witness account. Not to say that what those guys told me actually happened, but it's what they thought happened. I only reported what they told me."

"Did you do any follow-up?"

"Only what I describe in the story. The next day, I went over to the lockup right as some of the guys were being released. I asked them straight out if they had been taken up by a flying saucer. They couldn't remember a thing, not about flying saucers or anything else. My take on it is they were just too damn drunk, all of them. But I have to keep my personal opinions out of it."

"Well, you kind of snuck one in there with the sheriff's comment about Flying Saucer Beer."

"Yes, but he said it, not me. That was an exact quote."

"So you think the whole thing was some kind of alcohol fueled nightmare?"

"What else could it be? Those guys that go fishin' down there do a lot of drinkin'. That's what keeps those little bait stores in business. They couldn't survive only on worm sales."

"I see what you mean," Eller said. "Would it be possible for you to give me the witness names so I can talk to them myself? I figure I can find the names of those arrested at the Monroe County Sheriff's Office."

"Sure. I don't think they'd mind. They'll probably relish the attention. Let me look in my file here. Yep, I've got the names and phone numbers of all three guys."

It took Eller only one phone call and an hour to arrange a meeting with all three witnesses for dinner and drinks that night at Clyde's Place. He waited in his regular booth until they arrived. He noted as they walked towards the table that they looked sane enough and relatively clean cut. He stood up and put out his hand, "Buddie Eller."

"Hi Buddie. I'm Wade Brown, the fellow you talked to today on the phone. This is my brother Cliff and a longtime friend Jim."

"Have a seat," Eller said. "Thanks for coming out tonight. What can I get you before we order dinner? Beer? Wine?"

"I'll just have a club soda," Wade said. "I'm driving tonight."

"I'll have a Bud," Cliff said.

"That's good for me too," Jim said.

"The blue plate special is meatloaf," Buddie said. "I highly recommend it, but get whatever you want. Dinner's on me."

"Sounds good," Wade said and the others nodded in agreement.

"So, the three of you witnessed this UFO abduction reported in the paper."

"Before I say too much," Jim said, "I'd like to know what this is about. Are you another reporter?"

"No, I'm not. I'm a UFO investigator, but by day I teach over at the university."

"They're teaching about UFOs now?" Cliff said. "Man, the place sure has changed since I was a student."

"Probably not as much as you think. No, I teach math. This other work I do is on the side. Look, I will be straight with you if you will be straight with me. Yesterday I was on the phone with a colleague who asked me to look into the story you told the reporter to determine if what you thought you saw was what you saw."

"You're not from that show *Questers* are you?" Jim asked.

"Oh, no. That's not up my alley."

"That's good. I don't want anyone making a fool out of me."

"Would you feel better if I keep your last names out of my report?"

"That would be better. I don't know about the rest of you," Jim said and looked over at his friends.

"Well, let's keep it at that. So what exactly did you see?"

"I never saw a ship," Wade said. The others nodded in agreement. "I just saw this huge beam of light that brought these men down. We watched as they went into each RV and took the people out and beamed them up. There must have been a ship up there hidden behind a cloud 'cause I never saw it."

"So they looked human? The people from the ship."

"Yeah, they looked like you and me, except they were all wearing some kind of uniform that didn't look like anything I've ever seen," Wade said.

"It fit tight," Jim said. "Looked uncomfortable."

"How many of them were there?" Eller asked.

"About a half dozen or so I would say," Wade said.

"So what time did all this happen, and how long did it go on?"

"After midnight, and it must have lasted at least a few hours," Wade said and looked at the others.

"Have you all talked about this much since it happened?" Buddie asked.

"Sure, to each other," Jim said. "No one else."

"Not even your wives?"

"Particularly not my wife," Wade said and laughed. "Not her! She'd throw me out if I ever tried to tell her."

"So, after talking about it, did you come up with any other explanation for what you saw, a more terrestrial one?"

"Believe me if we could have, we would have," Jim said. "We tried, we tried really hard, but we can't figure anything out besides what it looked like."

"We did wonder if it could be some kind of foreign plot to take over America," Wade said. "Years back I would hear about such things, but I never believed it then and I don't now. Nobody here has got that kind of technology to beam people up. And what they did to those people. They didn't kill them; they turned them wild!"

"Yes, that was the other part of the story," Buddie said. "You say they turned them wild?"

"We'd been camping near those people all night," Wade said. "They weren't like that. They drank a few beers, sure, but then they went to bed. They were nuts after they were brought back down. We watched a long time, and when we saw some of the things they were doing, well it was disgusting."

"What were they doing?" Eller asked.

Wade look a little sickened. "Just say it was an orgy if I ever saw one, which I never had seen one until I saw them."

"And they had a couple of kids with them!" Cliff said.

"Then they started fighting each other. Beat each other up real bad," Jim said. "That's when I went up to my truck, got my phone, and called the sheriff. Heck! When the sheriff and his men got there these guys started fighting them."

"How about you? Had you been drinking?" Eller asked.

"Not like that!" Jim said. "A few beers, that's all. We weren't drunk if that's what you mean."

"Well, is there anything else any of you would like to add?"

"I don't have anything more to add," Wade said. "But if you figure this out, will you tell us? It's sort of driving me crazy. I feel haunted by the whole thing."

"Yeah, it sure puts a damper on going fishing," Jim said and looked at the other guys.

"Yeah, I won't go back there," Cliff said.

"None of us will, ever!" Jim said.

Eller had done a lot of interviews before and naturally had learned to judge people pretty well. These guys seem credible, he thought. They were careful in their descriptions, making a point to say they never actually saw a UFO only the transporting beam. They were not prone to exaggeration either, which is the first sign an investigator looks for in a witness. In fact, their most emphatic statements had more to do with the behavior of the returned RV campers than the extraterrestrials. He found it interesting that their motive in calling the sheriff seemed to have had more to do with this behavior than what they presumed to be UFO abductions. What could this mean, he wondered? They didn't describe the abductors as little gray men with great big eyes, the most common depiction of UFO aliens in the popular press. No, they said they looked like us. In fact Wade said that he entertained the possibility that they could have been some kind of invading international force, but then dismissed it because of the technology employed. Hmm, he thought. And they're definitely not seeking publicity or attention.

He shot off an email to Postremo.

Can't be sure exactly who they saw, whether it was extraterrestrial or not. But I'm convinced the witnesses interviewed are not lying or exaggerating. They saw what they saw. What struck me most was their reaction to the changes that occurred in the campers that were taken up. They were shocked, and these men did not strike me as easily shocked. I must presume therefore that the changes in the abduction victims was marked and showed a dramatic deterioration in their personalities and character. Tomorrow I will attempt to learn these victims' identities and track them down.

It was not difficult to learn who the victims were since their names had become a part of the public record. More difficult was making personal contact. Eller spent Friday afternoon making phone calls and all day Saturday driving to a few small towns and a nearby farm. He made five contacts altogether, but not in a single case was he able to speak with a victim. They had disappeared. In one case, the victim's wife had thrown him out after he repeatedly struck her. She had no idea where he had gone but was glad to be rid of him, she said, and shut the door in Eller's face. He was told that two of the victims dropped out of school and ran off to join the army. A fourth was in jail up in Detroit on murder charges. The fullest interview he was able to obtain came from the reluctant parents of one young man whose family had no idea where he was.

"It was drugs," the boy's father said from his recliner.

"It couldn't be," the mother said. "He was a star athlete. He never got into trouble."

"What do you think happened to him?" Eller asked

"It was drugs!" the father repeated loudly from across the room.

"He would never do that!" the mother insisted.

"What the hell else can explain what he did then!" the father shouted.

"You know he was arrested for fighting and resisting arrest," the mother said to Eller.

"That's not half of it! Tell him the rest!"

The woman started weeping.

"Tell him! Tell him!" her husband shouted.

"If you think it's so necessary to hang out the dirty laundry, then you tell him!" she said.

"Okay, I'll tell him!"

"Tell me what?" Eller said.

"He corrupted his little brother, only eleven years old. He musta poured beer down him to get him that damn drunk."

"Little Henry hasn't been the same since," the mother cried.

"Wait a minute. Was little Henry out there with them that night at Lake Monroe?" Eller asked.

"Yes," the mother cried. "That's when this nightmare all started."

"It was drugs. I'm tellin' you," the father said again. "What do they say? Look for a sudden change in personality and behavior."

"But why would Ben do that? He never did anything like that before," the mother cried.

"It's the only explanation!" the father said.

"So where is little Henry now?" Eller asked, thinking that at last he had found an actual victim.

"He sent him away!" the mother shouted, pointing her finger at her husband.

"I couldn't do anything with the kid. My brother will be able to straighten him out. He's a military man. It was either that or he'd end up back in the juvenile lockup."

"Where does your brother live?" Eller asked.

"If you think you're gonna interview him there, you've got another thing comin'."

"I think you better be leavin' now," the mother said before escorting Buddie Eller to the door.

"I'm sorry for all of your troubles," he said to the teary eyed woman.

"I hope things work out."

Eller fired off another report to Postremo:

Was unable to speak directly with the victims, but had a lengthy conversation with the parents of two of them. They confirmed the witness accounts. Their two sons suffered some kind of sudden and unexplained change in personality that led them to trouble. The oldest of the two sons whereabouts are unknown; the younger, only eleven, was sent to live with a strict uncle who the family hoped could provide proper discipline. I learned from relatives of the other victims that after the event they were drawn to one form of violence or another, putting two in the military, one in jail on murder charges, and another gone off to parts unknown effectively abandoning his wife and children. The wife said he had become violent, and she is glad to be rid of him.

This part of the investigation is over. The events reported in the newspaper have been confirmed. What is as yet unconfirmed is who was responsible and what their motive was. Please advise if you have further need for me on this. I will be more than happy to assist. I'm fascinated with this story.

Yours Truly,
Buddie Eller

Eller couldn't sleep that night thinking about the horror of what may have happened at that lake. And yet in another turn of mind he was mesmerized by the thought of UFOs only miles away. In his thirty years of investigation he had never seen a flying saucer although his curiosity to do so is what had driven him into this part-time profession. By 3:00 a.m. he had made a plan. The semester would be over tomorrow after he administered final examinations. He could assign his teaching assistant the task of turning in his computer-generated grades. He would pack a tent and a sleeping bag and head off for the lake the day after next. It was the only logical course of action if he were to find out what was going on.

Chapter 18

Wheels Turning

In the Southwest Quadrant of the planet Avian the rain had finally stopped its ceaseless pounding and the wind had subsided, leaving in their wake morning mists, soft breezes, and a verdant wonderland of all manner of leaf and flower. It was not the sight of it as much as the glorious smell of new life that had the effect to heal Roland's wracked brain, cauterizing old wounds and stanching the bleeding that had threatened to drown him in sorrow and rage. Recognizing the magic of this place in springtime, Sedwig kept Roland outside as much as possible although the temperatures were yet cool. He taught him the identities of flora and fauna, how to grow and hunt, all the essential tasks of living in this place. Roland, who had spent his years in universities and science laboratories, had never before felt such an attachment to nature's land. Like a tree that had just been released into the soil after spending years balled up, he grew new roots. He loved the place, wild and free and full of peace until his past life broke in. It was not Bryn who broke the spell but Lira, looking radiant as the suns.

"You be much better than when I saw you last," she joyfully proclaimed. "I admit I had my doubts that you would heal. But here you be a picture of strength and health. Sedwig, we be forever in your debt."

"Thank you." Sedwig said with a bow. "Can you stay with us for a while? I've made plenty to eat."

"Only for a brief visit," she said and looked over at Roland who sat upon a leafy tree limb grown close to the ground. "I tell you Roland now that I find you strong what we've learned as to the fate of the planet you hail from, although you look to me to have sprung new roots here."

"Happy I be I must admit."

"Let me give this reminder." Lira showed him the blue and yellow sapphire ring he had given Summer.

"Is she all right?"

"She be all right for now. I took it from her for her protection. This ring acts as a homing device that could have brought you to her if she had understood how to use it. I feared the Endron might capture her to take the ring to capture you. You be still very much in their hateful sights."

"I do not doubt, which is why I find so much solace here. Such a peaceful life it promises."

"No peace on Earth if the Endron have their way. We've learned they have been capturing and mind-stripping at a rapid pace. Their goal be enslavement and expansion of their occupation, which would destroy your planet."

"Expansion!" Roland said. "You say that as if they already occupy."

"They do so secretly we think in under earth bases much like the one we destroyed thanks to your keen observations. We believe those bases be their seat of operation to reduce the human species and steal the resources of your planet. If we cannot locate them quietly and take them out, we must advance a full scale counter invasion to protect."

Roland shook his head, the peace he had found having taken a respite. "A full scale war you threaten?"

"If necessary."

"Then what shall become of them and us?"

"Of that I be not sure," she said. "My watchers tell me your friends seek a remedy as do we. I ask you to meditate now that you be returned to yourself. The more minds at work, the greater the chance we can end this deadly problem. So I leave you now with a heavy burden, but a burden you be destined for. So with that, Roland, I say my goodbyes. If you need my help, you know what to do."

"Thank you for protecting Summer," he said.

"It be for you, as it be for her. I will walk awhile alone in the woods to strengthen myself before I journey back to the ship. Sedwig, please continue to take care of him. He be not as strong as he thinks. This place makes us all feel stronger than we be," she said as she stretched herself and then took a deep breath and disappeared into a nearby thicket.

"Why so Lira say you have a destiny to fulfill?" Sedwig asked. "What destiny be that?"

"I do not know what she means any more than you. What I do know is that when Lira speaks it is not to be ignored. I must find a way to avoid this full-scale war she threatens. All my instincts tell me that although the purpose be noble, it would bring disaster. They cannot know, these Earthlings, that they are watched."

"Why so if it be for their benefit? Would they not praise?"

"They do not think that way. Living as they do nestled in the cocoon of their atmosphere, they think they be masters of the universe. To be asked to think otherwise would make an enemy of the asker."

"In such circumstance that be not rational," Sedwig argued.

"Such circumstance, as you suggest, should compel their praise. That they would never accept."

"All right," Sedwig said. "If they not be rational, we be that for them. We begin in a logical way. First, state the problem."

"It seems unsolvable when I think how to state it."

"State it anyway."

"The Endron are abducting my people without their knowledge. They are using their mind-stripping technique not to probe for information but to unhinge them, to strip them of what keeps them stable as a means to undermine civilized life and turn human against human that they might exploit that weakness."

"I cannot see the logic. Would that not make your fellow Earth people a more aggressive foe, more difficult to subjugate?"

"At first perhaps. But once humankind lessens its own numbers through conflict and greed and becomes more unstable, it will be ever more difficult for them to organize for the betterment of the whole, leaving them defenseless in the wake of an Endron invasion, leaving them as an animal to be slaughtered or tamed under the whip of brute force."

"No remedy we have for mind-stripping," Sedwig sighed. "You be an exception only because the technique be aborted. Otherwise, you become like your father, only half the man you once were."

Roland shuddered to think of himself become a rapist. "I would rather have died," he said. "There must be a way. But even if we could find a remedy, how would we deliver it in mass to a people who fail to recognize the disease?"

"What destiny Lira must have imagined for you to leave you with such a problem," Sedwig said. "To avoid a mighty war you must find a cure for what has passed for centuries as an incurable condition, and if such cure be found, delivered to patients without their knowledge. A stubborn lot these Earthlings be."

"As are all of us," Roland acknowledged, "Stubborn and proud. Pride that be both curse and blessing."

"We go back to the cabin and have roasted vegetables in flaky crust. Perhaps if we eat and rest we can dream. Dreaming be necessary to find a solution here, if a solution there be."

"Why say you that Sedwig?"

"It opens the untapped mind. Something revolutionary we need. After you eat I will sing you to sleep."

Luc, on the other hand, needed neither song nor dreams to enter the recesses of his deep imagination. He had crossed that bridge years ago to the consternation of the more conventionally minded who shared his faith and sat far above him in the echelons of power. And yet he was not prevented from gaining admittance into the Vatican Library to see what he could find about the methods by which Pope Urban VIII was cured of his affliction as so beautifully described by Madame Conti. The fresco of Divine Wisdom casting the light of God upon the head of the trusting Pope had mesmerized Luc's imagination. What sort of hermetic magic could have pulled the heavens down, he wondered as he walked towards Saint Peter's Square? He recalled the conversation that had taken place between him and that glorious Madame just a few days after she presented her dramatic challenge.

"I'm gratified my teas have had a positive effect on Etienne," he had said to her.

"He's not entirely as he was, but he is much better," she acknowledged. "He certainly has gained control over his behavior that had grown quite offensive. Yet there is something about him that still seems—well, how should I put it—something in his character seems gone, missing."

"Maybe in time it will come back." Luc said.

"I fear that it will not if this is all we can do for him," she said. "The gentleness of his innate virtue is gone. He's become quite stern in his admonitions to himself and everyone else. He badgers his wife. He even had the gall to criticize me. It seems his high moral standards are ruling again, making him able to control what only a few months ago he could not. But it is not a natural virtue. I think those awful impulses he had been acting on are all still there. He has merely suppressed them, which is making him nearly intolerable to live with."

"I see," Luc said. "I bow to your astute observations. What was once natural virtue rules now by strength of force."

"Exactly! He's become a bully." She turned to Summer. "What about that creature, that angel woman who visited you? She had a touch of magic, no doubt. Could she not conjure up a more thorough cure?"

"Luc has done far more for Etienne than the people of Avian have done for their victims. They have no teas, no cure, not even Lira with all of her magic. They make them live as outcasts. Besides, Lira doesn't have half as much wisdom as she thinks. She took my ring!" Summer grumbled.

Madame Conti turned to Luc. "Summer has seconded my thoughts. It's up to you."

Luc was awestruck by Summer's high praise. He must learn the secret of Tommaso Campanella's magic.

The image of her he had envisioned in the shop window in Paris stayed with him, that pretty girl in the pink floral dress. He pored through book upon book in the Vatican Library to learn better what he could about Campanella and hermetic magic. At last he came upon "De Fato siderali vitando" in Campanella's 7th book of *Astrologia* (1629). The formula was there.

Seasoned UFO investigators learned years ago that one could not dismiss a news account based on a reporter's style since journalists often make light of what they do not understand. What mattered most was the substance of the reporting and whether or not it was true. Postremo made a quick phone call to Barry Short.

"Troubling news. My hunch proved correct. Mr. Eller writes me that what happened to your friend may have happened to those unlucky Indiana fishermen."

Barry sighed. "How much do you trust this Eller guy?"

"His published work is impeccable."

"Oh," Barry groaned.

"The only question I'm left with is what to do next."

"I bow to your expertise. What are you thinking?" Barry asked.

"I can see proceeding in two ways. I noted the incidents of reported abduction cases have grown very large although the documentation is scant. We could begin by doing a more thorough investigation of these cases to see if the incidents of abduction and what you call this 'mind-stripping' is in fact widespread. If this were only a research project, that would be my recommendation. But since lives may depend on our acting fast, I think we should take a more aggressive approach, which requires we accept the assumption and proceed from there."

"But proceed to do what? We can't fight these things alone!"

"Find out who or what we're dealing with. Some of us should fly over there. I would go myself if it were not such a long trip. We may need the cooperation of the military."

"Well, you're not likely to get it," Barry said. "Not now anyway. But I have a friend in Washington, a very fine investigator. Come to think of it, you met him in Geneva. Maybe I can ask him to drive over to Lake Monroe."

"Is he the man I met who confirmed the abductee's sighting?"

"The very one."

"Good then. He won't have to be convinced. Be sure to warn him that this could be very dangerous. I should tell you what I failed to tell you before, which Dr. Eller is well aware of. Lake bases have been talked about for years in the context of extraterrestrial invasion scenarios, but no claim has ever been substantiated. I had always hoped that like so many rumors this one would prove false. But if it is true, if there is some kind of underwater base at Lake Monroe that would augment what happened near Evian and could explain the ship you photographed at Serpent Mound. I determined from my maps that they are at the exact same latitude and in close proximity to each other. What this might mean, I do not know."

"I'll phone Stuart and get him on it straight away," Barry said.

Sedwig's reedy tune invaded Roland's dreams. He found himself back in the bucolic meadow where his mother, now only a girl, lay weeping. She looked up at him in recognition, her eyes large, reflecting both his image as a man and as the seed that had just invaded her womb.

In a woman's voice she said to him, "You must avenge this deed. Your father, whose mind was weakened by his enemies, could not resist his lower nature and left me as you see me now, my pretty dress in tatters. I was as the world will become, plundered and ruined; he was as the man who is robbed of his wisdom, destroyer of that which he loves."

The meadow that minutes before was all green and growing transformed into a rutted desert in the blink of Roland's eye.

"My dear son," she continued. "Let this seed in my womb turn into Earth's blessing. Make our world right again. Turn my shame into honor and restore honor to the lineage that had been your father's line."

Weeping, Roland said to his dear mother who looked now as pale and thin as she had the last time he saw her, "This I will do for you mother if it is the last that I do. You never blamed me for what was done to you, but you instead taught me the true meaning of love."

The flute song ended. Roland was nudged from sleep. "Be you all right?" Sedwig asked.

"I'm all right. I just had a dream of my mother that was most compelling. She asked that I avenge her, but in a way I do not truly understand."

"Revenge be not hard," Sedwig said.

"But making the world right again is. That's what she asked of me."

Sedwig said nothing, but instead resumed playing his flute, this time in a higher note on a different scale.

"You have altered it. It's quite pleasing," Roland said, eyes partially open.

"I merely adjusted it to lighten your dreams so that you might sleep."

"Music can do that? Alter my dreams?"

"Why yes!" Sedwig said. "Have you not noticed the effects of music on the soul?"

"I've had little time to consider such thoughts. Yet, your music does play on me like a balm."

"Ah, then you have missed much indeed. It soothes the soul; it harmonizes and balances. It keeps the psyche tuned, without which the whole personality can unravel."

"Tuned, you say?"

"Until the spring blooms added further pleasures to my bag of tricks, music be my only therapy for bringing you back," Sedwig declared.

In a spark of recognition, Roland's mind snapped back to his meeting with the timekeeper at the Library of Time. Did he not say something quite similar in principle at least? The universe is like a violin, he had said, subject to distortion. It must be tuned from time to time lest harmony fail. The consequence of many tunings being that the past is changed, very subtly he had said, yet enough changed that Roland could not be sure if what he saw in the building of the Serpent Mound had happened as it is now recorded in the Library of Time. Could the universe be likened to a human mind, he wondered? And could swift tuning harmonize it and alter it too, creating a new history, a new reality?

Roland sat up now fully awake. "Sedwig, can you get me to the Northeast Quadrant unnoticed? I must go to the Library of Time and meet with the timekeeper."

"I can get you there unnoticed if we go by ferry, but I should warn you that the timekeeper rarely meets with the public. He be a private person, I've been told."

"He will meet with me. We must leave as soon as possible. No time to waste."

"A ferry leaves in the wee hours every morning to carry workmen. It be just past midnight now. If you be up and ready, we can be at the dock in just over an hour."

Chapter 19

Lake Monroe

Barry's urgent phone call propelled Stuart out of his Washington DC condo in the middle of the night. He couldn't get there fast enough as he raced past Hagerstown, Morgantown, and on to Ohio full of fear.

He—with Natalie's help of course—had rationalized his whole UFO experience in Europe. What had happened there would not happen here he had told Natalie. Or had she told him? He could not remember. They both had agreed that America is just not the same kind of place as Europe. It has no Dante with his Angel Boatman, no legends of Zeus shapeshifting into a swan, no eccentric Madame Conti who decorates her apartment to look like an aquarium. Europe is ripe for confabulation. Americans, on the other hand, are made of sturdier stuff, their cultural roots far more grounded in the soil. "We're a practical people," Natalie had assured him, "not prone to such fantasies."

"Fantasy, she called it!" Stuart muttered as he tore down the highway. Together the two of them had all but ignored the brief onslaught of media stories about UFOs in Ohio, she chalking them up to sensationalist journalism. Privately, however, these reports had given him pause since he himself had actually witnessed the darn thing rise up out of the lake and take off, and he knew he had not been fantasizing. But it was the phone call from Barry Short that finally convinced him that sensationalist media or not, something awful was going on.

Though weathered, the "House For Sale" sign was still propped up in front of Barry's Delaware, Ohio house when Stuart pulled up. For Stuart, that sign served as a marker denoting that Neighbor Bill's house was next door. But for snoopers who were not welcomed in the neighborhood, the sign served as a red flag. In fact, that sign had turned Barry's house into a neighborhood nuisance since *Questers* had aired its program.

Stuart was not exactly in a panic when he pulled into Bill's driveway, but he was as near to one as he ever gets. He lay on Bill's front doorbell.

Yawning, Bill had just gotten up. Shadow was still inside resting, having been woken up at midnight by noisy teenagers who played I dare you games in Barry's backyard. "You got here fast," he said and looked over at the clock. "It's only eight. I didn't expect you would be leavin' until this mornin'."

"We need to get to Indiana right away. Particularly since that guy over there...uh..."

"Buddie Eller?" Bill said.

"Yeah, that's his name. Since this Eller fellow took off by himself to investigate. That's just plain stupid not to cover your back."

"He's alone?"

"That's what they tell me. What kind of nut would go off by himself after what just went down?"

"He's an investigator," Bill said. "Danger comes with the turf. If you can't handle the unknown, then you damn well ought to stay out of it. Leave it alone!"

"Investigator or not, you gotta use some sense," Stuart said.

"Look, I didn't mean to impugn your courage. It's just, well, it's a dangerous business. Look at what happened to your friend over there in Europe, and look what happened to Summer in my backyard!"

"Yeah, well, that's why I'm here! I witnessed one myself, the very one that took that friend of mine. If I hadn't been careful, it could have taken me up too. So that's all that I'm saying about this Eller fellow. You can't throw caution to the wind."

"Curiosity got the better of him, that's all. Say, come on in and I'll make you some breakfast, pancakes with maple syrup."

"Monroe Lake is at least another four or five hours from here, and then we've still got to find this guy. We better leave now."

"Calm yourself! You gotta eat, don't you? Then we'll go. You can sleep while I drive."

Over breakfast Bill updated Stuart about current neighborhood activity. "Cars just come creepin' on by like they don't think we notice. Sometimes they stop right in the middle of the street while some joker takes a photo with his phone. They don't care if someone's behind them just tryin' to get through. Friday nights are the worst. All these rowdy kids show up, jump out of their cars, and run through the backyard shoutin' 'lizard man! lizard man!' Shoot, my dog Shadow throws a barkin' fit every time."

"Yeah, well to them it's a game," Stuart said. "If they had been through what I've been through, they wouldn't think it so funny." He recounted the details of his own UFO sighting, how he had to keep the incautious Summer down and out of sight, and how Etienne froze up into a fetal position.

Bill sat quietly and listened while he made his own assessment of the man. Stuart's no hothead, he realized, he just sounds like one. In truth, he's scared to death. Bill diplomatically kept that thought to himself.

The drive over to Indianapolis was punctuated by Stuart's failed efforts to contact Buddie by cell phone. "He's not going to pick up," he declared just after they turned off Interstate 70 and headed south towards Bloomington.

"We can look for him when we get there," Bill said.

"We could be looking a long time. That lake isn't exactly small, and miles of forests surround it. Let me email Barry and see what he can come up with. There, sent," he said.

Ten minutes later he had a reply.

Claudio Postremo believes Buddie Eller can probably be found where the incident took place and suggests you contact the reporter who wrote the story. His name is Frank, and he works for the Bloomington newspaper. In a town that size, there can only be one.

Good luck, Barry

Frank was leaning back into his chair nearly asleep when Stuart phoned. Nothing had been going on in Bloomington for over a week now: no murders, no mayhem, no drunken student parties. He was bored and quite happy to take the call particularly when he learned that Stuart was a DC investigator come all the way to Bloomington to look into this UFO business he had reported. Maybe this could provide him a break into the national news service, he thought. At the very least it could be a great opportunity for a follow-up story.

"So you say Eller's out there right now?" Frank said.

"That's the information we got," Stuart said. "Thought he might be somewhere near the incident you reported, but we need a little intel to learn where that is."

"Oh, yeah, I know exactly where the incident took place. It's a little hard to get to so I tell you what I'll do. I'll take you out there myself. Okay, I'll look for you outside the building in about a half an hour. You should be here by then."

"He's going to provide door-to-door service," Stuart said to Bill.

"A newspaper man? Are you sure you want the publicity?"

"Beggars can't be choosers."

Standing outside the *Bloomington Times'* building was a guy wearing a black trench coat, jeans, and a fedora over straggly blond hair. A computer bag hung over one shoulder and his other arm held a worn-out leather briefcase. There was no need to ask questions. These men recognized each other like three peas in a pod.

Frank walked up to the window. "We can take mine or yours. I'm okay with either."

"Climb on in," Bill said, already taking a liking to the guy. "It'll be faster than switching."

Frank climbed into Stuart's SUV and immediately began to outline a plan. "The location is clear around the other side of the lake and near some wildlife preserve. I don't know how long it's gonna take to find this guy, but since we're starting out pretty late, I recommend we check in at the Panorama Inn and find someone to take us across the lake in their boat."

"It's that remote?" Stuart asked.

"Well, you can get there by car, but we may lose the light by then, and there's not much extra parking available at the RV camp so we couldn't leave it there for long. Besides, unless you've got an RV or are into camping outside, which I am not, there's no place to stay out there. I've got this thing about coyotes."

"Coyotes?" Bill said.

"Yeah, lots of 'em. I heard them the night I was out there for that story. Pretty freaky!"

"Do you have a number for the Panorama?" Stuart asked.

"I've got it right here in my notebook," Frank said. "I'll reserve us some rooms."

"The restaurant is next door and open until eight," the desk clerk said when they checked in. "I'd try to make it if I were you. There's no place else around."

"Oh, so you've got us captive out here," Stuart said.

"If you want to drive all the way back to the highway, I'm sure you could find somewhere that might serve you a sandwich. But let me tell you privately, it wouldn't be worth it."

"We'll take your advice."

"Good. You won't regret it. Lake trout's on the menu tonight."

"I wondered if we could find someone to take us out in a boat?"

"You can take yourself out. Step outside and go to your right. You'll see Bates Boats and Bait at the end of the pier."

Bates was not hard to miss with all the boats docked beside it. Nothing special about the place. Beer, bait, beef jerky, and various fishing and boating gear filled the shelves, along with a wide assortment of chips, salsa, crackers, and cookies.

"Are you sure you want to take her out this late?" the manager asked. "The least I can charge you is for a full half-day."

"That's okay," Stuart said and pulled out his credit card. "We just got here and want to look the place over. Anything unusual been going on?"

"Pontoon or runabout?"

"Which is cheaper?"

"That would be the runabout," the manager said. "Unusual you're asking? Can't say that I've heard anything. They tell me the fishin's been pretty good."

"I read something a while back about some men who were arrested. Disorderly and drunk, I think they were. The story mentioned something about UFOs."

The manager burst out laughing. "Yep, drunk and disorderly sometimes happens around here along with a few made up stories and excuses. They've got plenty of alcohol restrictions on this side of the lake. I believe the incident you're referring to happened somewhere over there," he said and pointed northeast. "I would say you've only a few more hours of light so I wouldn't try to take her too far. If you need her again tomorrow, I'll give you the full-day for the half-day rate to make up for what you're spending tonight."

"That'll be fine," Frank said and took the keys before the manager could hand them to Stuart. "We've got to be back before eight anyway. I just want to take them over to some of those wildlife and waterfowl refuge areas and check things out."

"Oh, you've got plenty of time to cross the lake and come back if that's all you're doin'. But you're not gonna find any UFOs if that's what you're lookin' for."

Frank revved up the engine and sped out into the lake.

"Seems like a pretty public place to be flyin' UFOs," Bill said. "People would have seen them, and apparently none of the Bates' customers have."

"Hey! You should talk," Stuart said. "You had one land in your backyard."

"What'd you say?" Frank asked, thinking the engine noise must have disturbed his hearing.

"That's what I said," Stuart said. "Didn't you see that *Quester's* special about UFOs in Ohio?"

Frank did a double take. "That was you?" he said to Bill as he studied him a bit more closely. "I recognize you now. So that happened in your backyard. Lizard man and all that. I thought it was all made up."

"In my neighbor's backyard," Bill corrected. "And it wasn't as public as you might think until that last day before they disappeared. They flew all over town in broad daylight. They got the whole town oohing and aahing until the media showed up and then they were gone. Before then they would hide themselves behind big, dark clouds. Beamin' things up and down was the only way we knew they were there, and I wouldn't have known that if it wasn't goin' on next door."

"Hiding behind clouds?" Frank said as he looked to the southwest.

"Yeah, it rains or snows a lot when they're around," Bill said, likewise staring up at the sky. "I don't know how they do it, but I know why. It's their cover. That's how they can be right here without people knowin'."

"We'd better get turned around and go back before those storm clouds get here," Frank said. "I just thought it would be a good idea to check to make sure Buddie Eller isn't stayin' at that RV camp before we have dinner and hit the sack."

"Don't apologize," Stuart said. "It's a very good idea. No use in wasting time."

Frank docked the boat and they quickly asked around. No one at the RV camp had heard of a guy named Buddie Eller.

"I'm not surprised," Bill said. "No sense makin' yourself a target when you're investigatin'. He's probably somewhere over in those woods."

"Tomorrow we can come back early and start looking around, but we'd better get back now. It's comin' in," Frank said.

And indeed it was. Before they were halfway across the lake the rain poured down hard. But it was not the rain Frank was worried about when he threw the boat into full throttle it was the clouds. He was quite relieved when they were at their table eating trout at the Panorama, but his sense of relief was short lived.

"What the...Did you see that?" he cried, when a bolt of lightning streaked across the sky startling him to his feet.

"See what?" Bill said.

"Out there! I thought I saw something silver descend," Frank said, now sitting back down.

Stuart put his fork down and looked out of the window. "You couldn't have seen anything. It's too dark out there, not even moonlight."

Frank was breathless. "I saw it when that lightning flashed."

"You're just spooked," Bill said. "That happens to all of us. Let's get to bed so we can get back out there early in the mornin'."

Stuart collapsed in his bed having gotten no sleep the night before. Bill dozed off like a baby. Frank, on the other hand, smoked his daily cigarette and drank a beer in an effort to relax while he studied the movement of the clouds when they were lit up by bolts of lightning.

Meanwhile, Buddie Eller, huddled on the edge of the woods near the RV camp, tried to combat the rain that had seeped into his tent and collected on the plastic ground cover that lined the bottom. There was nothing to do but haul the ground cover outside and empty it if he didn't want his sleeping bag to get soaked. He looked up from his work when a huge bolt of lightning and an accompanying clap of thunder distracted him.

"I see it!" he shouted to the thunder gods.

It had taken Buddie thirty years to finally see what he had been seeking all of his life: an authentic, unquestionable extraterrestrial ship. He ducked behind nearby shrubs on the edge of a cove as the ship ascended slowly out of the lake sending billowing waves against the shore. It was silver, he surmised, but in the glare of the midnight lightning, it took on a bluish hue. Eerie, he thought, as he watched this ghostly vessel rising farther and farther into the sky. He studied it as it soared until in a flash it disappeared as if it had gone behind a cloud or through a door.

When all went quiet and the storm clouds disappeared, he went back into his tent and broke out a bottle of beer in celebration as he detailed a full account in his notebook: size, color, trajectory, velocity, and duration. He turned off his lantern and went to sleep satisfied that what he had always believed had finally been confirmed. He had seen it himself.

He awakened to what felt like a cold hand resting on his forehead. He could not move. He was frozen in place as if he were paralyzed. Too afraid to open his eyes, he felt himself levitate. Was he dreaming? In a desperate act of courage he opened his eyes wide and saw that he was indeed rising in beam of light until he felt the hard floor beneath him after he was gently dropped. He still could not move under his own volition when hands reached down and picked him up. Then he heard someone speak.

"So you finally found us," the voice said. "We've been watching you for many of your earth years."

Buddie tried to speak, but no words would come from his mouth. The creature, nonetheless, seemed to hear his thoughts.

"Calm yourself! You're more inquisitive than most," it said. "We've measured you as highly intelligent among your race; and since we have you here, we are going to take some measurements to try to determine the depth of your mind. Hold still. This will not take long."

Buddie had no choice since he was unable to move. He felt himself being shoved into some kind of tube, a test tube, he thought. He could hear the soft whine of power being generated and then he saw eyes staring at him, eighteen sets detached from anything that looked like a face. He felt naked, and in fact he was. The eyes continued to bore in.

He felt stripped clean as if he were being skinned. He did not like it at all. And then it felt like holes were being bored into his brain. No longer frozen silent, he let out a scream that was not heard.

Years flew back, all of his thoughts and his studies. Backward they plunged from the current state of his thinking to the inception of thought. And then the numbers came. Buddie had been fascinated with numbers since childhood. He multiplied and divided and then added and subtracted. Finally, he counted what seemed very small toes. "This little piggy..." he could almost hear. Buddie had no past tragedies or emotional upsets to overwhelm him. He had two loving parents; a very stable childhood; and since he was more in love with his work than a woman, there was little upset there. I'm hallucinating, he thought, his mind still sharp enough to observe what was happening to him. Suddenly he dropped to the floor of the tube having been released from the hold of the eyes. The tube slid open.

The only thing he clearly remembered when he awoke in his tent the next morning was the residual chill from those cold hands. His head ached. He suffered an eerie but indefinable sense that he had been invaded. It must have been a strange nightmare, he thought, until he saw the celebratory empty beer bottle, read the notes he had taken, and knew he had seen a ship. But then his thinking stopped, replaced it seemed by deep hunger, a great urging like something primal in his being had been unearthed and underfed.

He carelessly threw on the clothes he had worn the day before and walked up to the road where he had left his car. Driven by pangs of hunger, he threw caution to the wind and raced along tiny lanes towards the best nearby restaurant he could think of. He ordered a western omelet with home fries and toast along with a stack of pancakes. He licked his lips. He was thirsty, nearly parched dry. He ordered a bottle of beer and several more as he chugged each down in nearly one gulp.

"That's him!" Frank said from another table. "That's Buddie Eller. I recognize him from his photo on the university's web page."

"Buddie?" Stuart asked.

Buddie looked up with his mouth full of pancake. "Yeah."

"We've been looking for you. Claudio Postremo asked us to find you and make sure you're okay."

"Yeah," he said still chewing. "I'm all right. Just hungry as hell." He took another swig of beer thereby emptying the bottle that he placed next to three empties that were already lined up. The waitress, who knew the routine by now, arrived with a fresh bottle.

Stuart knew something was wrong. A math professor, even if he's a UFO investigator, does not drink beer with his pancakes. "Do you mind if we sit down?" he asked.

Buddie stared at him as he stuffed his mouth with more omelet. Hearing no objections, they all three sat down.

"That was quite a storm last night," Frank casually said. "I watched the lightning from my window."

"It woke me up," Buddie said. "I saw it rise out of the lake."

"Lightning?" Frank asked.

"Hell no! A flying saucer! I've been waiting my whole life to see one. Now I have." He grabbed the fresh bottle of beer and held it up as if he were making a toast.

"I'm the reporter you contacted who wrote the story about the RV campers," Frank said.

"Yeah, I remember," Buddie said. "About those sorry guys who were taken up."

"Yes, it was about them. You checked out my story."

"Yep, I did. It is truer than shit."

"Did anything else happen last night?" Frank asked.

"You can have my story for your newspaper if you want it. I was over there camping," he said as he pointed out the window. "It was raining like the blazes, and when I went outside, there it was."

"Anything else?" Frank asked.

"Like what?"

"Any bad dreams? Anything strange you can remember?"

"Cold hands all over me," he shuddered. "I woke up with a splitting headache. Aspirin did the trick. Only I'm so hungry that I can't get enough," he said as he stuffed more pancake lathered in maple syrup in his mouth and took another swig of beer.

"Cold hands? Are you going back over there?" Stuart asked. "We'd kinda of like to see that flying saucer ourselves."

"Sure! I don't mind the company. I'll just stop off at Bates and get more beer."

"Oh, god he's been had," Stuart said to the rest of the guys once they were alone together in his SUV. "I've seen these symptoms before. The victims are prone to excess, and there's a marked change in their personality. Now, I don't know this guy from Adam, so I can only speculate, but he's not behaving like any math professor I've ever known."

"No one drinks beer with their pancakes," Bill said. "I ought to know. I've been makin' them for myself and my guests my whole life."

"You're right about that," Frank said. "What can we do for this guy?"

"Just stay with him," Stuart said. "There's no cure for this stuff, but I'm told my friend over in Europe has improved after regularly drinking these medicinal teas this priest I know makes. But that's for later. For now we need to stay with him and learn what we can about what's going on over here. Here he comes now with his beer. Bill, make sure we stay close behind him." Stuart opened his laptop before they got out of range of an Internet hot spot and sent a quick missive to Barry to inform him of Eller's condition and ask for further direction.

They followed his car around the lake and onto narrow roads that turned into footpaths, which took them deep into the woods. Eventually, Buddie pulled his car out of the forest darkness and into a small clearing and parked. He got out of his car and joined the others. "My campsite's just over there," he said pointing to a path in the woods that led to a rocky lakeshore beach.

Eller's campsite was a mess, so with the prospect of staying the night there the men pulled the plastic sheet and sleeping bag out of the tent to dry.

"You must have gotten pretty wet," Bill said as he wrung out the bag. "You either need a clothes dryer or a new one."

"Yeah, it's shot to hell. The lightning was tremendous. It threw an eerie light on that flying saucer I saw."

"Where was it?" Bill asked.

"I just came out of the tent to pour water off the ground cover when I looked up and saw it through the trees right over there. Here, I've written it all down." He took out his notebook and handed it to Frank.

"Right over where?" Stuart asked.

Buddie pointed.

"Does someone want to go with me back to my SUV and help me carry a tracking device I brought with me from DC?" Stuart asked.

"Sure," Frank said. "What kind of tracking device is it?"

"Advanced radar. If it catches a signal, it can follow it for miles up into the atmosphere just as long as the object stays below our satellites."

"This is pretty cool! What powers it?"

"A very large lithium battery. Without it this thing would be pretty light."

The two of them dropped the heavy device down gently, and Stuart aimed what looked like a small rooftop satellite dish in the direction Buddie had pointed. Once the contraption was setup and running, Buddie suggested they go back to the Panorama and have some dinner.

"Good idea," Stuart said, who was anxious to check his email. "Maybe we can pick up a few blankets from our rooms while we're at it. It feels like it's going to get pretty cool tonight."

The evening special was pork chops. Buddie had a double order followed by three pieces of pie. That's when all the screaming began.

In full view of restaurant patrons, a silver machine lifted up out of the lake and into the sky, then another, then another. Shaken customers gathered at the large picture window to watch.

"Look at that!" Bill said, "They aren't even tryin' to hide."

"Something tells me this is not a good sign," Stuart said. "I think we were better off when they stayed hidden."

Dr. Postremo would tell him later that his instincts were right. He opened his laptop and sent a missive to Barry updating him, and then he read what Barry had already sent back.

"Stay with him," Barry had written. *"Postremo is really sorry. He told me Dr. Eller had a very fine mind. Maybe we can do something for him later if the experiment Luc Renard is concocting actually works. I have my doubts though. Keep me posted."*

"There's a whole fleet of 'em," Bill said. "I wonder where they're goin'?"

"We've got to get back to that radar set-up," Stuart said.

They quickly stripped their beds of blankets and sneaked them out after the desk clerk joined the crowd gathered at the big picture window in the restaurant.

"That was good thinking," Frank said when they arrived back near the campsite already wrapped in their blankets as they were making their way through the woods. "It's already darn cold. Unseasonably so."

The three men huddled together inside Eller's tent while Stuart stayed outside to read the radar device as it continued to whirr. That's when the howling began.

"Look at that moon," Frank said as he peered through the split in the tent opening. "Whoever said the moon doesn't get these coyotes howlin' doesn't know what they're talking about."

"So that's what I'm hearin'," Bill said.

"Yeah, a whole chorus of 'em. You can hear better outside the tent."

Frank flung the tent open to a now clear, cold sky. The radar detector whirred as they listened to the howling that suddenly changed into high pitched hoots just as the whirring stopped and the radar detector started beeping.

"It's tracked another one going east," Stuart said. "They're clearly headed out to somewhere."

"Can you tell where?" Frank asked.

"The ones that took off earlier passed Cincinnati," Stuart said.

"I bet Wright Patterson Air Base is gettin' a lot of calls tonight," Bill said.

"It looks like their hovering due east of Cincinnati somewhere out in the boonies."

"Can you be more precise?" Frank asked.

"I've got the coordinates: Latitude: 39.0242357 - Longitude: -83.4296362. Let's get over there and see what's up."

Four men wrapped in blankets made a beeline for Stuart's SUV.

Chapter 20

Hocus Pocus

Luc combined elements of Campanella's formula with the universal principles circumscribed by one basic tenet: restore Heaven to Earth and Earth to Heaven through the force of mutual attraction. That combination is what underlays life, what fuels and ignites it, he learned from reading Hermes Trismegistus and other hermetic masters. When the two are severed, he reasoned, a kind of death occurs, leaving the victim in a state approximating zombiism.

That's how Luc came to understand Etienne's condition; and no amount of herbal tea, not even his own recipes, could cure that. Once untethered from his spirit through a process of personality destruction, Etienne had become equivalent to the walking dead. He was animated instead (if the word "animate" can properly be used in this context) by little more than the same base desire that might animate a creature with no conscience. Luc's task, as he understood it, was to restore the connection between Etienne's physical being and his higher spirit, thereby reestablishing his former personality that lay at the other end: body plus spirit creates soul. If Etienne was to become whole, Luc must devise a plan to draw down enough fire to ignite and make molten the blunt ends of the severed breach and fuse them together exactly as they had been. No small task, but one that would allow him a great deal of creative freedom that he rather enjoyed.

To achieve his ends he had to devise a plan that would draw the divine energy down from Sacchi's fresco. If he understood the principles correctly, earth magic would ignite life in the fresco's sacred image, allowing the mystical inspiration that animates it to burst into fire and touch down on the object of the magician's choosing: in this case, Etienne de Chevalier. More than that, he had to accomplish this task without the recipient's knowledge, since Etienne in his present state would certainly balk.

He met Madame Conti at the Palazzo Barberini less than a week before the summer solstice, the date he had chosen for the ritual to take place. Together they stood under the fresco of Divine Wisdom in the late afternoon to finalize his plan.

"It is good you were able to arrange the date with the museum on such short notice" he said.

"That was nothing my dear man. When they learned I would invite Rome's finest and all proceeds would come to them, they were delighted to accommodate."

"Have the invitations been sent? We do want a crowd," he said.

"They were sent immediately. I expect most of those invited to attend. They owe me that since in happier days my husband and I made generous contributions to their charities."

"You say it's your son-in-law who will perform the concert?"

"He's quite talented, but not yet my son-in-law. I do hope they marry soon, but you know how these young people are. He plays absolutely beautifully though. If earthly music can reach the stars, his surely can."

"Will he know what to play?"

"I've asked my granddaughter to select his most passionate pieces."

"And you're sure Etienne will attend?"

"Oh, yes. He will come to support his sister in her endeavor to promote the career of the man I hope she will soon marry. I simply told him I was sponsoring this concert to raise money for the purpose of restoration of the outside courtyard, which of course is quite the truth, just not all of it. He will do this for me, and of course, his sister. He would never come if he had an inkling of our plan. No, not him, at least not now. "

"He must be seated in the proper place," Luc said, as he looked nervously around the room. "Placement is nearly everything."

"Where would that be?"

He looked up at Divine Wisdom seated on her throne with her eyes averted as her mirror reflects the sun's light and sends it through her scepter to the Earth below. "Right there," he said as he walked to the spot in the room just below the fresco's globe.

"Good!" Madame Conti said as she bent down and marked an X with black tape. "That will help me know where to place the piano. And you had said something earlier about vases of flowers and candles?"

"Flowers, yes!" Luc said as he took a vile of rose vinegar from his pocket and sprinkled it on the designated spot. "The room must suggest earthly paradise. If you can arrange to have several live potted trees brought in, some assorted rocks, and granite and marble for their strength and beauty, that should do it. I shall bring laurel, myrtle, rosemary, and cypress to burn as incense. And we should have some kind of water feature, a fountain perhaps. Now the vases of flowers must be placed strategically, along with seven white candles of the purest type to represent the planets. I will use strings of white lights to mimic the constellations that were in the sky at the moment of Etienne's birth. For that I still need the exact time and place. The vases, I would estimate at least thirty, should be made of crystal to mimic the stars and the flowers should be of a pure white and fragrant type. Can you arrange all of that?"

"I shall try. The most difficult proposition here is to find thirty crystal vases."

Luc winked. "You are an amazingly resourceful woman. It certainly helped that you were able to arrange for this location."

"Yes, the museum was thrilled to learn I want to raise money for them. If they only knew what else I have planned, I hate to imagine what they would think. And yet it fits perfectly with the history of the place. Pope Urban VIII built this palace himself."

Luc looked around the room. "No one believes in that kind of history anymore. They treasure the beauty of the artifacts without correspondingly treasuring the inspiration behind them."

"So true," Madame Conti said as she looked up at the fresco of Divine Wisdom. "To most she is only an object of art."

"Tommaso Campanella knew better," Luc said.

"Dear man, that was four centuries ago!"

The men guarding the door of the Library of Time paid scant attention to the man who approached them dressed in plain spun cotton.

"It's an emergency!" Roland said. "I must see the timekeeper."

"He sees no one except under strict invitation," one of the guards said. "I shall not bother him now."

"Tell him the man is here who he took to Serpent Mound. He will know the place and the man, and I can assure you, he will want to see me."

"Would you have us lose our jobs?" the other guard said. "If you think yourself so important, get an invitation to an appointment. Without that, we will not let you in."

"How do I do that?" Roland asked.

The guards pointed to the Ministry of Justice, a place Roland knew well.

"You cannot show yourself there," Sedwig said as they walked away. "You be recognized by the Endronian representatives; and if that should be, I cannot protect you."

"Is this place all bureaucracy?" Roland said in frustration. "Nothing but rules and procedures that make no sense?"

"That's why I live in the Southwest Quadrant," Sedwig said. "I wish I could help you, but I have no influence here."

Roland looked up at the sky. "Their ship may still be nearby. She could make me welcome if she agrees with my plan."

"Indeed she could. If Avian had a queen, it would be Lira, so well thought of she be."

"Is there a place nearby I can privately meditate for a few minutes?"

"The Region Four port be all concrete and glass except, I be told, for a few courtyards tucked away inside buildings. I know of one I will take you to. It be inside the Ministry of Business so it be seldom used. Pull your hood down over your eyes and follow me behind as if you be my servant."

Roland followed behind in a deferential gait, past guards, through halls, and finally out of view of building occupants into a tiny courtyard overgrown with wild lycmthe. "Ah, heavenly," he said as he breathed in the fragrance. But before he could sit down to meditate, he was plucked away in front of Sedwig's astonished eyes.

"Lira had expected you may seek our help," Bryn said as he met the newly arrived Roland on their ship. "So I be monitoring you since your arrival at the port and saw an opportunity to bring you up with few to see. You must know it be dangerous for you down there. You were to stay confined in the Southwest Quadrant."

"That I know, which is why I wear this disguise. I seek a meeting with the timekeeper and need the help of one who can assist me. It is urgent that I see him, or I would not have left the pleasant home you have given me. I was just about to call you up for help by means of meditation when you so unexpectedly interceded."

"Urgent?" Bryn said. "Come have a meal with us. By way also, it be nice to see you so robust. Lira has told me you be on the way to recovery, but you look to me like you be already done."

"Thank you for your kind observation," Roland said as he followed Bryn to the dining room. "It was a long slog, I should tell you. And if it had not been for Sedwig..." he looked about. "He is still down there. He will wonder what happened to me."

"He will know and wait patiently. Here he be, Lira," Bryn said as the two men sat down with the lady already waiting at a table fully laid out.

"Did you expect me?"

"In a manner, yes," Lira said. "You forget that I have the gift, but I must say, with all my talent, I cannot comprehend this plan of yours."

"It's more idea than plan. I'm not sure it's possible. I must speak to the timekeeper to learn if it is possible."

"That can be arranged," Lira said. "But first you must describe this idea of yours."

"When I visited the timekeeper before, he told me something almost in passing that might save the Earth if it could operate at the level I have imagined. He explained that the events I was looking at in time past might not have happened as I was seeing them because on occasion due to one catastrophe or another, they tune time to rebalance and avoid chaos. He said such tunings are nearly imperceptible; but if there have been many, a past event might be altered to reflect a harmony that may not have existed in the time before the tunings."

"I see," Lira said. "What was be changed from what it had been." She mused on this thought for a while. "So you think these tunings could redress the harm that the Endron have done to your friend?"

"And to others if need be."

"Need be is no longer a question. Our investigation shows your friend was neither the first nor the last the Endron have harmed on Earth," Bryn said.

"Of that I am not surprised," Roland said. "I wonder and hope if such tunings might not put these victims back in harmony with themselves. It's the same principle."

"Hmm," Lira said. "I have little knowledge of tuning for that be kept quite secret, but what little I know its goal be to effect events that have gone helter skelter not individuals. But if it could be done, it might prove a cure to what others have thought an incurable condition. It would undercut the Endron's evil work. Yes! Yes! We must go see the timekeeper at once. Bryn, beam us down and keep an eye out in case we be detected. If the Endron should discover what we be about, all out war, I'm afraid. Oh, and yes, make us an invitation to an appointment with the timekeeper."

"I will fashion a cloak from the wheat stores that you might appear a farmer's wife," Bryn said.

"No time," Lira said.

"Follow me to the pantry. I fix you up, and make you an invitation." Bryn quickly emptied the largest bag of flour he could find, ripped it open and put it on the shoulders and head of his lovely wife. "There, you wear this beggarly dress well. Show yourself to no one until you reach the Library of Time."

Roland and Lira appeared among the fragrant lycmthe right in front of Sedwig's eyes, but he did not recognize her so poorly she was dressed.

"We will humbly follow behind you," Roland said. "You must lead us from this building and on to the Library of Time."

"We who? Who be she?" Sedwig said. "The kitchen maid?"

In a split second Lira dropped her cloak down and then restored it about her head and shoulders.

Roland gave a furtive glance. "I hope you were not seen. They have eyes everywhere."

"We be in the courtyard of the Ministry of Business, no worry," she said.

"I be honored by your presence," Sedwig said and bowed.

"You must not carry on that way or my disguise will be undone. Take us as we be your servants to the place of the timekeeper."

The guards were as they were, impolite and showing no respect, but this time Roland handed them his invitation.

"An appointment we must give you," one of the guards grudgingly said. "But it will be for tomorrow."

"Tomorrow!" Lira said from underneath her homespun veil.

"That be what I said! The timekeeper be at his dinner, and after that he go to bed."

"I demand you show him the invitation now and let him decide!" Lira said.

"Ah, and who should I say be here? The kitchen wife?"

"Your manners could stand much improvement," an angry Sedwig said. "If you only knew who you insult."

"All right. I will take it to him, but who should I say?"

"Tell him the man to whom he showed the Serpent Mound. He will remember," Roland said.

Within minutes they were admitted into the library, the timekeeper waiting inside the door. "I had a deep intuition you be back," he said to Roland and then looked over at what he thought was a kitchen wife. Lira doffed her homespun veil, letting her radiance shine.

"It be you!" the timekeeper said. "Such visitors. Please join me at my dinner table. I be about to serve my port. You must have some. It be very delicious."

"Why had you such a hunch that Roland be back?" Lira asked, aware as she was of the significance of such feelings.

"It be more than a hunch," the timekeeper said. "I be curious about this Serpent Mound we visited together and have been back since our friend here left. I have noted strange activity occurring and thought somehow there be a connection between his first coming and my discovery. If such be the case, I thought he likely would come back since I have knowledge that he needs. Such be the way of the universe."

"What strange things do you see?" Roland asked.

The timekeeper quickly drank the last of his port. "Follow me into the chamber and I show you."

A huge map of the Earth dropped down on the screen as the timekeeper honed in closer and closer until he reached Serpent Mound and focused in.

"It be still at this moment. Let me take you back a day. There!" he said. "That's what I see several times." Ships, many of them, appeared to dance about the site as if in preparation for something.

"Those be Endron ships!" Lira said. "What they be doing there?"

"It is an ancient site of worship of inhabitants that no longer live," Roland said. "And yet it has other ardent worshippers. I visited on my trip to Ohio. I was there for a celebration of the winter solstice. I could feel its power."

"I detect after some study it has more than religious power," the timekeeper said. "There be a deposit of iridium."

"Iridium!" Roland said. "That is very rare. How could it have gotten there?"

"That be my question too," the timekeeper said.

"A meteorite brought it perhaps," Lira said. "No matter, what matters be that explains the Endron presence."

"They mean to mine it!" Roland said. "And destroy the Serpent in doing so."

"That be my speculation," Lira said.

"I have something more to show," the timekeeper said. He drew back the focus so not only the Serpent Mound could be seen but also the valleys and fields around it and what appeared to be an elaborate crop circle in a nearby field.

"They've marked it!" Lira said. "They be about to commence. We have no time to wait. They be preparing to bring in more ships, perhaps doing more mind-stripping to disrupt the community and make slaves of them."

"It happens like that?" Roland asked.

"Yes, this be how they begin their conquests. At first imperceptible to most and then by small increments that grow so vast in number, if not size, that the whole planet and its people are subsumed, swallowed up in their mining operations, or if not be suitable for that, made as like ghosts confined inside the immaterial."

"Dead?" he said.

"Not quite. Some say worse."

"But there is no iridium on most of the planet," Roland said. "What do they want?"

"That be the first metal they take because of its value and rarity. But in the end they take almost everything. One might applaud their efficient operations if they be not so destructive and sly."

Roland nearly swooned as he thought of the meadows and farmland despoiled. "We must stop them!"

"Ask the timekeeper about your plan," Lira said. She sat down upon the floor to begin her silent meditation, but before she entered a trance she said, "If it could work, it would set the Endron back as well as restore those people whose minds have already been taken."

"Ask me what?" the timekeeper said.

"Can you tune the planet and thereby destroy their ugly work?" Roland asked. "More than that, restore the minds of those they have taken and mind-stripped?"

The timekeeper rubbed his balding head. "As you be aware, we do retune on occasion when events threaten the harmony. And their pending destruction of the Serpent would certainly do that even before their expansion of their operations. But restoring minds? I be not so sure. And yet neither I be sure that it would not work. It be something we have never tried. It be an experiment for I do not know the result."

"Then experiment we must do. Too much is at risk to do otherwise," Roland said.

Lira rose up from her trance. "I dispatched our ships to Earth," she said, "sending the fiercest of our men, the warrior outcasts."

The timekeeper turned to her. "How long this be going on?"

"Longer than we knew so undetected it be. We thought we were witnessing some natural course of de-evolution that had afflicted mankind. Now we believe they be capturing and mind-stripping for many years."

"I think not! I think not!" the timekeeper said shaking his head. "To tune for that duration would create too great an impact on the timeline. It could prove dangerous for stability. We mean to be subtle that none be aware. But no subtleness in this, I'm afraid, even if it can be done, which I'm not sure. What risk there be? What unforeseen outcome?"

"What is there to lose in trying?" Roland asked. "When you see what will happen without your intervention."

"In that you have a point," the timekeeper said. "It would be a tragedy to let Earth be despoiled, but the universe be greater still. We cannot risk that!"

"More than a tragedy an abomination!" Lira cried.

"And what is there to lose by trying?" Roland asked again.

The timekeeper looked at him quite seriously. "I tell you what there be to lose if this should succeed, of which I'm not so certain. Several years could be lost under such severe tuning. The effect of that lost time be unknowable in the current present, and it could ripple out and undermine universal stability. Everything could fail."

"If tuning not be tried then the outcome be certain," Lira said, "War! Such a terrible war would be fought with known consequences. It has happened in the far-off days of Earth legend, and nearly all be destroyed. It took thousands of years to repeople the planet, so it be written."

At this moment all Roland could think about was Summer. Not even Earth's ancient history— as fascinating as it would have been to him at other times—could move him from that subject. His eyes full of tears, he said, "But what of Summer?"

"That be your risk," Lira said.

"What choice do I have?" Roland said, his voice trembling.

"You have none unless you wish to leave the whole planet to suffer," Lira proclaimed in sadness.

"I will take it up with the Elders this evening," the timekeeper said. "No time left for further discussion. If it be possible to act, we must act now. That I will explain to them."

Chapter 21

Chasing Saucers

Stuart's SUV was equipped with a government issue GPS designed to work in tandem with signals picked up by his portable radar dish. He never imagined when this tracking system was installed that he would use it to chase flying saucers. He knew in what general direction they were headed but had no idea of their final destination since all that he had to work with were coordinates. Bill was attempting to solve that problem through a close reading of a map.

Stuart drove, Buddie slept, Bill studied the map while Frank came up with catchy titles for what he hoped would become a series of Pulitzer Prize winning stories.

"How about this? 'Saucers swimming with fish in Monroe Lake," he said from the backseat.

"No, that's too long," Bill said.

"You're right. How about 'Saucers fishin' in Monroe Lake.'"

"That's better," Bill said unenthusiastically.

"But not good enough," Frank replied. "It's got to capture it."

"How about 'Out of the depths and into the sky,'" Stuart said from the driver's seat.

"I don't know," Frank said. "Doesn't name the subject. Where are we now?"

"We crossed the state line into Ohio a few miles back. We'll be skirting around Cincinnati soon. But it looks like we've still got quite a ways to go."

"I got it," Frank said, "'UFOs over Ohio.'"

"That'll grab their attention," Bill said. "You know, I think I may have found somethin' here. What they're after, I mean."

"What's that?" Stuart said.

"There's some kind of uranium enrichment plant at a place called Piketon. It's out in the boonies in the direction we're headed."

"That's interesting," Stuart said. "A power source."

"Yep, that's what I was thinkin. They've been known to be attracted to high voltage power lines. So maybe that's it."

"Something to think about," Stuart said. "Could be their kind of gas station."

"Sure isn't anything else out there," Bill said. "Just a few parks and such. Mostly farmland."

"Any lakes?" Stuart asked.

"The only bodies of water I see on this map are Brush Creek and the Ohio River, but no major lakes."

"Well, let's just see where these coordinates take us."

"I got it! I got it!" Frank said chuckling. "I'll draw a cartoon. 'Fill 'er up!' it will say with some little bug-eyed space alien guy in a Texaco cap standing in front of power lines coming from a nuclear power plant. I bet *The New Yorker* magazine would go for that."

"You need some sleep," Bill said.

"Yeah, get some shuteye," Stuart said. "We'll wake you when we get someplace."

Frank obliged, leaning against the side window opposite Buddie who was ensconced in his blanket against the other side window.

In no time Stuart had steered his SUV around Cincinnati along the southern outer belt until his GPS directed him back into the darkness of fields. They were on the Appalachian Highway that stretched from Cincinnati to Parkersburg, West Virginia.

"I bet I was right," Bill said. "This road goes to Piketon."

"So you think their mission could have something to do with nuclear?" Stuart said.

"It's been documented that UFOs hang out around our nuclear installations. They've even been known to shut them down."

"That's pretty serious," Stuart said. "Never heard of it myself."

"Top secret," Bill said.

"We will see, but it seems to me that if all those ships we saw leaving Monroe Lake were headed to one of our nuclear facilities, we'd be seeing fighter jets by now."

Storm clouds moved in, heavy ones. Then single bolts of lightning flashed across the sky. Clouds lit up from behind discharging thunderous roars while casting an eerie light on the whole night sky. Ragged bolts of lightning started crisscrossing the firmament, lighting the road in front of them in a greenish glare.

Bill poked his head out of the window before the rain began and popped right back in, the cool night air having chilled him. "You might be right about that," Bill said. "Nothin' out there. The Air Force definitely would have scrambled some planes outta Wright-Patt if they thought a nuclear facility were being threatened. A place like that must have plenty of guards on the lookout. Unless, maybe those ships are hidin'."

"Hey, where'd you say this Piketon place is?" Stuart said.

"I'd say about 27 miles up the road due east."

"Well, this GPS just signaled that I will be turning north onto Highway 73 just up ahead."

"Man, it's takin' us further into the sticks," Bill said still studying the map. "There's nothin' around there in either direction. Of course, if they're hidin', that could be a good place. Whoa! What the hell?"

A huge bolt of lightning had touched down on the road in front of them with a roar of thunder. Frank groaned and repositioned his head but didn't entirely wake up. Buddie didn't utter a sound or move an inch. Stuart, for caution's sake, put on the brakes.

"Never seen it this bad," Stuart said. The lightning intensified, turning the sky, the roads, and the woods into an electrified scene the likes of which neither man had ever seen.

"It sure is lookin' strange," Bill said.

"And pretty damn dangerous," Stuart followed. "It's a good thing I have plenty of gas. I'd hate to get stranded in this."

Seven miles after the turnoff the GPS spoke, "You have arrived at your destination Latitude: 39.0242357 - Longitude: -83.4296362." The SUV slowed.

"Where the hell are we?" Bill asked.

"Serpent Mound State Memorial Park," Stuart read as he turned and drove up a dark, winding road that led to an empty gravel parking lot. "I guess we've got the place to ourselves."

"No cars at least" Bill said. "I don't like it."

"Me either," Stuart said. "I'll park somewhere less conspicuous."

"Yeah, we're sitting ducks," Bill said.

Stuart drove back down the entrance road and pulled the car way over to the side under some trees. The storm roared on relentlessly, hurling huge bolts of lightning from behind heavy clouds. Trees blew in the harsh wind, dropping branches right in front of them.

"Parking here probably isn't too safe either," Stuart said after a branch clobbered the hood.

"Yeah, I see what you mean," Bill said. "But at least we've got some protection."

"From what?" Stuart said. "What do you mean?"

"There up there," Bill said. "This isn't a natural storm. I've seen somethin' like this before, just not this intense."

Stuart thought back to descriptions of what happened at Jungfraujoch. "Yeah," he said, without adding more.

A strip of light became visible on the eastern horizon, breaking through the now dwindling clouds.

"Storm's nearly over," Stuart said. "Get them up in the backseat, will you? I'm going to gather some things. I've got crackers and beer. Make sure they don't forget their blankets."

"How long's this stakeout gonna last?" Buddie asked as they walked up the road towards the Serpent.

"As long as it takes," Stuart said. "My radar says they're around here someplace. They've got to show themselves sometime."

"It's starting to rain again," Frank said. "Let's get into that shelter house."

Bill pointed to fast moving clouds. "You know, they're probably hiding up there."

After huddling in his blanket and watching the rain for a few hours, Buddie spoke up, "I'm hungry as hell."

"I'm with you on that," Frank said. "Man cannot live on crackers alone."

"There's a town nearby," Bill said, holding up the map. "I think we passed through it when all the lights were out. It's pretty small, but they've got to have somethin'. We could go over there and get some breakfast." He looked at his watch. "Somethin' ought to be openin' up by now."

"You guys go on over," Stuart said. "I'll stay here and keep a lookout until you get back. Then we can switch, and I'll go."

"Sure you'll be all right?" Bill said. Stuart nodded and handed Bill the keys and they were gone.

Stuart wouldn't admit it to himself, but he is quite an urban fellow and felt pretty vulnerable sitting alone wrapped up in a blanket in an open-air shelter house out in the wilds of Ohio. From the corner of his eye he saw what looked like a gray shadow pass through nearby trees. He turned squarely towards the woods and stared hard. Spotting nothing, he thought he must be seeing things and rubbed his eyes as if that would return clarity to his vision. Looking east he watched the pale sun obscured by clouds rise higher into the sky. He thought he might climb up to the lookout tower platform when the others returned so that he could get a better view of the Serpent that lay prostrate before him. When he turned back to the woods, two gray shadows appeared and then were gone. He walked towards the trees both to satisfy his curiosity and ease his fear when he was confronted with a whole pack of coyotes, which at the sight of him approaching began to yelp in the strangest manner. He recognized the yelps as the same as what he had heard the night before in the woods near Monroe Lake. He froze in his tracks. Lacking the knowledge of an outdoorsman, he relied on his instincts. He didn't run but stared squarely back at them making it clear by his expression he was not their breakfast. They apparently read the message and ran off.

"They seemed almost stealth like," he told the others after they arrived back. "They were here, and then they were gone. I'm sure glad to be out of here for a while," he said just before heading to the car. "Man, they gave me the willies. Made my skin crawl."

"You'll be okay after you've had somethin' to eat," Bill said. "Get yourself the waffles with a side of bacon and you'll be fine."

Frank's eyes darted towards the nearby woods. "They tell me that they're more afraid of us than we are of them, but I've never wanted to test that theory."

"They're gone now; the sun is full up," Bill said reassuringly.

Stuart drove over to the Sunrise Cafe and ordered himself some waffles and bacon as Bill had suggested. When the waitress brought the check he thought it a good time to ask her about what had been on his mind ever since he sat down in the booth. "What can you tell me about coyotes around here?"

"Not many around here" she said. "I hear they're all over in Athens picking through the students' garbage."

"I just saw a whole pack of them up at Serpent Mound."

"Is that so! Thanks for tellin' me. I'll keep my cat inside."

"They eat cats?"

"They'll eat anything: garbage, cats, dogs, rabbits, anything they can find."

"Hmm," he said, while he considered that it probably had not been such a good idea to go into the woods alone to investigate those pesky shadows. If they had attacked, who would have been there to save him? Not smart, he thought. He knew what Natalie would think and determined not to tell her about his coyote confrontation. Not wanting to embarrass himself in front of this pretty waitress, he did not utter another word, only shook his head.

His mind drifted back to the others who he had left at the Serpent. Three of them together could handle the situation if those beasts should come back, he thought, and then he thought again. Bill, maybe. Frank, probably not. Buddie Eller in his current condition, a definite no. He quickly paid his bill and hightailed it back to the mound.

The grounds and the shelter house were empty. He hiked up the narrow, steep steps of the tower platform and looked far afield. Nothing came into view but the valley below, nearby woods, and far off fields. Directly below him was the Serpent, its coils outstretched from cliffside edge to cliffside edge. To get a full view of its length, he would need a plane or a helicopter, he surmised as he wondered who had built this mound and why.

"Bill, Frank, Buddie!" he shouted into the silence. "Can you guys hear me?" He looked out at the big, cloudy sky. Bill was right, he thought, they're up there. He called out several more times but got no reply until he turned around and saw a distant figure come out from behind an old stone museum that was closed.

"Are you okay?" the woman called. "I could hear your shouts all the way over at my farm."

Stuart scrambled down the steps and ran towards the lone figure. "It's my friends I'm worried about," he said to the woman. "They're missing! I left them here when I went to town to grab some breakfast." He looked about again. "I don't know where they are."

"Calm yourself," she said. "They're probably hiking nearby. Here, I've got my binoculars. Let's go back up on the platform, and I'll take a look."

"Who are you?" Stuart asked.

"Sarah. I live around here. And who may I be speaking to?"

"Sorry, I'm Stuart," he said, unsure how much he should tell her. "We just drove over here from Indiana. Got here before the sun came up."

The two of them mounted the stairs to the top of the tower and she focused her binoculars and began her search.

"I don't see anyone," she said. "That's unusual. There's usually someone hiking around. It's probably the weather."

"It's pretty chilly for this time of year," Stuart said, "And those storms could have kept hikers away."

"Yeah, and it looks like its gonna rain again. That keeps the tourists from comin' round. It's been real slow lately 'cause it's been raining for weeks. Suppose your friends took off on you?"

"They didn't have a car," he explained. "I had it. I drove into town for some breakfast."

"Oh, been campin' out. I'm surprised they didn't go with you."

"We took shifts," he said and realized as soon as he said it that it didn't make much sense. Shift's from what, she was probably thinking. How could he explain himself without telling her what it is all about, he wondered? "Look, we came over here on a kind of search mission and thought someone ought to be keeping an eye on the place at all times."

"What are you searchin' for?" she asked.

He sighed. "We followed these lights in the sky all the way from Indiana."

"All the way from Indiana?"

"Yes, we came over from Lake Monroe near Bloomington. They seemed to have come here, the lights, I mean. But since we got here, we can't find them."

"Funny you should say that. Those lights you mention. We've seen them too. There's been a lot of activity around here that we can't explain. It's got us concerned."

"Yeah?" he said.

"Yes! We've been trying to investigate but haven't gotten very far. It may be nothin' more than a lot of lightning; but for caution's sake, we've been stayin' away from the place a lot lately ever since we saw that crop circle across the road."

"Crop circle?"

"I can take you over to see it if you'd like."

Stuart followed Sarah back down the entrance road where he had parked his SUV and across the road into a nearby cornfield.

"It's hard to see all of it from this angle," she said. "You've got to go up in a plane to see the whole thing. My husband got a good picture of it."

"I remember something about crop circles from a UFO conference I was at," Stuart said.

"Yes, some people make that connection. And then we've been seein' all those lights. That's why we've been keepin' our distance. And now you!"

"And my missing friends," Stuart added.

"I wonder where they can be?" she said looking around as if she half expected to see them coming across the field. "If you'd like, I'll take you to meet my husband. He'll have some ideas about how to find them."

"Good, let's go. Nothing to do around here."

"Here's an aerial photo of that crop circle," her husband Seth said to Stuart.

"Interesting. Crescent moons within a circle."

"And look at how these two crescents form what looks like an eye that seems like it's lookin' down at that circle within a circle," Sarah said.

"You say you just saw it one morning?" Stuart asked Seth.

"Yep, it must have been made overnight."

"I've been trying to interpret its meaning," Sarah said. "It looks to me like the all seeing eye watching over us."

"Or watching you!" Stuart said. "Maybe there's nothing to interpret. Maybe it's more like a highway sign."

"Like a road marker," Seth said in partial agreement. "If that's the case, for who?"

"That's the question."

"I think you know more than you're tellin' us," Seth said.

"More speculation than knowledge, I'm afraid," Stuart said. "But there are certain facts. People going missing, and now my friends are missing."

"What really brought you over here all the way from Indiana?" Seth asked.

"I know this will sound nuts, but it's the truth. Ever heard of UFO abduction?"

"Sure," Seth said, "like the Betty and Barney Hill case." He paused for a moment and passed a glance to Sarah. "Are you trying to say—are you telling us that something like that happened over there?"

"Is that what you think happened to your friends?" Sarah asked, passing a return glance to Seth.

"Right now I'm more worried about that pack of coyotes out there in the woods."

"You heard them too?" Seth said.

"I did more than hear them, I saw them! Nearly scared the crap out of me, and right now I'm scared for my friends."

Seth and Sarah exchanged looks. Sarah said, "A few nights ago was the first time we've heard them around here, and then we heard them again this morning. And the storm clouds and the..." her voice faltered before it picked up again. "Go ahead, tell him Seth." Seth remained quiet so Sarah continued, "The nights have been haunted by strange lights."

"It's just lightning behind the clouds," Seth interrupted.

"No! It's something else behind the clouds," she shouted back. "You just don't want to admit it."

"They hide behind the clouds," Stuart said. "That's what one of the fellows told me who witnessed those events up near Columbus. It was all over the national TV. You must have seen that story?"

"Sure did," Sarah said, and asked Seth, "What do you make of this? Strange lights, UFOs, and now coyotes."

"Could be shapeshifting," he said.

"Sure sounds like it," she said.

"Shapeshifting?" Stuart asked.

"There's someone we need to talk to," Seth said. "Will you come with us?"

"I gotta find my friends," Stuart said.

"Maybe he can help with that too," Sarah said. "He knows more about what goes on around here than anybody."

The three followed a path that led from Sarah and Seth's front door across the field to the door of a house on an adjacent farm. They were greeted by a man whose heritage was made evident by high cheekbones, wise eyes, and dark hair pulled back into a ponytail bound by a woven ribbon. Stuart, desperate for help, told his story.

"It happened over at Monroe Lake in Indiana. That's what brought us over here. A group of campers were abducted from their RVs and taken aboard some kind of spacecraft. When they were returned, they were changed."

"What do you mean they were changed?" Charles asked.

"Their personalities were changed and not for the better," Stuart said. "It's as if they underwent some kind of reverse evolution and became impulse driven. That's how it's been described to me."

Sarah eyed Charles in recognition. Stuart caught the glance. "And then there's Buddie Eller, one of my missing friends. He is or I should say was a UFO researcher who became a victim of one of these Monroe Lake UFO abductions when he went out searching for their ships alone. We were trying to find him. Unfortunately they had taken him up before we did. He seems to have suffered a tremendous loss of intellect. He teaches math over at the university in Bloomington, but you would never know it now. Have you seen anything like this around here?"

"Oh yes!" Sarah said. "We've seen some people turn pretty strange."

"Your friends are missing right now, you say?" Charles asked.

"Yeah, I warned them about the coyotes, but they may not have been up to the task of fending them off if they were surrounded. That Buddie Eller I told you about is in pretty bad shape; and the other two, well, they're not exactly outdoorsmen if you know what I mean."

"Could they not have left and gone home or something?" Charles asked.

"They don't have a car," Sarah said. "He's got the car."

"You fear that all three were abducted?" Charles asked.

"I know this sounds crazy, but yes! But by who, those ships up there or coyotes? I don't know. I must be going nuts."

"They could be one and the same," Charles said.

Stuart looked puzzled.

"Shapeshifters," Sarah explained. "Coyotes are shapeshifters."

"Man, I must be losing it," Stuart said. "So what are you saying?"

"She's saying that those creatures up there in those ships may be shapeshifters too," Seth said.

Charles nodded in concurrence. "Thunder beings take many forms. It has been said that they will return to avenge the Earth. That day may have come."

"*O, wee, you, omg*" he chanted as he left his house and crossed the field walking under threatening skies towards the Serpent. Seth and Sarah followed, joining in the chant. "*O, wee, you, omg,*" the three of them sang.

How did I get myself into this mess, Stuart considered as he wrapped himself in his warm blanket and followed behind. This is nuts, truly nuts, he thought as he followed Sarah in the parade leading to the Serpent. He thought back to Natalie's assurances that what he had witnessed in Europe wouldn't happen here. Which down-to-earth Americans could she have been referring to?

Charles led them to the Serpent's head, its mouth open with a protruding egg. They gathered on the small lookout just above the head. "*O, wee, you, omg,*" they chanted. Lightning darted behind the clouds and thunder followed. Their chanting grew louder, "*O, wee, you, omg,*" the three sang in a raised pitch.

A bolt of lightning escaped from behind the clouds and touched down on the snake's head shaking the ground beneath them. Stuart wondered if they would survive the furious storm. Lightning strikes kill more than tornados, he recalled. And then something even stranger happened. Frank, Buddie, and Bill materialized in the center of the egg that rolled out from the Serpent's mouth as if the snake had given birth.

"Where'd you come from?" Stuart asked.

"What? We've been here," Bill said.

"*O, wee, you, omg,*" Stuart joined in loudly.

Chapter 22

Time Travel

"Unprecedented!" Lira said after Bryn opened and read a note just delivered by courier, "You be summoned before the Elders of the timekeeper, immediately."

"We never be in the presence of the Elders. I hardly know what they look like," she said. "But I be told they be lesser in appearance than one would expect. Still, they be great. What shall I wear? Bryn, can you make these men presentable?"

Thirty minutes later Roland and Sedwig dressed in Bryn's finest velvets and Lira wearing a silver dress and a golden shawl secretly beamed down to just outside the doors of the time library. The guards, after looking stealthily about, immediately let them enter and escorted them through darkened halls until a door opened to the well-lit room of the gathering of Elders. The timekeeper stood out as the only material form along with themselves in a room full of beings nearly invisible in their composition, almost shades.

"You shall sit while I tell ye what has been decided," the timekeeper said, impervious to the shock that the appearance of the Elders may have caused his guests. "After long consideration we have formulated an experiment that might safely do the trick. We shall tune the Earth out from under the influence of A major to the key of E minor. While such a tuning be far greater than we have ever before attempted, it has a significant advantage over anything else we could think to do. It will retune only minds."

The Elders mumbled something that sounded like amen.

Lira stood up, "Only minds? But it be the actions of the Endron that must be turned back. Their plot be far underway."

"As we speak the ships you have deployed already be foiling their plot," the timekeeper answered "The Alliance be capable to defeat the Endron without our help in this current battle."

"Yes! Yes!" the Elders softly sang out in unison.

The room darkened. A screen lit up near the wall on the far side of the room filled with real time action. A heated battle was seen taking place behind the clouds far above Earth.

"We be monitoring for hours," the timekeeper said. "The battle has ensued and the Alliance has clearly taken the upper hand."

The dense clouds opened for only a second or two but long enough for Roland to recognize what he thought to be the serpent below.

"Serpent Mound!" he said loudly, now standing up.

"Yes, it be fortuitous that you had given me these coordinates when we first met," the timekeeper said. "This place has great power. I learned it be the focal point of Endron planning for years, it being at the center of the Earth mind. I never would have guessed; it being where it be. But there you have it! Always a surprise when we look. We will tune here at the center so it ripple out like a wave to minds that have been touched."

"But if you not turn back the Endron's deeds!" Lira said, still not understanding.

"Their deeds be to strip minds! I grant these acts affected the course of events, as intended. But to change those events in time, to eradicate those events, as if to destroy, could destroy too much. We cannot risk such alteration for to do so would put the universe and all that we know at risk since what exists be dependent upon the last act. Ah me, picture a deck of cards collapsing. We cannot have that."

"Hear! Hear!" the Elders were heard to say loudly.

"Instead our plan be to restore only minds undone by them, and in so doing humanity be given a chance to direct its effort towards a future far superior to what the Endron planned. And if they succeed in charting a new course of action, that shall alter perceptions of the past much like Roland and I witnessed in the time machine when we looked at the harmonious history of the building of this Serpent Mound, harmonious no doubt after multitudes of tunings smoothed out human history. Who knows what it be without these tunings?"

"I'm confused," Roland said. "What it would have been, what it was, what it is? Are they not the same?"

"You forget the lesson I taught at our first meeting? The past be multiple, but what we understand of the past, what be recorded be the product of an accumulation of time-tunings to the human mind."

"So the past is no more than perceptions made in the present. Is that what you're saying?" Roland asked.

"So it must be for human minds to ponder and comprehend. That be what at issue here and what the Endron have sought to destroy, the proper balancing of the mind. Without that, humankind cannot make for themselves a future worth living. As has been always and always will be, it be up to the planet's inhabitants to rectify what be past; but if they be not capable, which be the Endron's goal here, well, we all know the outcome. The Elders and I cannot make outcomes or change history, we only rebalance and tune minds."

The band of immaterials at once stood up from their table gathering and clapped their hands in muted applause.

"What will be the precise effects of this mind-tuning, as you describe it?" Roland asked.

"Precise, you ask? Of that we cannot be sure since this has not been done before so powerfully. In the past it be so subtle a change as if the mood should swing from one day to next, so imperceptible it be. But this be not so subtle."

Roland asked the question that was burning inside him, "Will they remember? Will she remember?"

"That be what makes such a profound change in keys so problematic," the timekeeper said. "Memory will not be lost before the time of A major, that we know for sure. But the period between the time of A major and before our retuning to E minor, of that we be not entirely sure, but we know there must be memory loss for many. It be so abrupt on the mind, so extensive, but since it never be tried, we cannot be sure."

"What will this mean," Roland said sorrowfully.

Lira looked on him sadly. "It could mean several years be lost to those you love."

Roland looked into her eyes searching for deeper meaning. "You mean Summer will forget?"

"Perhaps, as if you never happened," Lira said. "As if she were never wed and came with you to Avian."

"Surely someone will remind her," Roland said.

"Remind? Only those who remember can remind," the timekeeper said. "Much may be lost to those on Earth. That be the danger of this experiment. We hope to limit to only those affected by mind-stripping, but be not sure how widespread the effects. Of course, we here be not touched and know the true history as will the Endron whose evil plans be foiled. But we be here and not subject to the wave that will be sent out across the Earth from that great serpent center once we begin our tuning. Unless, of course, our plan should fail, which always be possible; or it be not tried, the risk of loss too great."

"You know what that means for me," Roland cried out to Lira.

"You must find your strength Roland," she said sternly. "This plan we must try and pray it succeeds without ill effect. I know you suffer much. If she loses memory, the only remedy be you win her back; but be mindful she may have no knowledge, and there be risk that history will not repeat."

"But there is hope," he said. He studied the images on the screen once the clouds broke open. "Can you focus more closely? I see men."

At the head of the serpent were six men and one woman all chanting together, *"O, wee, you, omg."*

"What are they singing?" he asked.

"A powerful song from time past," the timekeeper said. "I hear it before as I studied this place's history. A summons I believe to the spirit that brought power to the place and caused it to be built."

"Wait! I recognize those men," Roland said. "Some are not of these people."

"It matters not who sings the summons; it be heard anyway. It may be..." the timekeeper paused for a moment in thought. "It may be their summons for return be what brought you to my time library to begin with. I never considered that. We may be an answer to their summons. This may be a greater plan than I be aware of. I like you may be only an actor, not the director I had imagined myself to be." He looked out at the table full of Elders, the wisest, oldest, and most powerful beings on Avian. And then he looked above them at the statue of the Bird Goddess who dangled from the wall opposite the screen that reflected images of Serpent Mound. Her mighty wings seemed to move in recognition of his recognition. "I never suspected!" he said in wondrous utterance.

Roland looked at Lira, eyes full of tears. "Before this tuning begins, can you put me down among my people to sing the summons of that which protects."

"Roland, you forget!" she said. "You have a place here with your dear friend Sedwig. Safe you will be and honored."

"My place is with them."

"Of course," she said and handed him her shawl. "Take this for your protection. Bryn will put you down."

Roland beamed up to the ship and shortly thereafter was set down again among the people who continued to chant "*O, wee, you, omg.*" There was little shock at his sudden appearance. Instead, Roland wrapped tightly in Lira's golden shawl embraced Bill and Stuart wrapped in their blankets and picked up the chant *"O, wee, you, omg."*

"Shall we begin?" the timekeeper said to Lira.

"Yes," she said, in a trembling voice. "This defeat being great for the Endron, but a magnificent achievement for us and for them." Roland's handsome, tear stained face filled the screen they stood looking upon.

Chapter 23

Roman Concert Night

The supervisor at the museum Palazzo Barberini was surprised by the look of the room after the young priest and his pretty assistant put on the final touches. Surprised is an understatement. Actually, she was disturbed by the disarray created by thirty crystal vases filled with white Madonna lilies scattered willy-nilly and the dirty pile of rocks and clay heaped up at the room's entrance. She could make no sense of the placement of an assortment of potted trees that looked in their rough containers as if they had just left a farmer's greenhouse, particularly the large palm that blocked the view of the grand piano from the front center angle. One touch she liked, however, was a rather interesting statue that had been brought all the way from Paris. Gitane Marie sat atop the piano, her crown glimmering under strings of small white lights strung in a seemingly haphazard appearance about the room. Of course, each of these items had been strategically placed according to Luc's carefully drawn plan to bring Earth to Heaven and therefore Heaven to Earth. But such a mystical implementation was quite impossible for the supervisor to comprehend.

Hand on her hip, she stood by the door like an agent of chic in her black silk suit and black pumps, a young women of about thirty who counted out the one hundred plus chairs that managed to fit rather nicely around vases, trees, and rocks with only a few chairs reserved in front for the family. The sight of each chair cooled her outrage at what she perceived as an indignity done to this magnificent room. Each chair would fetch the museum 1000 euros at no expense to it, she was told when she lodged a complaint with her supervisors. And besides, they claimed, Madame Conti is known to all for her eccentricities. Those who will attend tonight's event are well aware and would expect no less. The museum had no illusions that this great lady's generosity in putting on this fundraiser was only for their benefit. They assumed her other motive was to promote the career of her soon to be grandson by marriage to her lovely granddaughter, Cinzia de Chevalier. They lacked the ken to begin to imagine what her real motive was.

Cinzia and her fiancé arrived early so that he might have time to warm-up at the piano. Luc and Summer followed and made sure the placement of the crystal vases was just right, he having mapped them to the coordinates of the stars at the exact moment of Etienne's birth. Madame Conti trailed in shortly thereafter in the company of Hans Bueller and Barry Short. Hans, who was once Barry's nemesis when the two were archeologists in Egypt, was by now both Barry's and Madame Conti's fast friend.

"I'm glad you were able to attend," Luc said to Hans.

"Why of course! I would not miss such a performance."

"I was able to book Hans a seat on a high speed train. He tells me he was quite comfortable," Madame Conti said.

"Where is Etienne?" Luc asked.

"He should soon be arriving," she said. "Can I borrow Summer to help me greet my guests?"

"Certainly."

"Is this chair situated in the correct position for my grandson?" she asked before taking her position by the door.

He looked up at the fresco above and measured where the beam would fall from Divine Wisdom's scepter should it escape the painting as he had planned. "It's perfect," he said as he pulled a vile of rose vinegar from his pocket and sprinkled some on the chair. "Make sure he remains in this spot."

"I'll see to it. I'm putting him right between Hans and me."

"You will have him surrounded," he laughed.

"That's the idea," she said. "Barry, you sit there on the other side of Hans."

Hans patted the seat next to him. "Yes, sit here."

Barry was quite uncomfortable with the entire event. Too much hocus pocus, he thought. He had wished very much that Claudio Postremo could have attended to add some intellectual discipline to the mix, but Claudio thought it best he stay in Florence to make himself readily available should the men overseas, namely Stuart and Professor

Eller, need his help or his counsel. He had felt quite badly when he learned about Eller's abduction and its apparent effect on his intellect and appetite. Actually, Claudio suffered a bit from misplaced guilt. If he had traveled to America instead of depending on others, he reasoned, Buddie's fate could have been avoided. To make matters worse, he had not heard from either of these men for days. He wished Dr. Eller were in Rome so that he might benefit from Luc's hermetic experiment, which he placed more faith in than did his colleague, Barry Short.

Madame Conti and Summer moved to the door to greet guests who had begun to trickle in. Guests universally oohed and aahed as they entered the room. It was the fresco that caught their attention and not the decor, unless of course they were seated under a tree or too close to a vase of lilies whose fragrance was beginning to grow quite pungent. In those cases Summer would ever so slightly move their chairs to a more pleasing position.

The room nearly full, Summer asked, "Where is Etienne?"

"Here he is now!" Madame Conti said. She reached out and hugged him. "I was beginning to worry."

"I would never disappoint my Grand-mère," he said just before he kissed her cheek.

"But where is Juliette?"

"She sends her regrets. She had made a reservation well in advance of your invitation and thought you would understand. She has not felt well since giving birth and thought it best to go to the beach to help her recovery."

"Well, yes I do," she said hesitantly.

He greeted Summer with a whispered hello.

She nodded a response and turned to Madame Conti. "Go seat your grandson while I attend to the other guests. I think they're nearly all here now."

Madame Conti escorted Etienne to his designated chair but had a slight scare when he insisted on sitting to the left of Hans Bueller so as not to come between his grandmother and her date. Seeing Madame Conti in a flutter, Summer marched over. "You sit here," she said to Etienne, "and I'll trade places with Hans. That way he can sit next to your grandmother on her other side." The new arrangement effectively seated Etienne between Summer and Madame Conti.

She smells of fresh flowers, he thought. In fact the whole room smelled of incense and flowers now that the doors were closed. He leaned in towards Summer, not conspicuously, just enough to feel her body heat.

She pulled away ever so slightly. "I'm glad you were able to bring Gitane Marie from Paris. I love seeing her."

"It was no trouble at all," he said again leaning into her. "I had her packed up and put in my limousine."

"Oh, so you drove?"

"I should never let her travel out of my sight for a moment," he said with longing in his eyes.

"That's good," she said now looking right at him. "You look quite fit, much better than the last time I saw you."

"It is his teas," he said, pointing to Luc Renard. "They have given me back my energy."

"This reminds me of the day our museum opened in Paris—the lilies, the pianist—Remember?" she said.

"How could I forget," he said taking a full view of her. "Those were quite exciting times— the thieves and reporters— All of it."

"Signore e Signori" Madame Conti said to the gathered audience. "Thank you so much for coming out tonight and helping to preserve this beautiful palace." She paused for applause. "You know how much I treasure the beauties of Rome, and tonight you are in for a special treat." She waxed poetical for several minutes about the beauty of the pianist's original compositions and the magnificence of his skill at his instrument, and ended her speech by saying, "He will earn a place in the grand tradition of musical history. Mark my words!"

After a minute of silence, the artist opened with his own composition, a gentle, ethereal piece that in one moment dropped off only to soar in the next. It met with great applause that grew louder when he launched into a familiar piece, a Rachmaninoff *Prelude.* With that, the mood colored somber.

Luc rose and went about the room lighting seven long, white candles he had strategically placed while he anxiously looked up at the fresco to see if he could detect any alteration.

The mood of the music shifted again as if the intent of the ordering of the selections was to open every door behind which resides the full range of emotions, as if to trigger them all. The talented pianist's hands span the keyboard as he played Liszt's *Hungarian Rhapsody No. 2*.

Luc looked up and thought he detected a smile on the face of the goddess. She's turning her head, he imagined. She's looking down. She cannot resist the joy rising upward from the piano. It's the joy! he thought. They are all waking up now, he marveled, as the music breathed life into the faces of all the virtues that surround her. Tears welled up. "It's working!" he nearly shouted, although no one could hear him over the blazing sound of the music except Cinzia, who could read his lips from where she stood on the other side of the piano near her lover. She looked at Gitane Marie's impish smile and then directed her eyes upward toward the now animated fresco and offered a prayer for her brother. Eyes all met: Cinizia's, Divine Wisdom's, and Gitane Marie's. Three goddesses' powerful glance, Luc thought.

The pianist rose and took several bows to loud applause. He sat down and played Liszt's *La Campanella*, as if he wished those faces above him to know what this concert was about. Cinzia smiled and nodded just before he launched into a passionate rendering of de Falla's *The Fire Dance*, as if to conjure the brilliant flame that now soared like a bolt from Divine Wisdom's scepter, landing squarely on Etienne's head, knocking him back into his chair and onto the floor.

"Grand-mère! Grand-mère!" Cinzia cried in excitement.

"Fire! Fire!" other voices shouted. The pianist stood up. The audience rose from their seats and pushed their way towards the door, kicking up dust from Luc's strategically placed rocks and clay as they bolted from the room. Looking aghast, the young museum supervisor followed after them in her tight black skirt and clicking heels.

"There's no fire in here!" Barry shouted over the din of the fleeing crowd. "This man needs a doctor. Is anyone here a doctor?" He put his arm around Summer. "Are you all right?"

"I might be burned a little bit, but I'm alright," she said as they both looked at a blackened spot upon her shoulder.

"Is there a doctor here?" Barry shouted again.

Luc looked up at the fresco. The figures were still and lifeless as they had been before the concert began. It's over, he thought. Had his magic worked? Had it been too strong?

The startled pianist sat down and began playing Debussy's soothing "Sarabande" while Etienne lay on the floor unconscious and Madame Conti cried. She brought his head up into her lap and checked his pulse. "It's a little fast but seems normal enough."

"We need to get this man to a hospital, someplace where he can get some help!" Barry shouted.

"As long as his pulse is fine, I do not think that will be necessary," a man said who had stayed behind the fleeing crowd. He looked at the burn on Summer's shoulder. "A cooling ointment is all you need dear. It will feel better in the morning."

Madame Conti looked up. "Oh, Doctor Lombardi. So nice to see you here tonight. Could you take a closer look at my grandson?"

He bent down and put his ear to Etienne's chest and his hand on his pulse.

Debussy had worked its balm. Etienne, though groggy, began to regain consciousness. "What has happened? My head!"

"The fall knocked you unconscious," the doctor said. "Head injuries are not my specialty, but I can say with complete confidence that this looks like a mild concussion. Go home and rest. Tomorrow you will be fit as a fiddle."

Luc helped Etienne out to a cab. Cinzia grabbed the Gitane and carefully wrapped her in her shawl before tucking her in the taxi that sped off to Madame Conti's apartment at the Piazza del Popolo.

"He will be more comfortable in my room," Madame Conti said as she placed the treasured statue on a high shelf next to a window. "I will have my maid prepare us an evening snack while I get him settled in." Twenty minutes later she was back in her living room. "Summer! He's calling for you. Could you please speak to him?"

After Summer had left the room, Madame Conti went over to the table and filled a plate with cheese and bread, poured herself a glass of wine, and sat down next to Hans. "I believe he has forgotten that he's married. I mentioned Juliette's name several times and he would only look at me vacantly and ask for Summer."

"I'm not surprised," Hans Bueller said, "She's a very sweet girl."

"You've missed my point entirely."

"It's temporary amnesia, that's all," Barry said.

"Well, he remembers me, and he remembers you, and he remembers Summer. He even asked after Gitane Marie. If it is amnesia, it is a rather selective type."

Luc rummaged through his memory to see if he could recall any mention of Pope Urban VIII suffering amnesia after undergoing his cure at the Palazzo Barberini. His mind went blank. "I'm a bit fuzzy myself," he said, feeling a headache coming on. "All this excitement has rattled me, but it had to be the blow to his head that caused his amnesia, selective or not. I never anticipated that strike from Divine Wisdom's scepter would knock him off his chair like that."

"Her scepter! Do you really believe that's what caused him to fall?" Barry said.

"What else could it have been? We nearly had a fire," Madame Conti said.

"It was those lights, those cheap, blasted lights Luc strung about," Barry said. "I saw it all happen. I heard a big pop, saw a spark, and there was Etienne sprawled out. They shorted out, that's all! It must have started in that strand hanging above him."

"I'm sure you are quite incorrect," Madame Conti said.

Luc stood up obviously rattled. "Barry, I know you've been very uncomfortable with my work in hermetic magic, but you should try harder to minimize your prejudice, particularly after what has just happened."

"What are you telling me?" he snorted. "You know I have two very good eyes."

"Now, now, Barry," Bueller said.

"Oh, shut up Hans."

"I saw it for myself!" Luc said. "The music breathed life into that fresco. I saw their faces animate. And then that bolt of flame exploded from her scepter." Clearly fatigued, he nearly fell back into his chair. "Madame Conti, could you please fetch Summer. My head is splitting, and I should get her back to the hotel."

"It's about time you thought about Summer. I can hardly believe this!" Barry said, stood up and walked towards the door of the apartment. "A man of such fine intellect. Maybe tomorrow the truth will become apparent to all of you," he said before stomping out.

"My, my," Bueller said. "I haven't seen him z'is angry for a very long time, not since Egypt." He looked piteously at Luc. "He used sometimes to rage at me too about our little disagreements."

"Is everything all right?" Summer said. "I heard a lot of yelling."

"It's all right dear," Madame Conti said. "Luc and Barry had a little argument."

"You sure were loud, but fortunately not loud enough to wake Etienne. He's out like a light."

"Hmm, that's just what we were arguing about," Luc said. "Was it a light or a flame?"

"What?" Summer said. "What are you talking about?"

"Oh, nothing much," Luc said. "We should get back to the hotel. All of this planning has kept me up for days."

Summer grabbed her bag. "I'm feeling exhausted too."

"Here dear, you can take the rest of this ointment with you," Madame Conti said.

"Madame Conti," Luc said before leaving, "I must apologize for my behavior."

"Never mind that. Can I will call you a cab?"

"Thank you very much but not tonight. A little walk will do us both good."

The hotel where the three were staying was just across the Villa Borghese Gardens from the Piazza del Popolo, approximately halfway between Madame Conti's apartment and the Palazzo Barberini. Luc and Summer had just climbed the steps to Borghese's Pincio Gardens when they spotted Barry sitting on the terrace that overlooks Piazza del Popolo. The air was cool and silky as if a fresh wind had blown into Rome when the three sat down together and further discussion ensued.

"I don't know why you two are arguing over this now," Summer said. "We all knew about this experiment."

"An experiment is one thing, magic is another," Barry said. "He's asking me to believe that a spell he cast animated figures in a two dimensional fresco."

"What did you think was going to happen?" Luc asked. "You

obviously had no faith in my planning."

"I didn't think it would work. You're right about that."

"But it did!" Luc said.

"There is an obvious and simpler explanation. That's all that I'm pointing out. And we still can't be sure of the outcome just yet."

"It burned me too," Summer said. "Oh, god, it's starting to smart."

Luc inspected the wound. "It looks pretty bad. Do you know how it happened?"

"Well, it must have happened when that bolt struck Etienne. I was sitting right next to him."

"Etienne wasn't burnt, was he?" Barry said.

"Only a little," Summer said. "I could smell it in the bedroom. His hair was singed. I think we probably overlooked it because of his other injury."

"You must have taken the brunt of the flame then," Luc said, looking at the girl. "When we get to the hotel I'll put my own salve on it. Do you mind me asking what he said when you went in to see him? Did he seem, well, did he seem changed?"

"Ah, yes. He seemed more like the princely man I had once known."

"I take it then that he continued to deny he's married," Barry said.

"Yes. It was quite awkward. He not only has no memory of his marriage, he has no memory that we split-up. I didn't know what to say given his condition so I said nothing."

"Hmm," Luc said. "He may have been affected in ways I never anticipated."

"I bet tomorrow he will remember," Barry said.

When he arrived at his room at the hotel Barry had a message to phone Claudio Postremo. He thought it a good opportunity to commiserate with someone who would understand his point of view.

"Something happened all right. The guests thought it was a fire." Barry said. "You should have seen the toast of Rome push and shove their way out of that room. Oh, Etienne? Well, he fell back in his chair and cracked his head. Now he's suffering from a case of amnesia. The doctor said it is only a mild concussion so I expect him to recover his memory soon. The funny thing is how selective his memory loss is. He remembers me and everyone else who was there, but it seems he has no memory of his wife."

"Some men would call that a stroke of good luck," Claudio chuckled. "How did it happen?"

"On that point there is disagreement. Luc thinks his magic the cause. He swears Divine Wisdom came to life under the music's spell and shot a bolt of lightning from her scepter that smacked Etienne on the head and knocked him over. But that's not what I saw. I saw a strand of cheap, white Christmas lights short out nearly causing a fire. They must have delivered a powerful shock when they exploded above his head. In fact, the whole place panicked after a couple of people stood up and shouted fire. It was quite a sight!"

"Yes, yes, I suppose what you saw is the possible cause," Postremo said. "But is it not equally possible that a bolt of lightning coming down from that scepter could have shorted out those lights? That what you saw was only a secondary consequence?"

"I'll be darned! You really do think that Luc's magic came to fruition."

"I'm only suggesting."

"Well, in American parlance we say the proof is in the pudding. We will see."

Chapter 24

Song of Morning

"*O, wee, you, omg,*" Charles chanted, while the others lay sleeping on the cliff that overlooks Brush Creek. He watched as ship after ship rose up from an undisclosed cave as if exorcised, flew over the ledge where he stood firm-footed, and disappeared into a murky predawn sky. The storms had abated. Counterfeit storms, he thought as he marveled at the simplicity of the disguise. A great battle had been fought behind those fearsome clouds, a battle undetected by most of the people who lived nearby.

He knew those people well. For them Serpent Mound was only a relic of some ancient past. It had no potency they could detect. Coyotes who had recently come in packs and roamed the woods nearby were to them only what they seemed. They lacked the imagination to sense what was going on. The crop circle, that for a short time drew their attention, would soon grow over with weeds and be forgotten. The battle that had just been fiercely fought to save the minds of mortal women and men was hidden from those who lacked eyes to see. And his chant, "*O, wee, you, omg,*" to them was only a queer set of rhythmic words whose power went unnoticed by those who do not understand the universal determinants of word and song.

"*O, wee, you, omg,*" he continued to chant, hoping his song would help mend the disruption to the universal order and would aid the Great Spirit. "*O, wee, you, omg,*" he chanted again. It was for him to assist, knowing that he drew upon an ancient tradition that he was now the living bearer of.

Gradually the others began to wake. Seth and Sarah immediately resumed their song. "*O, wee, you, omg,*" they chanted.

"I've been watching them leave," Charles said. "I believe all their ships are going."

"Where'd they keep those ships?" Sarah asked.

"I saw them rise up from that gully. There must be some hidden cavern down there."

"Hard to imagine," Seth said, "unless it was newly made."

"Perhaps it was there all along and required only an entrance to be excavated," Charles replied.

"That makes sense," Sarah said. "Otherwise, we would have seen it before."

"We must find this place and destroy it so that they never return," Seth said.

"That we will do once this tragedy is past."

"Oh, my head," Stuart said, as he woke up. He wrapped himself tightly in his blanket and looked over at his friend who had appeared out of nowhere the night before.

Roland, as if he felt Stuart's eyes upon him, immediately sat up and warmed himself in Lira's golden shawl.

"Where'd you ever get that blanket?" Stuart asked in mockery.

"Tis a gift from a great lady," Roland said. Still dazed from sleep, he looked up at clear skies. "What's going on? What happened?"

Charles looked at him curiously, realizing now he recognized him from a past encounter on winter solstice eve. "The battle is over. I've been watching their ships withdraw one by one. Did you perhaps come here with the other side?"

"So to speak," Roland said. He thought back to where he had been before he found himself on the edge of this rock. The Library of Time, he remembered. My memory seems intact, he thought. She has not escaped my mind. He looked about where he was. "Are these others all right?"

"I'll wake them," Stuart said as he shook his three companions in adventure. "Fellas, are you doin' all right?"

Bill and Frank recovered quickly from a rather deep sleep. Buddie Eller took more time to regain full consciousness. But when he did he was a different sort of man than Stuart had met at Monroe Lake.

"Where am I?" Buddie asked as he looked around.

"You're at Serpent Mound in Ohio," Frank said. "We drove over here from Monroe Lake."

Buddie rubbed his head as if by rubbing it he might stir up memories. "I remember driving to Monroe Lake. I remember setting up camp.

Then I draw a blank. How did I come to be with you Frank? You are Frank, aren't you? The reporter I spoke to from the *Bloomington Times*?"

"Yes, the one and only." He pointed to Bill and Stuart. "These guys learned from some Italian scientist they know that you were going over to Monroe Lake alone to see if you could find the UFO responsible for the abduction I wrote about in the paper. They contacted me to help search you out."

"I remember some of it now. I was in contact with Claudio Postremo who had taken an interest in that abduction story, but beyond that I remember nothing. I have to assume you found me because here I am."

"We did," Frank said, "but not before you were abducted."

"I was abducted?"

"Were you ever!" Stuart said. "You were not only abducted, you were mind-stripped."

"I was what? I have no memory of this at all. Nor do I remember meeting up with you."

"I can offer a likely explanation," Roland said. "Mind-stripping alters the mind dramatically. You become almost another person, the person you might have been if you had no superego and little intellect. You've been restored, which means the experiment is a fantastic success."

"What experiment do you mean?" Charles asked.

"It's hard to explain," Roland said. "Think how profoundly musical notation can change the tempo and mood of a piece of music and correspondingly the mood of its listener. Well, the timekeeper I met at a place called Avian says the universe is governed in much the same way. He and the Elders learned the secret of retuning, which can alter the direction history is taking if it has grown too chaotic and needs a slight nudge in a more harmonious direction. In other words, retuning can change human mood enough to change the course of actions they choose to take. They've had Earth in their sights now for thousands of years and claim to have done minor tunings over the course of history to reset us, keep us in line, so to speak. But their work had recently been undercut. The Alliance learned the Endron have been employing a technology known as mind-stripping to produce an entirely different outcome. Rather than creating a mood conducive to harmony, their goal is disruption, conflict, and enslavement. Just before I left Avian, the Elders had proposed a far more radical approach than standard tuning to reset the Earth to what it had been before the Endron had begun their dark work. They proposed to change Earth's key A major to E minor in an experiment they could not guarantee the outcome of. If what I see here in Buddie Eller is representative, I would say the experiment is a resounding success. And yet, he has noticeably forgotten so much."

"Something like amnesia," Eller said as he continued to rub his head. He turned to Frank, "And those other men, those men you wrote about whose families I talked to, are they likewise restored?"

Frank turned to Roland who was clearly far more expert in these matters than he.

"If the experiment was as successful as it appears to be from your example, yes, they've been restored."

"And they won't remember who they've been or what they've done these many months?"

"By your example, I would say no, and that's the hitch," Roland said.

"Boy, that could be tough," Frank said. "One of them got himself put away for murder. Imagine him waking up in his cell a new man with no memory of who he had been or how he got there."

"The Elders debated this very question. Their business is harmony, not disruption, but the situation on Earth was so dire and heading towards such a catastrophic conclusion that it had to be averted regardless of the cost."

"*O, wee, you, omg,* is powerful medicine," Charles said. "Those were the words spoken to me to put to song. *O, wee, you omg,*" he repeated and went silent.

"It was the right song," Roland said, as he stood at the head of the Serpent, his golden shawl shimmering. "And this is the right place to sing it. The timekeeper told me that this Serpent is the Earth mind. And isn't it a wonder how and when he should find this out."

He considered that the timekeeper had only recently learned of the existence of the Serpent, this knowledge having been lost even to him and to the Elders. But not to them, he thought, as he looked over at Charles and his friends. He remembered the night of the winter solstice, the Serpent lit in a ring of fire. What brought me here? Was it fate? Something greater and wiser than the Elders?

"Wait just a minute," Sarah said. "Who are these people with all this power? Who are these Elders, and who are these Endron, and what is this Alliance you speak of?"

Before he could answer a great shadow swooped down, and like a predator bird swooped Roland up and carried him away.

"Where the hell did he go? What happened? Is it another ship?" Stuart cried.

"*O, wee, you, omg,*" Charles began to chant again, but it was too late.

Stuart, Frank, Buddie, and Bill did not stop to ask questions but ran straight for their car. In the few short minutes before they sped away, Stuart shot off an email to Claudio Postremo.

About to leave Serpent Mound. Things are crazy here. People disappear then reappear. If we don't make it back, I want you to know they just now took Roland. Swooped down and took him up before we could do anything to stop it. Revenge, I think. Eller has returned intact although he has no memory of being taken. Nothing we can do but get out of here before they come back after us. I'll write you more later I hope! Stuart

Chapter 25

Get Away

Buddie Eller reached his head through the open window and craned his neck upward when he spotted another ship. "There's one right up there!" he shouted over the din of the engine and the deafening wind as Stuart raced south on Highway 73. "Now it's gone. Where did it go?"

"Oh, shit! I don't know," Stuart shouted back. "All that I know is we gotta get outa here fast. Can you close it up? The noise is driving me nuts."

"I want to see!" Eller said.

Frank patted Buddie on the shoulder and reached over and closed the window. "I think right now we need to focus on escaping this place before whatever came after Roland comes after us."

"I hate missing the opportunity," Eller said.

"Just look out the window," Frank said. "Here I'll help you."

Buddie, Frank, and Bill trained their eyes on the sky through the now closed windows while Stuart kept his eyes on the road. There was nothing left to see. Apparently, Buddie had seen the last ship take flight from its hiding place below the Serpent Mound. When the vehicle full of men arrived at the Appalachian Highway and turned west towards Cincinnati, Stuart finally slowed his pace as he mixed in with trucks and other vehicles moving steadily along as if nothing unusual had happened.

Frank and Buddie were eager to arrive home so they could get on the phone and reconnect with the families Eller had ferreted out in his follow-up investigation of the men and boys who had been abducted while camping at Lake Monroe. After all, that event had led both of these men on the odyssey that led not only to Eller's abduction but to an entirely new understanding of the universe, a universe that excited their imaginations, stimulated their moral sense, and propelled much of their conversation. They reasoned that if the universe is the great conductor who draws forth from the stars and planets grand music and we are the choir, should we not become more cognizant of the songs we sing? They hoped to reconcile those victims of abduction with whomever they may have wronged while under Endronian influence.

"You're being too optimistic," Stuart counseled. "You can't say anything about Endronian influence. It won't work. The public will think you're nuts. Or if they believe you, well, hell, what would they do?"

"I see your point," Eller said who for years had concealed his side projects for those very reasons.

"So what are you saying Stuart?" Frank asked. "We do nothing?"

"You either do nothing or come up with an explanation people might believe."

"Like what? The music of the spheres was out of adjustment and now it's back?"

"That's no good. It's got to sound more familiar than that."

"I've got an idea," Eller said after considering the problem. "The father of one of the victims was convinced that the changes in his son must have been caused by drugs."

"Bingo!" Stuart said. "That works every time."

"Yes, but what kind of drug could have had such lasting and profound effects?" Eller asked.

"You're right. Maybe we're going to have to invent one. Frank, you're a newspaper reporter, aren't you? Maybe you can write a story sourced from a hot tip you got from *moi*, a government investigator whose name you pledged not to disclose. You got it when you were doing a follow-up investigation of these men whose behavior grew bizarre after the disruption at the camping site. Hmm, I think I can come up with something."

"Ha! Sort of like an X-file," Eller said.

"I like that," Frank said.

"I don't!" Bill said. "I've been waiting nearly my whole life for this thing to bust wide open. And here's our chance, and you want to make up some phony drug story."

"Be careful what you wish for," Stuart said.

"Why? It's time everyone knows the truth."

"Man, I've gotta tell you. I know a lot about human nature, and I wouldn't count on universal peace breaking out if people learn we're being monitored by alien forces who are trying to take control."

"Their intentions are benevolent," Bill said.

"Guardian aliens, you think? Then what about Roland? What happened to him? And what about the Endron? They don't sound so benevolent. If you ask me, what we've learned is we're in a hell of a lot more danger than I had ever imagined."

"The Endron were defeated!"

"This time!" Stuart said. "I'd advise you to keep a lid on this until we know more about what we're dealing with. We don't want to cause a panic. And believe me, widespread knowledge of what we've learned would cause a panic of monumental proportions."

"I have to agree," Eller reluctantly admitted.

"I get it," Bill said. "Barry Short once said somethin' like that. He said droppin' themselves down among us might be like jumpin' into a lions' pit. We'd pull out all our military hardware and likely be defeated."

"Barry's a wise man. I've known him many years now," Stuart said.

"So maybe the best I can do is prepare people for the inevitable when it comes," Bill said.

"Yeah, yeah" Stuart said. "Unfortunately, that could be sooner rather than later. But you've got a good idea there," he said, wholeheartedly believing that anything Bill could do or say would be better than the truth, whatever that might turn out to be. "Prepare them not to panic if you can figure out how to do that. Maybe tell them stories, those kinds of 'what if' scenarios that get people thinking but don't make them scared. So if the time ever comes that they need a resource, they'll have something to draw from so they might react with more curiosity than fear. Fear poisons men's souls. I saw a lot of that in combat."

"Right on," Bill said. "That's what I'll be doin' from now on, preparin' them."

Roland had no knowledge of what had transpired in Rome, he having found himself transported onto a ship he had no acquaintance with, moreover, locked up alone in a steely gray, windowless compartment. He assumed by his circumstance that he had been taken prisoner by the

Endron until a short, squat fellow he knew to be Martian greeted him.

"We only agreed to hold you temporarily," the fellow said. "Bryn asked that we get you out of a pinch. You be captured if we had not quickly interceded. Oh, my," he said as he turned away and wiped his nose.

"I guess I should say thank you then if my situation was as precarious as you say."

"Indeed. It be like a hornets' nest out there. We be landing immediately to keep you and ourselves out of it. Hold on!"

"Hornets' nest on Mars?" Roland laughed.

"We do have them," the stout Martian said as the ship shook them both. "But I be metaphorical, and you do not understand. You must read little poetry in your line of adventure."

The ship plunged as if it had been dropped fast down an elevator shaft. Roland pressed hard to the floor before sliding across it and slamming against the wall. "I presume we've just landed," he said.

"I told you to hold on," the Martian said as he helped him up. "The doctor who treated you earlier has agreed to take you in whilst we plan your departure and concealment."

Roland found himself in the same glowing rock hanger he had been brought to some time ago with Summer, but he had little memory of it given his condition at the time. Two stout men escorted him to the doctor's quarters where he was greeted gingerly when he arrived.

"Could this be the same man?" the doctor said and began to circle him. "You look, well, you look quite different."

"I presume I'm the same man," Roland said. "Just restored."

"Remarkable! Yes, there seems to be quite a bit of restoration going on. First you and now Earth."

"Oh, so they've told you," Roland said.

"Bryn and I be quite good friends, and then there be our proximity to Earth to think about. No one yet knows the full repercussions of the interference. Like you, for instance. Bryn tells me they did not consider that they should never have let you go back when they agreed to it. So here you be. You look quite remarkable. To be quite honest, I never expected that you would recover."

"I think you were not alone in that," Roland said. "So Bryn has told you I'm not to be on Earth. Did he happen to say why?"

"It would be far too easy to capture you there. Believe me, the Endron are mad as hornets. That, Bryn should have known. I do not know what he could have been thinking. The other reason be a little more subtle, and they could not have known until the experiment be done."

"The time-tuning you mean?"

"To the extreme, they tell me. It proved quite disruptive."

"And why should that be a determinate as to whether I be back on Earth."

"You know too much, and you talk too much. Given the level of disruption, Earth people might actually believe you. They need an alternative explanation if we are to remain safe. If the Endron be like hornets, humankind be like surly beasts: large and aggressive and very warlike. We monitor them, you know. But we are told you be different. You have evolved genes. So I'm glad to be of your acquaintance and mean no insult."

"I suppose you are right about being large and warlike, but not all are like that. They too are evolving."

"But to what? Hornets or more like us?"

"Or perhaps like the birds of Avian," Roland said.

"Ah yes, they be a race. That be for sure. Bryn will come unnoticed and take you back to spend your days."

Roland was not too sure he liked the sound of that. Two days hence he was taken aboard a cargo vessel loaded with red glowing rock headed for the free trade zone. They would stop for resupply at Avian, he was told, and there he would be let off. Three days later he was bundled up along with empty water containers needing refill and dropped gently into a flower-like landing platform on the planet that was to become his permanent home.

Chapter 26

Disruption

Barry rolled over and buried his head in his pillow in an attempt to block out what sounded like his hotel room telephone. Then he considered that it was probably Luc phoning to make amends. After a fretful night's sleep, he was quite prepared to offer his own humble apology. He rolled back over and picked it up.

"I do believe Stuart is quite terrified," Postremo said without further introductions.

"What? Stuart?" Barry asked, feeling slightly confused and let down.

"I just received his email. I'm sad to report he does not sound good, although much of what he wrote is quite vague."

"What?" Barry asked full voice this time.

"Sorry to have awakened you," Postremo said, assuming that was the cause of Barry's bad temper.

"Don't be sorry. I thought you were somebody else. What's this news you're calling about?"

"Stuart must have written within the hour if I've got my time zones correct."

"It's generally six hours earlier in the Eastern United States."

"That's what I thought. He wrote to say they were just escaping the Serpent Mound. Evidently, they spent the night there."

"Where? There aren't any hotels."

"That I do not know. His note is abbreviated. He says they took Roland."

"Who took Roland? What was Roland doing there?"

"I do not know that either. He says here that they swooped down and took him so I assume he was referring to a ship of some kind."

"That man is a complete mystery. I haven't known his whereabouts since he left my house in Ohio in another spaceship or some such contraption. Hmm, Serpent Mound? Well, there was some kind of a ship hanging around there when we were down there for the winter solstice. It's out in the middle of no man's land so I suspect there had to be a reason, which might explain what Roland was doing there. But I thought Stuart was someplace in Indiana?"

"He was! He and the others were at Monroe Lake. As I said, his message is vague. He does not say what brought them to Serpent Mound, only that they are leaving for fear that they too might be swooped up. The good news here is he says Buddie Eller was returned and is now mentally intact. The most troubling news is he thinks this Roland fellow was taken out of revenge."

Barry sat up on the edge of his bed. "That doesn't sound good." What will I tell Summer, he thought to himself. "Look, I'm going to go out now and try to ascertain Etienne's true condition. It was impossible last night to tell for sure, but if Eller's okay there's a possibility—well, we'll see."

Privately he thought that if Eller is restored and if Etienne is restored, the cause had to be more than shorted out light bulbs. He truly owes Luc an apology, he thought. But then again he wondered how Divine Wisdom's scepter could have affected Buddie Eller who was thousands of miles away in Ohio.

"I don't know what to report to Summer at this point," Barry said to Luc over the hotel phone. "She's been through too much. Damn it anyway!"

"Say nothing for now. No need to alarm her about Roland at the same time she is coping with Etienne's memory loss. It never occurred to me that the scepter strike would cause him to forget his marriage, worse to believe he is still engaged to Summer. Oh, I forgot. You don't believe the scepter strike ever happened."

"Luc, I want to apologize for my argumentative behavior. The cause of all of this couldn't be just light bulbs. At this point I'm open to anything that could explain what's going on. I have another bit of news to report about Buddie Eller, that ufologist over in Indiana who was recently abducted and mind-stripped. Well, Stuart wrote Claudio that Mr. Eller is now fully recovered from that event, which I find interesting in light of what went on here last night. Yet he was there not here, so I don't know how Divine Wisdom's scepter would explain his recovery."

"Nor do I. For now I think we should pay Etienne a visit and ascertain the full effects of last night's experiment."

"I can be ready in about twenty minutes," Barry said. "Meet you in the lobby."

The scene at Madame Conti's apartment was terribly domestic, so much so it made everyone but Etienne quite uncomfortable.

Only slightly embarrassed, Summer said, "He phoned, so I came over early. I didn't want to awaken you."

Madame Conti looked exasperated and drew Luc aside. "I'd like some fresh flowers. Can you accompany me to the flower vendor in the piazza?"

"Certainly," he said. And the two immediately left, leaving Barry alone with Etienne and Summer.

"Can I get you some tea?" she asked.

"Coffee, if you've got any."

Etienne immediately stood up. "Sit down," he said to Summer and looked over at Barry. "She's been taking care of me all morning. Actually, I am feeling quite well. I will make espresso for the three of us. I should not be long."

"And how are you feeling?" Barry asked Summer.

"I don't know. He's forgotten everything and treats me like we're still engaged. I don't know how to tell him the truth or if he would believe me if I did."

"Quite remarkable. Otherwise, how is he? Do you think the experiment a success?"

"He's very much himself again. So to answer your question I'd say a resounding yes!"

Etienne returned and served the espresso in a most gentlemanly manner, which led Barry to concur with Summer's estimate that he had been restored to his old self. As far as the other problem, he felt sure he should extract Summer out of this awkward situation as soon as he could.

As Madame Conti picked and sorted among the cut flowers in the piazza she confided her concerns to her now favorite confidant and priest. "I do not know how to address the problem. Yes, the experiment was an enormous success. He is my grandson again, but he has forgotten his wife."

"The amnesia should only be temporary."

"I should hope so! I'm beside myself. His wife is the granddaughter of one of my dearest friends. What shall she think? I've tried to remind him most subtly in my remarks, but he seems not to know what I'm talking about."

"Something happened outside the scope I had envisioned. You are not aware of this yet, but another man we know who was abducted and mind-stripped was likewise restored to himself last night. But he was some forty-seven hundred miles away in the state of Ohio in the United States."

"I don't understand."

"Neither do I. And even worse we are told that Roland was also there in Ohio and was swooped up by some unknown party and taken away."

"If he should be returned here, he would not be pleased to see his wife taking care of my grandson and neither would Juliette. I am sorry I must ask this of you, but you must remove Summer at once."

With this remark, the scene was set. Madame Conti and Luc returned to her apartment with flowers in hand. Luc made excuses as to why the three visitors must leave so that Etienne could continue to rest and recover. Etienne was none too pleased, but Summer was relieved to be put on a train that very night heading for Luc's townhouse in Evian.

The following day, after Etienne showed no progress towards remembering his wife, Madame Conti confided in Luc while her grandson was resting in his bed. "I must call Juliette's grandmother immediately," she said.

"You could wait," he counseled. "You might give him a few more days."

"I can wait no longer. She is such a dear friend. She has a right to know," she said and dialed her phone.

"You are asking about Juliette?" Juliette's grandmother said. "I'm sorry to report she has gone off to the beaches in the South."

"I became aware of that the night of the recital. Actually I wanted to speak confidentially with you about my grandson."

"She hardly has her figure back and she's off! She should have attended your recital."

"And where is the baby now?" Madame Conti inquired.

"With my daughter, the baby's grandmother. I promise you she is earnestly looking for a wet nurse. You cannot imagine how distressed she is that Juliette has had a complete breakdown and has forgotten her obligations. Postpartum depression, the doctors call it."

"I'm sorry to hear this news," Madame Conti said. "Is there anything I can do?"

"It might help if you should send your grandson to find her and remind her who she is. My late husband always said that it takes a firm hand to keep an unruly wife in order. He never used force with me, of course. I never would have given him cause!"

"I should hope not on either account," Madame Conti said. "I do not know how to tell you this that will not startle you, but we are having a little problem here too. My grandson, who kindly came to Rome for my charitable event, fell down and hit his head. He's lost a good deal of his memory, most especially his memory of Juliette"

"What?"

"I've been nursing him for several days now, and as of yet, I've seen no improvement."

"Mon dieu! What do we do?"

"Perhaps if we sit them down together his memory will be refreshed," Madame Conti said.

"To be sure! I must bring her to you at once. They have obligations!"

Harrumph! Obligations! Madame Conti thought. She could not help but be reminded of how much of her family's fortune had already been spent bailing out Juliette's father. Apparently, the need is present and growing. "Good," she said with less enthusiasm than before. "You bring her here, and we will sit them down together."

"I will have my driver fetch her and bring us to you directly."

"I will be expecting you then." She turned to Luc. "Have you returned Summer to Evian, or wherever you are going to send her?"

"I did so last evening," he said, much relieved that she was gone. For he could not be sure how Etienne would react when faced with the truth of his situation given what he had seen of him that blustery night when he had arrived at his door in a state of irrational despair that very well could have led to acts of violence. Then his attention turned to the role he had played in this fiasco. Could his awakening of Divine Wisdom have brought on such a calamity for Juliette, Etienne, and Summer? Had it all been his fault? He would never know for sure how powerful and far reaching his magic had been, but evidence notwithstanding, he swore to himself and Madame Conti that he was done with hermetic magic. "It's far too potent, dangerous, and out of my control once launched," he admitted. "I will stick to my teas."

Chapter 27

Reconciliation Or Not

Stuart stopped at a roadside café to relax, have a cup of coffee with a donut, and write Claudio Postremo a rather lengthy email. He had been driving alone long enough after dropping the other fellows off to pull his thoughts together. He recounted all that had transpired in greater detail. He related what Roland had told them before he was swooped up. And then in a circumspect manner, which is characteristic of his trade, he cautioned Postremo as he had Bill to be careful what and to whom he reported any of this. His thoughts turned to Natalie and his home in DC where he was now headed. What he would say to her? He loved Natalie and wanted to be happy with her for the rest of his life. Fearing that she might think him a crackpot, he knew better than to tell her too much.

He rehearsed several variants of the story he could spin as he drove across Ohio and West Virginia, each time guessing her reaction to the most dramatic parts. By the time he crossed into Maryland, he had concluded that he should reduce the tale to its bare bones, leaving out the parts most likely to offend, frighten, or not be believed. The story he ended up telling her was how he, Bill, and a local Bloomington reporter chased down an eccentric math professor and UFO buff, Buddie Eller, first to Monroe Lake and then to Serpent Mound. He told her about his run-in with coyotes but left out the part about shapeshifting. He described Charles and his chants, Eller's personality change, and how Eller once recovered had lost all memory of who he had become and what he had done under the influence of what seemed like some kind of spell. He did not mention Roland. Nor did he tell her about space aliens and universal music. None of that. Instead he told her that some backyard gardening genius had hybridized a powerful new variety of weed that Eller and others had succumbed to, leaving them with an extreme case of personality disorder, a Jekyll and Hyde effect, he called it. Thankfully, in Eller's case the effects wore off rapidly. In other cases it could take longer, even months he explained, depending on the potency of the weed, how much the victim had smoked, and over how long of a duration.

Natalie believed the story just as he thought she would. Her concern rapidly shifted to the need to eradicate this very lethal weed, and she laughed nearly to tears when Stuart over dinner imitated Eller eating while under its influence. Later that night after Natalie was asleep, Stuart typed up the drug story he had invented in the manner of a classified report with redacted names and all and sent the hot tip on to Frank.

Meanwhile in Florence, Italy, Claudio Postremo calmly read Stuart's second missive, fully agreeing with his assessment. He had determined years ago while doing research for his latest book, *Blindfolds Lifted* that humanity was not ready for such revelations but needed instead to evolve in their own time without the obvious interference of even the most benevolent extraterrestrial guardians. Humanity most particularly was not ready for revelations about the threat posed by the Endron; a race that without the Alliance's help the Earth was totally unprepared to defend against. News of them, their goals and methods, sent Postremo himself shivering. Better they all stay behind the clouds, he thought. As for the Endron, he could only hope they were soundly put back. And Roland? He wished the best for him but believed there was nothing to be done on his behalf.

He got up from his desk and went out onto his sunny patio to await Barry, Luc, and Summer who had agreed to stop off in Florence on their return trip to France. A 'powwow' he had called their meeting, a word he now associated with this foreign place called Serpent Mound, a place he was disposed to visit as soon as possible. He was quite sure all three would agree with Stuart's assessment and plan a strategy to minimize the impact of what had just transpired.

"Where is Summer?" he asked when his housemaid led only the two men out onto the veranda.

"She returned earlier," Luc explained. "Madame Conti asked that I put her on a train since Juliette and her grandmother were to show up sooner than expected. It was quite awkward. I pray for them all."

Shaking his head Postremo said, "It makes one wonder how many cases of disruption are occurring as we speak. Evidently a man named Charles of Native American descent was performing his own ritual at this Serpent Mound just as these ships belonging to the Endron were leaving some kind of concealed, underground base. Stuart credits him for having some part in driving them away."

"What was the nature of this ritual performed?" Luc asked.

"Stuart wrote that Charles and some others repeated a chant, '*O, wee, you, omg.*' Roland informed them that yet another strange ritual was being performed on a planet he called Avian. He called it time-tuning. This Roland fellow equated the ritual with some kind of alteration in musical notation. But I must confess I have no idea what that could mean."

"Roland is an advanced thinker," Luc said. "He knows what he's talking about."

"I do not doubt that," Postremo said.

"That battle behind the clouds Stuart wrote about reminds me of what Roland and Summer experienced at Jungfraujoch last year," Barry said.

"Yes, it's chilling," Postremo said. "A night of heightened strangeness in a year of heightened strangeness. The question remains, what caused what?"

"I think that ambiguity is something we're going to have live with," Luc said. "And believe me, I have a vested interest in knowing all the facts. But there is no clarity here."

"Precisely," Barry said. "Which is a good reason to keep what we know to ourselves."

"Agreed," Postremo said. "The fact is we don't know enough to provide the confidence that would be needed for the public to begin to peacefully take this in."

"Should we inform the military?" Luc asked.

"No! No! That could be worse than informing the public," Postremo said. "They might only stir things up. I'm afraid we should depend on this Alliance that Roland told them about."

"We know about Etienne and we know about Mr. Eller," Luc said. "I wonder how many other people might have been abducted and mind-stripped and now find themselves like Etienne, returned to lives that have been turned upside down?"

"Well, I don't know, but there must have been many if the activity we know about was taking place as far removed as Indiana. And that is just what we know about," Postremo said.

"I think that's what Luc means," Barry said. "Won't someone take an interest if possibly thousands of cases like Etienne's become known?"

"I'm sure you're correct," Postremo said. "But who would ever guess the true cause? Even if we tried to tell them, would it solve anything?"

"Most people would never believe us," Barry said.

"Yes," Postremo said. "They will find another explanation or explanations that better fit the current thinking...."

"Of what is possible and what isn't," Luc said. "I think you're correct. We should leave this alone. But still I wonder?"

"Whether it was Divine Wisdom's scepter or a shorted out light bulb?" Postremo asked.

"Yes!"

"Well, of course I was not there and cannot know for sure, but I think the former," Postremo said. "In fact I believe there was some kind of correspondence between all three events. A great light show in the sky and chanting at the Serpent Mound seems to have born a relationship, in my mind at least, to the flaming scepter and grand music at the Palazzo Barberini. And there was this universal retuning that Roland spoke of. Maybe all three worked together. Their common bond being music."

"But I knew nothing of this retuning," Luc said. "How could what I did be conceived as a contribution in that case?"

"Those fellows down at Serpent Mound wouldn't have known anything about universal retunings either, or whatever Roland called it," Barry said seconding Luc.

"I think the ways of the universe are beyond our understanding if we choose to confine ourselves to causal logic, or at least to our perceptions of logic," Postremo said. "Something greater was at work."

"Extraterrestrials you mean?" Luc said.

"Maybe if you perceive them as the first cause, which I doubt."

"Well, magic," Barry said. "Luc here believes in magic."

"Only as method, not as cause," Luc said.

"Maybe what you see as a correspondence is only a coincidence,"

Barry said.

"That's certainly possible," Postremo said. "But think about this. Roland said this Serpent Mound is the Earth mind. I can tell you that Rome is the Earth's soul."

"Mind and soul," Luc said. "I see what you mean. Hard to believe this was only coincidence."

The chauffeur had brought the car around to take the couple back to Paris. Etienne opened the door for Juliette and followed after she slid in. Madame Conti handed him his priceless statue carefully wrapped in her best shawl. "It will be all right," she whispered in his ear although she had grave doubts.

"Yes, Grand-mère," her dutiful grandson answered with his words but not his heart.

The grandmothers had established a truce between the couple, but not a happy one. Juliette for her part was uncomfortable with this new situation. This man sitting next to her was a complete stranger, not the strong if sometimes brutal man she had married. His obsession with accommodating her every command made him weak in her eyes. And yes, his behavior was as slavishly accommodating as it was false, for if he allowed himself to act on his true feelings, he would have been miles away. The position he found himself in was incomprehensible to him although his grandmother tried in vain to explain it more than once. How could his life have come to this, he would ask and ask again.

Chapter 28

The Yellow and Blue Stars Of Albireo

Summer managed to switch to the right train once she arrived in Milan, which required a feat of concentration given her state of confusion. She knew she had been banished to Evian, although Luc never put it that way. Had she been abandoned, she wondered, her mind awash in loss.

She recalled Etienne grim faced when she was rushed from Madame Conti's apartment, as if the truth of his predicament had begun to assert itself over the comfort of his amnesia. She remembered the pain in his eyes when he took her hand and told her to be strong. We must both be strong, she had thought, but for very different reasons.

She had not seen Roland since she was forcibly returned to Earth well before his recovery. The image of him weak and weary remained in the forefront of her mind. She pulled out his note that she kept pressed to her heart and read and wept.

Know that there are no words to fully express how much I love you. Carry that in your heart when you think of me no matter what befalls us. And remember too that I want nothing but your happiness. If the future should fail us, you are free from any constraint or obligation to me to seek out what brings you joy for joy is all that I want for you.

Her mind cast back and forth between their fates. Etienne will find no peace, she realized, only the satisfaction that comes from fulfilling his duty. And I alone and Roland very ill.

"May I sit here?" a well-dressed woman asked as she joined her in her empty compartment. "Do you mind if I sit across from you?" the lady repeated. "The compartment I be assigned is far too crowded."

"Oh, please do," Summer said. "I'm rather lonely here." She could not help but notice the woman was wearing a rather large hat whose brim dropped low, nearly concealing her face. "What a beautiful hat you are wearing."

The woman responded with only a question. "You be going to Paris?"

The accent was familiar, Summer thought. "No, I'm returning to Evian. And you?"

"I be only a tourist here. I just visited Milan."

"I just came from Rome," Summer replied nonchalantly as she turned and looked out the train window. She noticed something peculiar in the mirrored reflection she saw of herself and the woman. Startled, she studied the portion of reflection that revealed the exposed part of the woman's face. "You remind me of someone I saw there?" she said when she turned towards her.

The woman blanched. "I have not been in Rome for many years."

"No, that's not what I mean. I should say you remind me of something I saw, a painting, or to be more precise a fresco on the ceiling of the Palazzo Barberini."

"Nor to my knowledge have I ever been an artist's model."

"Of course not," Summer said. "The fresco of which I speak is nearly four hundred years old."

"As old as that?" the woman said, smiled, and doffed her hat.

"Lira! It's you! You pop up out of nowhere!"

"You say you see me in Rome?"

"No, but you do look like her. Ouch!" she cried, feeling a sharp sting from the burn on her shoulder.

"I do not mean to startle you."

"I'm used to that. No, it's not you, it's this burn." She pulled off her cardigan sweater and showed Lira the burn mark on her shoulder.

Lira reached over and touched the mark, instantly cooling it with the tips of her fingers. "Yes, it be a very bad burn," she said as she continued her soothing touch. "How you come by it?"

"I was just at a concert in Rome where the music seemed to bring this fresco I was speaking of to life. It was as if the scepter that Divine Wisdom held burst into flame and struck me. But one of my friends thinks it was only a short that sparked in lights that were strung around as decoration."

"You look distressed. It be the pain from the burn?"

Summer began to weep. "You know why I'm distressed. You took my ring and you took my Roland." She looked up, "Where is Roland? Is he safe?"

"He be safe enough now."

The train slowed for a passenger stop. "I have something for you," Lira said, her own eyes now full of tears. She pulled a blue and yellow sapphire ring from her bag. "I can keep it from you no longer. It be not mine to take, fates be. Let me see your hand," she said just before sliding the ring on Summer's finger. "See, it fits perfectly."

Summer held up her hand and delighted as the late afternoon sun coming through the coach window illuminated the gorgeous stones.

"I give it back. It be yours."

Grateful, Summer pressed Lira's hands.

Lira never returned after leaving the compartment in search of bottled water. Summer gazed at the ring throughout the rest of the trip to Evian feeling connected to something of far greater value than itself. She felt at peace.

Roland had been transferred from the landing base in the Northeast Quadrant to the idyllic home Sedwig had made for him in the wilds of Avian's Southwest. It was summer there and as beautiful as he had left it. But as much as he had grown to love the place, all seemed changed now that he felt himself a prisoner.

"Seclusion be necessary for your safety," the magistrate had said when he ordered his deportation from the Northeast Quadrant. But Roland believed it was rather their safety that most concerned them after the Presider had made the case that Roland had breeched the etiquette of high secrecy by revealing too much about the Alliance's existence and intentions to those who should not know. The Presider went so far as to castigate Lira and Bryn for having transported him to Serpent Mound at such a critical time and at such at a critical place. Neither was present to defend themselves, and Roland was unable to offer much in his own defense for there was no defense to make. He admitted to the charges, saying only he meant no harm and was unaware of this particular application of high secrecy protocol and apparently so were Lira and Bryn.

Sedwig tried for days to entertain him with his flute song in the fragrant meadows and shady groves as they leisurely hiked from village to village and inn to inn. When that did not improve his mood, Sedwig ordered up purposeful work for both to engage in. But Roland remained lackluster, and his appetite scant even after several weeks of Sedwig's efforts.

"I cannot stay here any longer," Roland finally admitted.

"You miss her too much?"

"Like one of our two suns would miss the other if they were parted," he sighed. "I hear her call to me in a sound so soulful it makes me weep. I know not how she is, and I'm given no way to find out."

Sedwig began playing a mournful tune on his flute.

"Aye, you be telepathic," Roland said. "That is the song that I hear with no way to know."

"Unless and perhaps you would see her through the timekeeper's machine," Sedwig said. "His cameras record the present as a moving record of the past. If we go there...."

"Can we? Do you think he would see us?"

"If we go illegally perhaps, much like we did before, disguised as workmen. That would at least get us to the Northeast Quadrant. But as for the rest, we be indebted to the goodwill of the timekeeper."

"We should try," Roland said. "What else is there?"

"But if you be found out, no more soft melodies out here. A hard cell shall await you."

"We must try," Roland repeated now resigned and intent.

A few days hence the men left on a ferry carrying workmen to the Northeast Quadrant. They determined that Sedwig alone must make a request at the door of the timekeeper lest the guards recognize Roland's disguise.

"I come to see the timekeeper," Sedwig said, while Roland awaited word over a glass of mead at a nearby pub.

"He has no appointments today," one of the guards said.

"I beg you tell him Sedwig be here with a message."

"You may give me the message, and I will take it to him," the other guard said. "That be the best I can offer without an appointment."

"Let me think how to write it. I be back shortly."

"Those guards would give me over to the authorities if they should learn I am Roland."

"So might the timekeeper," Sedwig cautioned.

"I think I have his goodwill to count on. Hmm, how shall we compose this message without giving me away to guards? Put it in your hand. Write, that I have come from Serpent Mound with a request. The guards will not know who 'I' is, but the timekeeper will. The mention of that place should be enough to wet his whistle."

"Wet his whistle? What say you?" Sedwig asked.

Roland laughed. "I forgot. You are not proficient in our idioms. Well, it usually refers to taking a drink," he said as he lifted his cup of mead to his mouth. He licked his lips. "But my meaning here is to stimulate his curiosity enough that he will see me. Go now and see if this will do the trick."

Roland waited alone for Sedwig's return near thirty minutes later, aimlessly drinking his mead and another, unaware that curious eyes were upon him. At last Sedwig returned to the pub with a cloaked person beside him who looked about furtively before he took a seat.

"Tis dangerous you be in such a public place," the timekeeper said. "I hear you become a fugitive in the wilderness. I be very sorry to learn such. Yet I know how frightened the people be that the Endron find out that they protect you, and they be frightened too by your treachery in revealing them to a species unable to understand."

"Some would understand," Roland said. "Those who I spoke to understand. But I'm not sure about the others. They are a people who believe they make their own way in the universe and imagine themselves kings of their planet. They would never believe what I have said anyway, so do not fear. Others are far more humble in their understanding of their status, and very fine students they would make."

"Such as you be, Lira has told me."

"Such as I was," Roland said, head bent in modesty. "But now I break with that and seek to break the rules. I must know how she is and if I should go back."

"After it be done, the retuning that is, I watch intently to see how things unfold," the timekeeper said. "Prayers are still sung at Serpent

Mound as this man called Charles has drawn many people to him to sing his chant. This be good I think. As for the others who you know, I watch intently to see how they sort it out. The woman you call your wife is in a water town."

"Evian!" Roland said.

"Sad methinks. She spends her days by the lake with her books. When she be not there she stays in a place with a holy man."

"Luc!" Roland said. "Do you see another man who is a friend of Luc?"

"The one who travels with this Luc? He be gone now. I see him fly over the sea."

"Not in Italy?" Roland said.

"No, near that Serpent Mound. But the most peculiar thing I see many miles from water town—Well, see it not at first until I trace a brilliant light traveling the distance between a city of lights and water town—It be a statue that seems alive."

"Gitane Marie! In Paris!" Roland said. "Say why you be curious?"

"Her light mesmerizes. In it be pictures for those with eyes to see, methinks. I see her, this statue, casting blessings on the woman that be yours. She seeks to heal her. At least that's what I see. This place, this Earth you call your home be, well, very exciting in its confusion. I think to study it a very long time."

"And how did the retuning go? What is the outcome?"

"Better than hoped. We see it as success. Still confusion, but it rests mostly with those who were changed back from what they be under the influence of the Endron. As for the others not so afflicted, we see a mighty drop in armed conflict, murder, and mayhem. So, I say, confusion but far more harmony than what be before, for a time at least. So what say you? Why you ask?"

"I must go back!" Roland said. "You see why. That woman you see is everything to me. She is the moon to my sun on a planet with only one sun. And that confusion you find so exciting, well, it is that. The people are on the cusp of great knowledge, which makes it a very exciting place to be. Here is too placid for me. Beautiful, orderly, far too orderly it seems, but missing a certain fascination in its lack of drama. I seek her back and that drama too. Oh, me! What shall I do?"

The timekeeper shook his head sadly and whispered, "The magistrate will never let you go, methinks. If only you could steal away without him knowing. You must seek out Lira and Bryn. Only they have the power. I have none of that kind. If I had a ship and crew, I would board you in a barrel and take you out of here this very day, so grateful I am to you and so enamored with your life there."

"Can you make an appointment with Bryn and Lira?" Sedwig asked. "You could seek to convince as you are convinced."

"I will," he said. "I go back now. How shall I find you?"

Roland looked at Sedwig. "I shall find you, tomorrow," Sedwig said. "It better you know not where we be."

The cloaked personage got up from his chair and made a slight bow before he departed.

"He be of good heart," Sedwig said.

"So passionate a man for his age," Roland agreed. "So where do we go until tomorrow?"

"I've got us rooms at the inn. You be disguised as my servant if you don't mind."

"I am humbled. You've been such a good friend to me in my infirmary of all kinds, head and heart."

Sedwig made his way to the inn along the canal path. Roland trailed behind, head bent in servile respect until a bag dropped over his head and he was plucked up.

"Roland!" Sedwig cried when he turned back and saw him there no longer. He followed their path back to the pub, hoping to see him stopped at a shop window that might have caught his eye. But he was nowhere to be seen. Sedwig inquired with the pubkeeper if his friend may have returned. The pubkeeper shook his head. He then ran back to the Library of Time. His voice was so urgent that the friendlier guard left him at the door and sought the timekeeper, who immediately brought him inside when he discovered him there.

"He's gone!" Sedwig said. "He be following behind in his disguise as my servant, but when I looked back he had disappeared. Had you made contact above?"

The timekeeper sighed. "Not yet. It must be the Endron," he said. "They have their spies here. They must have found you out."

Sedwig began to weep while the timekeeper held back his tears. "He be a strong man," the timekeeper said, "with a destiny yet unfulfilled. Do not weep. He will return someday a hero. Do not weep," he repeated as he himself dissolved into tears.

"Quiet!" a voice said inside the ship's hold. "Bryn does not know what I do, and it be best to keep it that way. I already be the target of the Endron wrath. No need to amplify."

"Lira!" he said.

"Shush! Be quiet."

In a low whisper he said, "What will you do?"

"I seek to return you, but no one must know. If it be learned I returned you to Earth, you be not safe and neither be I. So I must ask if you can to obey such terms as I require."

"Yes, anything!" he said.

"You must return to the quiet life you had before you discovered your true origins. A plain man, a scientist you must be."

"That will not be hard for me. It is who I was for most of my life."

"You must pledge your friends be silent."

"I don't think they would mind," Roland said. "In fact, they might even be relieved to forget that part of me."

"And here be the hard part. You must protect Summer from the Endron. They not forget, and if they find you out, woe to her and to you and to me. There be risk, and if you stay here among us such risk be avoided. But I tell you something. I saw her on the train to Evian. She at first recognized me not. I give her back her ring as a gift, which truly moved her. A sad emptiness haunts her soul, safety but no life, and if you can fill it...." Lira went silent, not wanting to cry again.

"Lira! You be right. No risk, no life. I will try to fill her soul with gladness. I swear, I pledge to you to keep your covenants as long as you choose."

"She be valiant, passionate, and fearless. Up to the task. But before you commit, you must know all that you give up, your destiny if you would stay here with us."

Lira waved her hand and Roland felt himself enveloped in a strange robe of feathers. She waved her hand again and a mirror descended.

"What's that?" he said startled at the sight.

"That be you in the future if you stay here with us."

He lifted his arms under the weight of the robes. As he lifted, his body ascended to the high ceiling of the room in the lower deck of the spacecraft.

"What's this? I could fly if not for these walls," he said.

"That you could without any need of device. You must know this. If you return, you make this sacrifice. You give up your lordship to which you were born."

"I?" he said in wonder.

"You! That be your future here, Lord of Avian. That be what you give up. You must decide."

"And there?" he said.

"There you be what you can become in a place of little understanding."

He thought for a moment and said, "Here my destiny be given. There my destiny to make. I give you my pledge."

He swooned, and when he recovered he found himself on the doorstep of Luc Renard's townhouse in Evian. She answered the door. Tears of joy surpassed anything Luc had ever witnessed. "We must celebrate this miraculous event," Luc said, "with bottles of wine, my favorite soup, and I will bake a magnificent cake."

Later that evening they phoned Barry. Told him the news and swore him to silence. He said he would come soon to join the celebration.

The following day, Luc, Roland, and Summer wandered out into the meadows and woods that surround Evian. She skipped off the path and into the wild flower fields until Roland drew her back and led them into the woods and to the very lake that had swallowed up Etienne. They stayed back this time, concealed in the trees as they watched birds overhead dropping into the lake to catch a bug or two. They listened to the sounds of croaking frogs. They stood there a good thirty minutes and watched. No saucer descended into or arose from the lake. It is truly over they thought and returned to the fields they had just walked through.

Luc invented the poem he would write that very night. Roland watched as Summer stopped to examine a flower or two and seemed to pirouette, as she would turn suddenly to follow the flight of a bird, her hair a mesh of golden radiance in the sunlight. What animates her he wondered, until he answered his own question. She is the harp upon which nature plays. Nothing could be more perfect, he thought. He smelled mint in her hair and his heart pounded. He was quite sure of his decision. What would his life be without his beating heart, he thought, no amount of power or worshipful eyes could have made up for the loss.

Across the seas, Neighbor Bill sat on his front porch drinking his morning coffee while reading the newspaper. Shadow was out in the front yard looking for the perfect spot when Paul and Andy came riding up on their bicycles.

"Boys, you're here just in time for breakfast. I was gonna make me some pancakes. You want some?"

"Sure," Andy said.

"Can you tell us more stories about what the future will be like?" Paul asked.

"Sit down to breakfast," Bill said. "Like I was tellin' you last night. If you boys train for it, you might be flyin' across the universe on windsails and makin' friends with all kinds of intelligent extraterrestrial people who aren't that different from yourselves. They'll be able to tell you wondrous tales about all kinds of things you didn't know about."

"Tell us some!" Paul said.

Fini

By Linda Oxley Milligan

MMXX

Author Biography

UFOs Over Ohio is the sequel to *Cygnus* and the fifth in a series of adventure novels by Linda Oxley Milligan. Earlier works are *The Blue Nile Adventure*, *Gitane Marie: Through the Eyes of the Black Madonna*, and a novelette for young readers, *The Shadows that Haunt the Walls*. Milligan's novels draw on her love of travel as well as her background in folklore and literature. She seeks to take the reader to many of the places she has traveled offering distinct insight that is the product of both a folklorist's eye and a vivid imagination that draws from the history and mythos of ancient places.

UFOs Over Ohio reflects her folklore fieldwork: the legends and sighting reports she gathered, her group analysis, and other perspectives on the subject of UFOs that resulted in a dissertation, oral papers, and published articles. "Fieldwork involves spending time just listening to people, researching the media many beliefs are drawn from, while trying to understand the place UFO beliefs hold in culture," she says.

Milligan's academic work remains as objective as possible. As to her own beliefs, she claims herself an agnostic, noting that while hard evidence as to the existence of UFOs remains elusive, nonetheless, there are witness reports and a body of evidence that cannot be easily dismissed. She argues that the field is begging for more research to be done by those in the scientific community able to go beyond cultural studies like her own.

Also By Linda Oxley Milligan

The Blue Nile Adventure
Gitane Marie: Through the Eyes of the Black Madonna
Cygnus
The Shadows that Haunt the Walls: Paul's Story

If you enjoyed this novel, please consider writing a review of the book on Amazon.com.

Thank you,

Linda